Praise for *The Someday Daughter*

"A compelling, beautifully drawn exploration into the frailty and fortitude of a girl simply trying to succeed, love, and thrive. I'm proud to live in a book world where Ellen O'Clover is writing contemporary young adult fiction. *The Someday Daughter* is a forever treasure."
—Laura Taylor Namey, *New York Times* bestselling author of *A Cuban Girl's Guide to Tea and Tomorrow*

"Heartbreaking, romantic, funny, and smart, Ellen O'Clover's *The Someday Daughter* is a modern road map for figuring out where you truly belong. This beautiful and compassionate book has a permanent place in my heart. You'll be with Audrey every mile of her journey."
—Betty Culley, author of *The Name She Gave Me*

"Warm and heartfelt even as it addresses difficult, complex truths, and packed with memorable people and places (not to mention one very enchanting dog). I loved watching Audrey develop the courage to face—and maybe even enjoy—the unknown."
—Julia Drake, author of *The Last True Poets of the Sea*

"One of the best depictions I've ever read of the beautifully messy coming-of-age experience. Seamlessly weaves together a complex mother-daughter relationship, mental health struggles, and the softest, sweetest romance. An achingly relatable story. I couldn't put this book down!"
—Kaitlyn Hill, author of *Love from Scratch* and *Not Here to Stay Friends*

"A fast-paced and emotional story about figuring out who you really *aren't*, after a lifetime of being told who you are. A surprise gut-punch punctuated with a promise that life might not be predictable, but it'll be what it'll be. Perfect for anyone who, like me, has spent years chasing the high of *The Truth About Forever*."
—Samantha Markum, author of *This May End Badly* and *You Wouldn't Dare*

Also by Ellen O'Clover
Seven Percent of Ro Devereux

The Someday Daughter

Ellen O'Clover

HARPER TEEN
An Imprint of HarperCollins Publishers

To anyone who's ever wished they were different.
I'm glad you're here just as you are.

LOS ANGELES

1

There's a zipper pull pressed directly into my spine. It's matte white, sharp-cornered, a spiteful metal rectangle. I know because I spent eight sweaty minutes wrestling with it backstage, trying bitterly to tug it over the waistline seam of the flouncy, floral dress Magnolia set out for me. I got it settled between my shoulder blades seconds before Mags burst into my room and now it's back to haunt me, piercing my vertebra like a punishment. Or a warning.

"That sounds like a good question for Audrey," my mother says. She looks over at me, and in the hot stage lights dust motes float like pollen between us. "Honey?"

I lean forward in my blush velvet chair, the perfect aesthetic accompaniment to my mother's mint-green one. Try to swipe at the zipper. Miss.

"Hmm?" I haven't been paying attention, which is off-brand for me. But there's something impersonal about this, personal as it's meant to be. With two thousand people staring up at us, it nearly feels like no one is. Ten people, sure. Five, even more pressure. But two thousand? They may as well be fake—a soundless sea shifting in the dark beyond the glaring lights.

My mother laughs, the rehearsed titter that's as familiar to me as the sound of my own name. "Laz asked what we're proudest to share on the tour this summer."

I look at him. Lazarus Leblanc: media darling, beach-chic tastemaker, he of the laminated eyebrows. My mother's Malibu neighbor, and the exact kind of Los Angeles Ken doll to moderate an event like this. I'm 90 percent sure his legal name is Scott.

"Proudest," I repeat. Laz cocks an eyebrow, tilts one ankle so his snakeskin boots catch their polish in the light. We've known each other for a lifetime, and not at all. "Hard to say." It's the easiest truth within reach. Because really, I left everything I'm proud of back at school. I boxed it up and hoisted it into a windowless container that'll ship directly to my dorm in Baltimore mid-August, first day of freshman orientation, the minute my life picks back up. This is an interlude—this tour, this summer, this conversation on this stage—an exercise for my mother's pride that has absolutely nothing to do with my own.

"Understandably so," Laz says smoothly, "when there's so much to be proud of. What about you, Camilla?"

My mother preens. I brace myself, watching every shift of her body like the adjustment of so many jewel-colored feathers. The level setting of her freckled collarbones. The blonde hair she tips over one shoulder, so lustrous it could be liquid. The calculated angle of her smile: the warm one, the one that invites you right in.

"I'm proudest to share my relationship with Audrey." It's the worst thing she could say, and the inevitable thing. She isn't looking at me but instead at the audience—that dark, faceless sea. "To throw open the doors to our bond, and get real with our friends across the country about what it means to share a relationship as mothers and daughters, as parents and children, as women."

Finally, she looks at me, our mirrored blue eyes meeting across the glossy, echoing stage. I can tell I'm supposed to be honored she's called me a woman in front of all these people. Me, six months past eighteen. But I know what they don't: that I have never been Camilla's equal, and that she will never see me that way.

"She's grown up with all of you," my mother says, sweeping a delicate hand toward the audience. Her smile broadens. "And now, this summer, you'll really meet her. Get to know her. See her the way I do."

I have bristled down to my marrow, every cell inside me growing spikes to keep this out.

"How *special*," she says. She leans back, letting her words settle in the rapt, reverent air. "What an undeniable thing of beauty."

Applause rises from the audience for absolutely nothing. The wall-to-wall screen behind us illuminates and I turn to see my own face, gridded out like a gallery. Photos of me stretching back over a decade, my mother's social media handles bolded in the upper corner of each one. Me at seven, holding a palm-sized turtle in Camilla's sloping yard. Me at eleven, casting a backward glance from the steps to my dorm at the Summit School, the year she launched Saint and sent me to boarding school. Me two days ago, robed and capped, standing next to Ethan at graduation.

All those Audreys compiled like postage stamps for my mother's collection. I don't recognize myself in a single photo.

I blink up at the screen. I lean back so the zipper gnashes my bones. I think, *Who are you?*

And then I run.

2

The alley behind the theater smells like hot garbage. When I spill sideways through the metal door, my foot lands in something wet enough to splash me, though this is Los Angeles and it hasn't rained in weeks. Horrifying. I suck in a lungful of trash air and collapse against the door as it whooshes shut, zipper pull promptly gouging my spine.

It's muggy as murder out here, moon rising over the smog haze of downtown LA. Inside, my mother is doing damage control. Magnolia is probably on a rampage already, hunting me down one hallway at a time. I've got maybe thirty more seconds to myself, so I smash my eyes shut and start counting my fingers.

Thumb to pinky, thumb to ring finger, thumb to middle, thumb to index. I repeat it quickly, over and over, counting out loud.

"One, two, three, four." Breath of disgusting air. "Five, six, seven, eight." Another breath, and a steadying swallow. "Nine, ten, ele—"

"What are you doing?"

For a moment, I don't move. I stand suspended—hand lifted in front of me, tips of my thumb and middle finger pressed together, zipper pull lodged into my skin—like maybe if I don't open my eyes, I'll still be alone.

But then the voice comes again, a pointed little cough. I open my eyes and lower my hand.

"Conjuring a spirit?" I can only see half the guy's face, one knee jutted into the yellow cast of a streetlamp. He's leaning against a dumpster, and moves even farther into the light to get a better look at me. "Don't let me stop you, if so."

"I'm clearly not conjuring a spirit." My voice is as acrid as the garbage keeping us company back here. The last thing I need, after being paraded like a prize calf by my mother, is some stranger joking around with me in a trash pit.

The guy steps into the glow of the streetlamp and, finally, I place him: one of the interns staffing the tour. I saw him backstage before the reading, huddled over an enormous video camera.

"Not super clear," he says. His hair is dark and curly, tied at the nape of his neck with a few pieces shaken loose to scrape his jaw. It makes him look like some kind of colonial pilgrim. Or Tarzan. "I didn't realize magic would be part of the show." He tips his head toward the theater's giant marquee, just visible at the end of the alley: *Camilla St. Vrain: "Letters to My Someday Daughter" Anniversary Tour.*

"It's not magic." I reach for the zipper, trying to twist it so it isn't jutting into me. "It's a centering practice." I can't quite reach, and I spin so my back is facing him. "Can you help me with this?"

Silence. I glance over my shoulder, and he's watching me with his eyebrows raised. "What?" I say.

"Do you need to be naked for the next phase of the conjuring?"

"I don't need to—" He's smiling when I turn around, lopsided and easy-looking, one crooked canine visible in the dim light. "I'm sorry, what are *you* doing back here?"

He huffs half a laugh. "I'm not answering until you tell me what a centering practice is."

"I don't need to explain myself to you." And I certainly don't need to explain my finger counting, the habit I haven't quite been able to break, the quickest way to calm myself down when I'm worked up—by my mother, by her demands of me, by anything. "Just help me with the zipper."

I turn back around, hands on my hips. For a moment there's nothing—just the hot, motionless air and the distant honks of evening traffic. Then I feel fingertips on my back, cool and light, and finally—*finally*—relief from the zipper. The guy takes two steps away from me before speaking again.

"That was rough in there."

I straighten, smoothing my hands over the floral skirt as I turn back to face him. "I don't know what you mean."

"Really," he says flatly. I don't like how he's looking at me, like I just showed all my cards and have no way to clutch them back to my chest now. "So it's typical for you to flee mid-event like you just remembered you left your flat iron plugged in?"

I feel my face scrunch into itself, rake my eyes over his dark hair. "What would you know about leaving a flat iron plugged in?"

"Little sister." He lifts his phone, dark-screened in the space between us. "I'm out here because she called."

My own phone buzzes in the depths of my dress, and I reach into the frills to find it.

ETHAN WOOD: *How'd it go?*

His name is enough to make me remember: I need to get out of here.

"Look," I say, glancing up, "um—"

"Silas," he supplies, watching me patiently. As if it doesn't smell like a landfill on fire back here, as if he has all the time in the world.

"Silas," I repeat. I gesture at myself. "Audrey. I've—"

"I know who you are."

I wince. "Right. I've got to go."

"Where?" he asks, glancing toward the dark end of the alley. There's a town car waiting there, sleek black and sleeping, ready to whisk my mother away. "Driver's still inside."

"No," I say. I open my phone to call a rideshare and in my peripheral vision, Silas shifts. "Like, *go* go. Go home."

"To Colorado?"

I look up at him. I shouldn't be surprised when people do this, when they've read enough of Camilla's Wikipedia page to see where she sent me to school. But still, it grates: I don't know this person at all, but somehow he knows where home is to me. I don't answer, just look back down at my phone and start to call a car.

"Hey, don't," Silas says. Our eyes meet, and there's something there—like this matters to him. "We're just getting started."

The *Letters to My Someday Daughter* tour has barely begun. There are nine more cities to visit, eight more weeks of travel, so much more money for my mother to make. And yet.

"I'm leaving."

"No." An icy voice rises from behind us, and there she is: Magnolia Jones herself, haloed in the light from the doorframe. My mother's assistant, and the most tenacious woman to walk the earth in four-inch stilettos. "You most certainly are not."

3

I wake up in a ten-thousand-square-foot, concrete-and-glass mon-
strosity in Point Dume. It's the last house on the block, butted
up against the nature preserve, so if you step through the sliding
back doors and look left, there's just scrub grass and ocean to the
ends of your eyeballs. It has a gated driveway, a manicured lawn
with stone steps down to a private beach, a chef's wet dream of a
kitchen that's never been cooked in. It's a gilded fortress. It is, of
course, my mother's house.

No place for children, is how Laz always described it—usually
with a highball glass in hand, sun hitting his green eyes as he
perched on the back patio. I have this perfect memory of him in
white linen pants, framed by Camilla's infinity pool. He'd walk
across the street from his house for afternoon drinks, every bit as
groomed as he was at last night's show, though his only audience,
those days, was my mother.

He'd say this in front of me, that the home she'd made was
not intended for me. I knew it already; it was impossible not to
know—the house had a meditation studio, an infrared sauna,
blown-glass objets d'art scattered like so many seedlings. But no
place for me to keep my brightly colored chapter books, and no

snacks in the pantry unless I wanted raw almonds, which I didn't. My dad's apartment in Venice still had my first-grade drawings taped to the refrigerator. Taped, because it wasn't magnetic. And still there, maybe, because he so rarely was. But at Camilla's house I'd always known to make myself small and neutral enough to creep chameleon-like through her monochrome rooms.

The only color in the house is the sea; every room was designed to let it in. The entire back wall is glass from floor to ceiling, like we're in a display case for the ocean to observe. This morning the water is a moody blue, shadows moving across it like specters cast from the clouds. Rain today, maybe.

I've been watching the ocean since before the sun rose above it, tracking its churning waves from black to navy. It's light enough now that the room around me has come into focus: last night's floral dress draped over the desk chair, my phone screen-side-down on the cold marble nightstand, the frayed edge of a book just peeking from my open backpack on the floor.

I stare at the only visible triangle of its cover until my eyes blur. A physical reminder, incontestable, of the last thing I did before flying to Los Angeles. The same thing I always do.

I went searching for my mother in the one place I can always find her: the airport bookstore.

Sometimes she winds up in SELF-HELP, but usually she lands in the broader NONFICTION. Often at the back of the store, past all the new hardcover fiction and the spinning shelves of airplane neck pillows. Finding her in airports is more of a compulsion than a choice, something I always do before flights, like a nervous tic or maybe a good luck charm. There have been a couple of times over the years I couldn't track her down—in the Jackson Hole airport when I met my dad for Christmas sophomore year, or during one never-ending layover in Des Moines. But almost always, tucked between the *R*s and the *T*s, there she is. Camilla St. Vrain: *Letters to My Someday Daughter.*

It's a thin book, which probably factored into its popularity. One hundred and twenty pages, easy to rip through on a cross-country flight or a long afternoon at the pool. The book's newer editions have a subtitle, added by her publisher after a few years: *Rewriting Your Inner Narrative Through the Transformative Power of Kindness.* Most versions have Camilla's face on the cover, frozen in time at twenty-nine, when the book was published and became an instant bestseller. She's wearing a blazer in the photo, its lapels framing her flat, gold necklace. Under the picture: *Camilla St. Vrain, PsyD.*

I've heard her explain the book's philosophy hundreds of times—often enough to wear it like a tattoo on the inside of my forehead, often enough that I can pull up the words from nothing.

Ladies, she always begins. *Let's stop being so mean to ourselves, shall we? Let's change that little voice inside that tells us we're unworthy. Let's each of us speak to ourselves as if we're someone innately deserving of kindness. Someone we're obligated to protect, to convince that the world is beautiful and good. Someone like our own hypothetical someday daughters.*

Of course, I wasn't around back then. Camilla didn't have me for another seven years; when she wrote the book, she had no idea how to talk to a daughter. But millions of women ate it up. My mother was so successful at writing about being a therapist that she didn't need to actually *be* one anymore. Her fans were loyal and hell-bent on bettering themselves; she did speaking tours, book clubs, conferences. She changed people's lives, or at least that was the claim.

And here I've always been, the real daughter Camilla St. Vrain holds at arm's length, like a tissue you've trapped a house spider inside. Something to be contained and feared until you can get it to the trash can.

They had three copies at Denver International, two hardcovers and one paperback with a neon USED sticker half-covering the title. The airport was test-driving a new trade-in program: buy a book at the start of your vacation and return it to another airport at the end for half your money back. The next day, I knew, there would be twenty-fifth-anniversary editions on those same shelves, smelling of fresh-cut paper and sporting a film-grain photograph of Camilla and me on my fourth birthday. The next day I would be in Los Angeles to begin an entire summer promoting it with her.

I pulled the used copy of *Letters* off the shelf. It was a first edition, no subtitle, just the title written out in self-confident capitals. When I cracked it open to a middle page, the margins were full of annotations, someone's reactions and reminders and starred sentences left there for anyone to find.

I glanced up instinctually, breathing through a hot flush of secondhand embarrassment. Who would return something like this? I flipped to another page, where the reader had underlined *We are the determiners of our own self-talk.* How mortifying to take this book so seriously you'd mark it up for yourself, save a sentence like that.

I snapped it shut, took it over to the register. Bought it for $6.79.

Ethan was waiting for me between our gates, thick textbook splayed open in front of him on a high-top table halfway inside a coffee shop and halfway into the terminal.

"Find anything good?" he asked, looking up as I pulled out the chair across from him. But I'd already buried the book between folded jeans in my suitcase, hidden it from the world just like everything else about my relationship with Camilla.

"No," I said, accepting the coffee he nudged toward me. "It's all tabloids and beach reads in there."

"Mmm," he said softly, and tucked his chin to turn back to the textbook. We'd graduated the day before, me with the *S*s and Ethan with the *W*s, wearing matching black robes and gold-tasseled caps. He was flying to Pennsylvania, where we should have been going together. Already studying for the summer pre-med intensive we were both accepted to back in March. His family was tucked away at their gate, giving us the privacy of one last hour together before we parted for a summer that was supposed to be spent side by side. Camilla, of course, had taken a red-eye back to LA after the ceremony.

"This is interesting," Ethan said. He looked up at me, then spun the textbook so I could read it right side up. "The first unit's on biomedical ethics, and they're talking about this case study from the seventies, this man who presented with thoracic pain. . . ."

His eyes were on the book, pointing me through a diagram. But I just watched him: dark lashes through his square-framed glasses, the soft lines of his pale cheeks, the cut of his shirt collar. He smelled like piney deodorant and the fancy Kiehl's soap his mom always sent in her care packages—the familiar way he'd always smelled, since we met in junior English when we were paired up for our midterm assignment.

We were supposed to take turns verbally arguing our thesis angles for *Frankenstein*, work out the kinks before putting pen to paper. Ethan told me that *Frankenstein* was Shelley's reaction to the body horror of giving birth and losing her baby, herself the motherless daughter of a woman who died in childbirth. I stumbled through an argument that I knew wasn't nearly as compelling, feeling like a fool until he intercepted me on the steps of the humanities building after class and asked if I wanted to join forces. That's exactly how he said it, too. *Join forces.* He meant, did I want to go on a date. He was wearing a burgundy cabled sweater and those same thick-framed glasses, his teeth perfect white and braces-straight. I almost couldn't believe my good fortune that this person thought I was his match.

We spent the year and a half after that editing each other's papers, holding up flash cards for one another on our favorite couch in the library. He became a student EMT because I was one, too, and when our shifts overlapped, we sat up together in the student center with our navy-blue uniforms on, watching old movies on his laptop. Ethan came from a family of New York lawyers and wanted to be a neurologist. I came from my mother and wanted to be a real doctor in the way she was not.

We chose the summer course at UPenn because it was the obvious option: a résumé-builder that kept us together for the last few months before college. Ethan is going to Yale, and I'll be at Johns Hopkins—a fewer-than-five-hour drive for weekend visits. But for just a little while longer, he was right there across from me: steady, reliable Ethan. Poised over a textbook to share something he knew I would care about, because he's the one person who always knows.

I took a breath. I took a minute to mourn what Camilla had stolen from me.

4

FALLON MARTIN: *did you vom?*

My phone pings with a text, and I lift it off the stone step. I've
made my way down to the very bottom of the ocean staircase, my
feet buried in the sand. I snuck outside when I heard Camilla start
to stir; it's chilly out here, the morning whipping with storm wind,
but still preferable to being near her and that copy of her book.
Fallon's sent me an article, too: *Camilla St. Vrain Tour Off to a
Shaky Start as Daughter Audrey Suffers Food Poisoning.*

Food poisoning. I have to hand it to Magnolia; it's a smart
story. Why else would national darling Camilla St. Vrain's historically self-composed daughter flee the stage in the middle of a
sold-out event? Why would anyone?

Curdled carbonara's easier to grasp than the truth of the matter: that seeing all those photos, the person Camilla's made me
out to be for her six million social media followers, felt intolerable.
Not difficult to tolerate—intolerable. Full, simultaneous rejection
from my body and my brain. So, in a way . . .

Yeah, I reply. Spiritually.

Fallon responds immediately. explain

If I were to explain, it would sound like this: That photo of me, seven years old, holding a turtle on this exact beach, was taken by my dad. I'd never have held out a baby turtle to my mother, because she'd never have touched something like that.

The one of me on my first day at the Summit School was taken without my knowledge; I was eleven and walking into my new dorm building and she called my name so I turned around. In the photo I look focused and serious, the perfect face for the caption she posted—a gushing rush of emotion about her pride, her big-brained daughter, her mini-me so self-actualized at just eleven that she was ready to live in Colorado, live at school, make academia her entire life. I didn't feel that way then. I felt terrified. I felt alone and unwanted. But she told me how excited I was, how brave I was, how much I wanted this—told the whole world, too. And eventually I did feel those things, though I don't know who chose them for me to feel: my own mind, or Camilla's voice that lives inside it.

Then the last photo: Ethan and me at graduation. Ethan, the embodiment of a life I'd made without her, still somehow there on her social feeds like he was hers, too. Nothing was mine to hold sacred; nothing belonged to me fully enough that she couldn't abscond with it and turn it into a layer of her brand.

And now, the very worst of it: this summer. The biggest thing she's ever ripped out from underneath me and taken for her own.

She stole my summer on a Thursday morning while wearing a matching lilac workout set. Scallop-edged sports bra, high-rise leggings. She'd sent me a set of my own; mine was seafoam green but, critically, had the same Saint logo emblazoned across the boobs. It was still in the flat-rate shipping box Magnolia mailed it in; I wore pajama shorts and an oversized T-shirt I'd stolen from Dad in middle school.

"Find your sit bones, honey." My mother pulled her feet together in front of her, legs bowed wide, extending her spine. "And close your eyes. Thumbs to third eye center."

I crossed my legs and watched her breathe, ribs expanding over the lip of her yoga pants. We did this every Thursday: Weekly Flow. A name that sounded decidedly menstrual to me, but was actually an hour of one-on-one yoga over video chat. Exactly as torturous as you'd imagine.

"Namaste," my mother murmured, her eyes fluttering open. She always smiled at me dreamily through the screen before adding, "The light in me honors the light in you."

Great. Weekly Flow was the only way we kept in touch while I was at school, sixty minutes per week of Camilla bossing my body into various contortions that required zero conversation. But the light in her always honored the light in me, so. There was that.

"I'm going to go," I said, reaching to shut the computer. "Have an exam tomorrow." It was early May, the heat of finals season, and I resented the loss of the last sixty minutes.

"Just a moment." She sat up taller, and I let my hand drop from its grip on my laptop. She had that look—the *I need to tell you something* one. The *This school across the country will be perfect for you* one. The *Maybe spending Christmas with your father makes more sense* one. I bit the inside of my cheek.

"*Letters* is turning twenty-five this year," she said, like her book was a human being. "And they want to do a national tour for the anniversary edition."

The door to my dorm room swung open, and Fallon walked in with an armful of textbooks. *Sorry*, she mouthed, waving a hand at Camilla on-screen. She crept over to her desk, out of sight of the camera, and shot me a *what is it this time* look.

"Congratulations," I said, because it had always been my mother's favorite thing to hear. "I'm sure that'll be great."

"Yes, well." She cleared her throat, smiling in a way that would almost seem nervous if I didn't know her so well. "I'd like for you to come with me."

Over the top of my computer screen, Fallon made a choking noise. Our eyes met across the room, and she screwed up her entire face in a caricature of shock. Because, truly, *excuse me?* I hate surprises. *Hate* surprises from my mother.

"What?" I pulled my legs out of their careful fold. "I'm going to UPenn this summer."

"Well," my mother said, "I wonder if that could wait."

I snorted, laughter licking up my throat like fire. She was the most ridiculous person. The most unreasonable, unthinkably privileged person. Nothing existed outside of her own expectations, and there was nothing the world could do but fall in line.

"No," I said, so sharply that Fallon hunched into herself. "It can't wait, Mom. It's a program for rising freshmen. It has a seven percent acceptance rate. I'm going with Ethan."

"Honey, you're already in at Johns Hopkins."

"And that precludes me from having any other goals?"

"No, but you certainly don't need to spend your whole summer studying. That's what the next four years are for."

I tipped forward, elbow buried between my thighs, to pinch the bridge of my nose. I needed the Penn program—not just to be with Ethan, but to set myself up for the fall. Johns Hopkins Hospital takes one incoming freshman for its fall ICU shadowing position, the most coveted premed placement on campus. I needed Penn on my résumé to land it, but my mother would never understand that, or care. The only way to get her to listen was to frame things through the viewfinder of her own desires.

"Why do you need me there?" I asked flatly, not looking up.

"You're the most important part, honey." I lifted my head, met her pixelated gaze. "On the anniversary of *Letters to My Someday Daughter*, touring live for the first time with my *someday daughter*."

Fallon mimicked vomiting, and for a minute we stared at each other over the computer screen. Being a pawn in my mother's speaking career was nothing new; Camilla had built an entire empire on her *someday daughter*—me. The world thinks we have some idyllic, beatific bond, when the truth is all Camilla actually has time for is running her Saint wellness retreats and curating healing gemstone product lines.

"It'll be wonderful," she continued. "Eight weeks, ten cities, plenty of room to breathe and explore between each one. Like a summerlong vacation."

This pitch was a case in point of how very little she knew me. The last thing I wanted was a summerlong vacation, and the thing I wanted even less than that was a summerlong vacation with her.

"If you're worried about running off course before college begins, I'll hire someone." Her evergreen, tried-and-true solution: just hire someone. "I'll find a professor to tour with us, take you to local hospitals so you can keep learning about medicine."

I was still looking at Fallon, who shook her head in sheer disbelief. *Find a professor?* What did that even mean? People had jobs; they couldn't just pick up everything because she wanted them to.

"And besides." Camilla's voice softened to something almost

vulnerable, and I finally looked back at her. "This summer is our last chance, Audrey." She said this like someone was dying, like there was something sinister at stake. "You'll only get busier from here."

I've been busy, I thought. *So have you.* But then—

"Please," she said. Didn't look away from me. "I want to share this with you."

I felt something shift in me, reluctant and squishy and too shameful to name. She wanted me with her, and I didn't want to need that.

I really didn't want to.

But now, here I am. Alone at the beach, over a month later, and about a million miles away from Fallon.

I'd thought I could do this summer. Thought maybe Camilla had meant it, that flickering moment over video chat: *I want to share this with you.* But it came through last night with full-sun clarity: she only needs *me* to share with *her.* And she only needs me to do it so this tour succeeds.

But I don't explain that to Fallon, because these aren't things I can ever say out loud. Not even to my closest friend, my roommate since the sixth grade. These feelings, at least, get to be mine, and mine alone.

I'm cutting out, I tell her instead. First class at Penn isn't until Wednesday, so I should be able to make it. You packed?

really??? she replies. how did camilla take that?

Then a selfie: Fallon's blunt blonde bob and dreamy expression, flanked on both sides by an airport gate.

packed, she sends. airported. melatonin and benadryl on tap so I can sleep through this interminable flight instead of thinking about how my one precious life is suspended in midair above the atlantic ocean!!!

I smirk, glancing up as a seagull screams overhead. The beach is empty, like it always is, but full of motion: wind shifting loose sand higher up the shore, waves licking at the waterline, tiny mole crabs peeking their domed heads above the dunes. I've spent the last seven years in Colorado, and the whole earth has a different rhythm on the coast.

Commercial planes never crash, I tell her. 1 in 1.2 million chance.

Fallon's going to Uganda for the summer to dig wells and repair critical infrastructure. She'll study civil engineering at Colorado School of Mines in the fall, farther from me than I care to think about. *The Colorado bug bit me,* she said, the day we submitted our applications side by side in the library's cavernous reading room. *No going back to 'Bama now.* Her whole family is in Montgomery: happily married parents, ten-year-old sister, older brother playing football at Auburn.

Fallon replies, 1 chance too many!! and then my phone starts buzzing in earnest. Dad-o, the screen says. But I know he'll only try to talk me out of what I'm about to do—so I send him to voicemail, take one last breath of salt air, and stand to face the imposing edifice of Casa Camilla.

There's a box on the dining room table that wasn't here when I got up this morning, set at one end of the great glass slab with its top cut open. I can hear Mags and my mother talking in the kitchen, their voices drifting toward me like the warning music in a horror movie.

I open the box's top flap to find, no surprise, that everything inside has the Saint logo embossed onto it in bright, unmissable white. The first bubble-wrapped layer is glass water bottles with crystals at their bottoms, no doubt intended to purify your H_2O—as if supergluing a sparkly rock to a jar imbues it with healing powers. I push them aside to get at the small stack of velvety bags beneath, each embroidered in gold Saint stitching and bound by a slim, shimmering rope. When I pull one open I let out an unintentional yelp. It's a vibrator. A Saint-branded, lasciviously matte black vibrator.

"Audrey?" my mother calls. "Is that you, honey?"

I drop the vibrator, pressing my palm to my shorts like it scalded me. "Yeah."

"Would you like to join us for some coffee?"

Boy, would I. I press my eyes shut, quickly count off four fingers, and make for the kitchen.

They're seated next to each other at the island, which is so massive it's more of a continent. Magnolia is forty-five to my mother's fifty-four, but they both look a decade younger, many thanks to the frequent procedures that Camilla calls "treatments." I've known Mags forever; she's been my mother's assistant since the book came out, since all this began, since she was only twenty. She's Camilla's best friend and ultimate groupie. They're only more intimidating when Laz is with them, when their power trio feeds off its own chaotic energy like a pack of circling tiger sharks.

"Good morning." Camilla smiles, and I have to look away. She's in a cream-colored cashmere sweater with short sleeves, already made up in pale pink lipstick and dark mascara. As usual, she seems to glow at me across the room. She's the supernova that everything else falls into. "Do you feel better after a good night's rest?"

I reach for a jar of cold brew on the counter. This is typical: the charmed, chipper tone, like nothing untoward happened last night. When I look at Magnolia, I can tell she's bracing herself for what I might say next.

"Not particularly." I lean against the lower cabinets, take a sip of coffee. We're separated by the white expanse of the island but they're both turned to face me, like this is some kind of tribunal.

"Mmm," my mother hums, a vaguely sympathetic sound. There's a minuscule wooden bowl of salt next to her coffee mug: she's the only person I've ever seen salt their coffee, just another of her incomprehensible habits. "Your energy is a little stiff, I have to say."

I blink. "That's not a thing."

"What isn't?"

I'm—okay. I'm not doing this with her. "You can't read my energy field, Mom, and honestly I just came in here to—"

"Well," she cuts me off, "I'm telling you that I'm reading it right now, and it's stiff."

I wonder why? I nearly snap.

"Maybe you need to take a moment before we leave for the airport," she continues. She lifts a green smoothie to her lips, and I wonder who made it. "For some earthing therapy. Take your shoes off, go walk around in the yard. Ground yourself."

We stare at each other. I grind out, "I've been outside for the last hour." I wouldn't go barefoot through the yard in a million years—what, so the soles of my feet can get covered in crushed ants and grass clippings? I suck in a breath. "And I'm not flying to San Francisco with you."

She looks at Mags, which sends a hot spark of fury up my spine. I barrel ahead. "I need a flight to Philadelphia."

"Why Philadelphia?" Camilla asks.

My turn to look at Mags. "You didn't tell her?"

"There's nothing to tell," Magnolia says. "You were overwhelmed last night, but you'll feel better next time. Always lots of nerves for the first show."

I laugh, a bitter noise that makes me hate myself, hate the person she makes me. "I wasn't nervous. I just don't belong here, doing this. My real life is waiting for me at UPenn, with Ethan, and I need to get there before classes start on Wednesday. You can do the tour without me." I shift the coffee cup in my hands. "You always have before."

"This isn't like before," my mother says. Her fingers are wrapped around the smoothie glass, and she leans toward me on her elbows. "I want this summer to be for us, Audrey. If you're missing Ethan, let's fly him out for a bit. What about the Miami

23

stop, hmm? At the end of July? We can stay awhile, hang out on the beach." She smiles, wiggles her shoulders like we're just a couple of chums, happy dancing together in the kitchen. "Eat some fresh *oysters*?"

One time. *One* time she made me try an oyster and I said I liked it.

"No," I say, pushing away the image of Ethan and me at the beach, reading side by side. A whole summer together is better, cutting across the quad after class, studying in coffee shops when it rains. No. "I'm not doing this. You can't make me."

For a moment, there's silence. I watch her weigh what to say next: I'm eighteen, is the truth. She *can't* make me do this. This isn't like sixth grade, when she flew me to Colorado and left me there. When she made a decision on my behalf and I was powerless to stop it, no choice but to watch her recede across the autumn-dappled quad, my tears blurring the aspens into auburn flames.

I can do the leaving this time. I can be the one to walk away.

The doorbell rings, and all three of us turn toward the front of the house.

"Before you decide," my mother says as Magnolia stands, "I thought you should meet Dr. Stone."

"What?" Mags moves toward the front door, and when it opens, two voices rise to the house's cavernous ceiling. *"Mom."* I'm still wearing what I slept in: pajama shorts and an enormous *Summit School EMS* T-shirt. I haven't brushed my hair. I have my own agenda for this conversation, and it's being grenade-bombed, and before I can say another word Mags is coming back into the kitchen with the woman I've spent weeks reading about on the internet.

"Dr. Sadie Stone," Mags says, gesturing toward her. Dr. Stone is shorter in person than I was expecting. Her headshot on American University's biology department website is unflinching and unreachable, as intimidating as I expected from the youngest professor on campus. She's the bargaining chip my mother used to get me to join this tour in the first place.

"Good morning," Camilla says, smiling at Dr. Stone over her smoothie. "Thanks so much for stopping by."

Dr. Stone says something that sounds like a cross between "of course" and "thank you," a muddled whisper that floats straight up to the ceiling. Her chin is tipped nearly vertical, taking in the house in all its shocking splendor. She has light brown hair swept into a neat bun and wears a pale blue T-shirt with dark jeans. In any other context I'd be tripping over myself at the chance to work with her.

"This is Audrey," Camilla says, a gentle attempt to hook Dr. Stone's attention. "My daughter." They look at each other, and Dr. Stone holds my mother's eyes for just a beat too long before finally turning to me. I watch her compose herself, blinking apart the stunned set of her face. My mother does this to people, traps their attention like a moth to flame. Makes it hard for them to see anybody else.

"Audrey," Dr. Stone says. She extends a hand toward me and I truly cannot believe this is happening while I'm in my pajamas. This woman has published in the *New England Journal of Medicine*. "Sadie. It's so nice to meet you."

"You too," I tell her. Her grip is firm, squeezing my palm tightly before she lets go. "I'm really, um. Honored that you're here. But the truth is—"

"Would you like some coffee?" Magnolia interrupts.

Sadie's gaze flickers between us, tracking the tension in this marble hull of a kitchen. "Yes," she says finally. "Please."

"Mom," I say. Everyone turns to look at me. I don't want to do this in front of Dr. Stone, but there's nowhere else to do it. Our flight leaves in four hours. "I'm not going with you."

My mother draws a breath, her eyes flicking to Dr. Stone. She doesn't want to do this in front of her, either. "Audrey, you can't go to UPenn."

"Yes, I—"

"I already pulled the tuition, honey." She holds my gaze, and the kitchen hazes out around her—like my whole brain has gone static. "Weeks ago, when we scheduled the tour. There's no place for you there." Her voice gets smaller, fades until I can barely hear her at all. "Your place this summer is with us."

6

It's Ethan, in the end, who convinces me to stay. There are only two hours between my conversation with Camilla and our scheduled departure for LAX, and I spend the first one on hold with the Penn admissions office. It's a stilted roulette of *Yes, hi, I'm calling about the Pre-College Biomedical Sciences Intensive* and *Please hold, let me transfer you* and *Yes, I was enrolled, Audrey St. Vrain* and *Not seeing you on the roster, please hold* and *No, wait, I—*

Anyways, my mother was telling the truth. My place at Penn has been filled. *I'm sorry, sweetheart,* someone named Yvette finally told me, her words carrying through the line on a big sigh. *We've already got a wait list two pages long. I can add you to it, but with classes starting in just a couple days . . .*

It didn't occur to me that Camilla would do this, though I realize that was idiotic—wishful thinking I should know so much better than by now. When my mother told me about the tour, I said I'd take care of notifying Penn—which I didn't do, because I wanted to hold my place there for a gigantic and likely-to-come-in-handy "just in case." But she'd circumvented me to seal my fate.

And so I spent my remaining hour pacing the shoreline down

the steps from the house, gaming this out. The one time I glanced up I could see all three of them watching me: Sadie Stone, Magnolia, and my mother standing in a line in the glass-cased living room. I moved closer to the ocean, away from them.

I had the UPenn syllabus pulled up on my phone. The maroon-and-navy logo beamed up at me like a swift kick to the ribs.

WEEK 1: INTRODUCTION TO BIOMEDICAL ETHICS

WEEK 2: GOING CELLULAR—HUMANS AT THE MICRO LEVEL

WEEK 3: NONTRADITIONAL MEDICAL THERAPIES

WEEK 4: EMERGENCY MEDICINE AND TRAUMA

WEEK 5: INFECTIOUS DISEASES—THEIR CAUSES AND CURES

WEEK 6: HUMAN ANATOMY INTENSIVE (CADAVER DISSECTION)

I wanted to reach two-handed into the bright rectangle of my phone and grab on for dear life. *God*, I wanted this. I'd worked so hard for it.

We'll review the readings together every day, Ethan had told me, backpack in his lap as we sat in his parents' car on our way to the Denver airport just a few days ago. *And I can send you my lecture notes and give you the highlights from all the labs.*

Getting the ghost of the Penn program over video chat is better than nothing, but it's not what I want. I want to be where Ethan is. I want to work with professors who *haven't* seen me in my pajamas. I want the summer I planned for.

So I pick up the phone, and I call him.

Ethan answers as a particularly breathy gust of wind buffets the side of my face, and I can barely hear him. "Audrey?"

"Ethan, hi." I turn my back to the sea, pull up the hood of my sweatshirt. "Hey. Can you hear me?"

"Hardly," he says. But even through the wheeze of the ocean,

his voice has the tug of a magnet. He sounds like my real life—
like the version of it that makes sense. "Where are you?"

"At my mom's house," I say. "On the beach. Look, this—"

"What happened last night?"

I hesitate, stare up the sloping lawn. There's definitely a storm
rolling in; the sky's almost the same gray as the house's concrete
exoskeleton. The thing is, Ethan never would have done what I
did at the theater last night—he's a committer down to his toenails,
through to his bones.

In the English class where we met he'd read the entire syllabus
before the semester even started, then reread every book along
with the rest of us. It wasn't because he wanted to be better; it was
because he didn't want to miss a single thing. That's how he does
everything—completely. There are the world's ideals, and then
there are Ethan's. He'd rather not do a thing at all than do it only
halfway, and I don't want to show him the part of me I can't hold
to that standard.

"I just realized that this is wrong," I tell him, not exactly a lie.
"I shouldn't be with her this summer, talking about some self-help
book; I should be at Penn. But I called them this morning and my
place is gone. I won't get off the wait list by Wednesday."

There's a pause. When Ethan speaks again, his voice is clearer,
like he's moved the phone closer to his face. "They didn't hold
your place ahead of applicants who were wait-listed?"

"I know." I rub my forehead, wrap my sweater farther around
myself in the whip of a wind gust. "Camilla pulled the tuition,
apparently, so I'm back in the general pool."

"Okay," Ethan says. His voice is even; in all the time we've
been together I've never seen him upset. "Okay. So it'll have to be

the tour, and studying with Dr. Stone, and we'll talk through the Penn coursework together as we planned."

"Or," I say, drawing a breath, "I could come anyways."

He's quiet. I turn around to squint over the ocean. It looks angry, churning navy and gray.

"What do you mean?" he asks finally.

"I could rent an apartment." It's the plan I've cobbled together while pacing the beach for the last hour. "In Philadelphia. Maybe a long-term vacation rental? I could talk to my dad. And study with you between classes. Go through the coursework together, like you said." I pause, tuck loose hair behind my ear. Swallow. "Or I could stay with you, even."

"What about the ICU shadowing position at Hopkins?" Ethan sounds confused, but his voice is patient. *Help me understand*, he always says. When he's tutoring at the student center. When we're working as EMTs and someone's hurt in a way we can't see. And now, apparently, to me. "Isn't the application due next week?"

"It is," I say.

"If you come here but aren't enrolled at Penn, how will you describe your work this summer?"

I close my eyes, feel the storm wind in my eyelashes, try to breathe around the truth. Which is that he's right, like so many times before. When I don't speak, he keeps going.

"I don't think they'll choose you without something tangible on your application. The physician visits you have planned along the tour with Dr. Stone make more sense—and, I mean, if they'll write you recommendations?" I hear a rustle from his end of the line, picture him reaching for his computer. "I looked into Dr. Stone, too. Did you know she published in the

New England Journal of Medicine? The research coming out of her lab is . . ."

I let his voice wash into the sea, the rising wind. Ethan is the one person in my life who consistently knows what I need and makes sure that I have it. If he thinks I should stay, I should stay.

I open my eyes. Wish for the ocean to swallow me whole.

7

The noise coming from under Silas's seat can only be described as *croaking*. Low, gurgling, somehow both wet and crackling. When I finally rip my gaze from the reading Ethan's sent me to glare at him, he has headphones in and his eyes closed.

"Silas." Magnolia is sitting a few seats past him, Google Calendar pulled up on her tablet. She's not having any of this, either. "*Silas.*"

"Mmm?" He pulls out one earbud and raises his eyebrows at her. The croaking sounds again, melancholically determined, and he jumps a little.

"Oh, shit. Puddles."

Half the people at our gate watch as he doubles over, pulling a soft-sided dog crate from underneath his seat. In all the commotion his phone slips from his lap onto the floor, plane ticket illuminated there on the screen: SILAS ACHESON. The croaking intensifies when he crawls onto the nubby airport carpet and sits cross-legged in front of the crate's zippered flap.

"Hey, girl," he says. His hair's tied back again, mostly hidden under a green baseball cap with *GG's Gardenshare* embroidered on it. He nudges up the brim and unzips the carrier. "We don't need to share our bad attitude with the whole airport, do we?"

With one mollified little croak, a hopelessly wrinkled animal emerges from the bag. It's—um. I watch Silas lift it to his chest and run a hand over its back. Okay, it's a dog. It turns its furrowed face toward me, cloudy gray eyes finding mine from beneath the canopy of a prominent forehead wrinkle.

"Hey," someone says, a pair of white leather sneakers appearing next to Silas. We both look up to find Dr. Stone reaching down to pat the dog, backpack slung over one shoulder.

"Oh, hey," Silas says, glancing at me in the same moment Dr. Stone says, "Have you met—"

They stop simultaneously, looking at me and then at each other, and I realize they were both about to introduce me.

My eyes flick between them. "You know each other?"

Silas glances at Dr. Stone and unfolds himself from the carpet, one hand on the dog and the other held out to steady himself. "Sadie's my bonus mom," he says incomprehensibly, offering absolutely no context.

When he reclaims the seat next to me, she settles on his other side. I'm mortified about how Dr. Stone and I met, especially now that I'm staying on the tour for real, and more mortified still when she says, "I used to look after Silas and his sister when I lived in Michigan."

"Like a babysitter?" I say, and Silas looks at Sadie.

"Sort of," she says, and the dog lets out another rickety yowl that makes me physically recoil.

"It's okay," Silas says, though I can't tell if it's for my benefit or the dog's. He looks up at me. "Puddles has some flight anxiety." She's pressed against his T-shirt, one of her paws half-tucked into its pocket. She's the size of a butternut squash and completely tubular, as rotund at the front as she is at the back. Every inch of her fur is wrinkled. Her squat black face is silvery and solemn-looking, and as we stare each other down she lets out a demure little burp.

"Why?" is all I can think to say.

"Why what?" Silas adjusts the dog against him, leaning back so one of his shoulders bumps mine. I shift in my seat.

"Why did you bring that here?"

"*That?*" Silas repeats, hiking his eyebrows so dramatically he looks like he'll give himself a headache. Next to him, Dr. Stone stifles a laugh. "*She* is my dog."

He says this like it's a complete explanation. But we aren't at a backyard barbecue, we're in the domestic terminal at LAX with twenty minutes until boarding. We're at the start of a two-month book tour. I'm at the end of my rope, and he's going to get all of it.

"Yes," I say, "and *we* are working this summer, so why is it here?"

"First of all," Silas says, turning so we're facing each other, "*it* is a *she*, and her name is Puddles. Second of all, she's eleven, and you can't leave an old lady behind. Third"—he looks down at the dog, rubbing one hand over its grubby head—"she's incredibly polite and you'll barely notice her."

I blink at him. Wild tangle of his hair, hideous rubber hiking sandals strapped to his feet, threadbare T-shirt stretched across his shoulders with a streak of slobber shimmering at the collar. Noisy, vaguely fish-smelling dog already snoring against his chest. *This.* This is what my summer will be.

"Fourth," Silas adds, looking back up at me, "we aren't just working this summer."

"Excuse me?"

That's exactly what we're doing. If I can compartmentalize this summer, file it away how Ethan did—*it's something tangible for your application*—I can get through it. I'm here to learn, to land the ICU position, to stay focused and keep my head down. And Silas should be, too. He's here with two other rising sophomores from American; they all won some media scholarship to staff the tour. Camilla went to American three decades and a full lifetime ago. She likes to *give back to her alma mater* frequently and with as much fanfare as possible. Silas is the videographer; there are two others managing photography and digital media who are running so late I'm concerned they'll miss the flight.

But, no—I'm not concerned. I don't need to concern myself with anything this summer except studying with Dr. Stone. Dr. Stone, who's apparently known Silas since he was a kid.

"I mean, we *are* working," Silas says. "But also seeing the country, right? Eight weeks of travel. I couldn't let Puddles miss out on that."

Eight weeks. Hearing him saying it out loud turns my stomach all over again. San Francisco, Santa Fe, Austin, Chicago, Denver, Nashville, Miami, Boston, DC. And at the end, a pinprick light in a two-month-long tunnel: Baltimore. My life back. It's so bleak—so goddamn *long*—that I can't even respond to him. But Silas, apparently, is happy to carry a conversation all on his own.

"Speaking of working," he says, though I've already turned back to my reading, "where's Camilla?"

"She's hiding." I don't look up. "Probably in the corner of the Starbucks with giant sunglasses on."

"You riding with her in that lush first-class cabin?"

"No."

"No?"

"*No*," I say, finally looking up at him. "I'm reading, okay?"

"Reading what?" He says it so easily, so casually, that ridiculous dog snoring away on his chest like a baked potato.

None of your business, I want to say. Instead, I bite out, "An article."

He nods. "Heard of 'em. What's it about?"

"Is that Puddles I see?" A voice booms through the gate, and we both look up. A short, dark-haired guy in a black Adidas tracksuit is cutting toward us, pushing a silver suitcase in front of him. "My favorite girl?"

The dog starts quivering on Silas's chest, a full-body tremor that makes her nub of a tail jitter so quickly it practically blurs. The guy scoops her away from Silas and holds her up like Simba in *The Lion King*.

"Ravishing," he tells her. "You look absolutely stunning today. There's never been a more beautiful pug."

I'm watching in horror as Puddles licks the guy's entire face—mouth included—when a girl sidles up behind him.

"Hey." She swipes one hand over Puddles's head before dropping into the seat between Dr. Stone and Magnolia. She's taller than the guy and much more angular, wearing black platform boots and a leather minidress. "Cleo," she says, nodding at me across Sadie and Silas. She points up at the guy holding Puddles. "And you've met Mick."

"Oh, sorry," Mick says, finally holding Puddles at a distance so he can see me over her wrinkled head. He's half laughing, his face wet with slobber. "You're Audrey."

"I'm Audrey," I say flatly. When I turn back to my article, Mick takes the hint, brings Puddles with him to sit down. But Silas presses on.

"Why aren't you sitting with her?"

"What?" I look up at him, five shades past exasperated. His T-shirt is covered in dog hair.

"Your mom." This morning's rain has come and gone—a cloud parts outside, sending sun into his eyes. They're so light brown they nearly shine gold, flecked with the same green of his baseball cap. "Why aren't you sitting with her in first class?"

"Would you want to?" It's out of my mouth before I've thought it through. Next to Silas, Dr. Stone looks up at me. "Spend an hour and a half trapped next to her in a hurtling metal tube?"

Silas's eyebrows lift just the tiniest distance. What I don't tell him is I'm the reason we're in this airport at all: if it were up to Camilla, we'd be flying private all summer. But those tiny jets terrify me. The fragility of them, their propensity to fall out of the sky. It was one of my conditions, that we fly commercial, and now my mother has to disguise herself at a public airport. Now I have to field questions about how, no, I don't want to sit next to her in first class.

"Okay," Silas says slowly. "What's the deal with you two? I mean, this feels maybe related to what went down in the alley at—"

"Silas." He glances back at Dr. Stone, who's watching us with an inscrutable look on her face. "There'll be plenty of time to interview Audrey this summer, okay?" She meets my eyes, but I look away. This isn't how I want her to know me—the flustered daughter of a woo-woo celebrity. "Let her breathe."

I can feel Silas look back at me. I stare at the same word in my article until my eyes burn.

"Sure," he says finally. "Yeah, okay."

8

"Sadie Stone and Audrey St. Vrain." Dr. Stone presses the inter-com button with one finger, her chin jutted forward to speak into it. "We're here for Dr. Osman."

There's a crackle of static, a chirped, "Come on in," and then the door buzzes open. It's fifty degrees but clear in San Francisco, and we're standing before a rainbow-painted door on a steeply angled street in Cole Valley. Dr. Stone pulls it open for me and gestures me through.

I glance at her as I step forward. She's wearing a simple black sweater and forest-green barrel pants, her hair wrapped in the same bun as usual. When I met her in the hotel lobby thirty min-utes ago, she was crouched on the floor with Puddles's front paws on her knees, their faces nose to nose. All three interns were there, too: Silas, Mick, Cleo.

"We're going for breakfast," Mick had said, his black hair gelled into an oil-slick wave. "Want to come?"

I was freshly showered, hair still drying over my shoulders, wearing slacks and a button-down. I was carrying the leather briefcase Fallon had given me for my birthday, deep navy with *Audrey St. Vrain: Definitely going to save your life one day* embroidered in pink thread on the inside flap. Couldn't he tell, just from looking at me, that I meant businesses?

"We can't," Dr. Stone said, saving me from responding. "We're meeting a pediatrician this morning."

She stood up, and Puddles leapt at her ankles. The dog got snorty when it was animated, huffing excited breaths through its mashed little face. I took a step backward to keep its slobbery maw away from my pants, and Dr. Stone looked at me. "You ready to go?"

I nodded. I could feel the three of them watching us as we left, and resisted the urge to look back. Magnolia had pushed our next *Letters to My Someday Daughter* show until Friday night "to give Audrey time to recover from her food poisoning," which meant the interns had three days in San Francisco with nothing to do but explore. I, on the other hand, had my first appointment with Dr. Stone and plenty of time with Mags and Camilla to look forward to, going over talking points so I don't bungle the next show like I did in LA.

Now, Dr. Stone and I stand next to each other in the ascending elevator. I clear my throat.

"Dr. Stone, there's dog hair on your pants."

She glances down, brushes at it. This is why dogs don't do it for me: the hair, the smells, the fluids. I'm already in my briefcase, pulling out a pocket-sized lint roller and handing it to her.

"You come prepared." She takes it with a smile. "And please, call me Sadie."

"You can never be too prepared," I say. "I'm, um. Surprised Silas brought the dog on a trip like this."

For a moment there's just the sound of the roller, squeaking faintly. She hands it back to me as the elevator doors slide open, and the distinct smell of Doctor's Office wafts toward us: antiseptic, hand soap, adhesive. I breathe it in, feel my shoulders relax.

"Silas got Puddles when he was fourteen," Sadie says as we step into the hallway. The floors are pale wood, morning sun glancing across them, and our heels tap us toward a door marked *Rainbow Pediatrics*. "It was the year after his mom died, and Puddles was already six. She really needed a home, and Silas really needed a dog." She meets my eyes briefly and reaches for the door handle. "Your mom okayed it."

I feel like I've been put in my place, checked so thoroughly and simultaneously so gently that I can't even muster a response. Silas's dead mother—and my living one, who knew about this and agreed to travel with a pint-sized slobber farm all summer. Silas motherless at fourteen.

"Sadie freaking Stone!"

A woman in a white coat peers over reception at us, arms stretched out like she wants a hug. Sadie beelines for her and they embrace over the desk, swaying back and forth like a slow dance. I hang back, taking in the room: board books on low tables, kid-sized chairs next to parent-sized ones, a tank full of clown fish gurgling beneath the window. And, overshadowing all of it in my brain: Silas with his goofy laugh and his uncomfortable familiarity and no mother.

"I got a shot."

I look down, where a little boy is suddenly standing next to me. He's in a dinosaur-printed T-shirt and khaki shorts, bright red sneakers with Velcro. He thrusts his bicep toward me, white *Star Wars* Band-Aid a highlight against his dark skin. "See?"

"Wow," I say, crouching in front of him. He puts his arm right in my face, so I take his elbow to inspect the Band-Aid. "Did it hurt?"

Our eyes meet and he scrunches up his nose. "Nah. It was like a little pinch."

"You must be brave," I tell him. "I'm so scared of shots."

"Really?" His voice is soft and imprecise in that kid-specific way, so it comes out like *weally?* "I used to be 'fraid but that's when I was four."

"How old are you now?"

"Five," he says proudly. "For my birthday my dad got this huh-*yuuuuuge* balloon that looked like a basketball because at summer camp with Micah we always—"

"Liam, honey." The boy whips around, his arm slipping out of my fingers. A tall man drops a hand onto his shoulder and smiles apologetically at me. "Let's let this nice lady get back to her morning, okay?"

Liam looks at me, smiling shyly as he leans into his dad's legs. "Okay."

"Good job with the shot," I say, offering him a high five as I stand up. He slaps my palm, all enthusiastic energy. "I hope I can be as tough as you next time I get one."

I turn toward Sadie as they leave, find her and the doctor watching me.

"Well," the doctor says. She's smiling, arms crossed, her dark hair pulled back with a knotted pink headband. "That was charming."

I flush. I don't want her to find me charming; I want her to find me impressive.

"My mom always took me for ice cream after shots," Sadie says as I pick my way around the scattered chairs toward reception. "Even if it was nine o'clock in the morning."

I glance at her and don't say what I'm thinking, which is that Camilla doesn't even eat dairy and I can't recall a single time she's taken me for ice cream.

"I'm Audrey," I say instead, reaching a hand over the reception desk. When the doctor takes it, her skin is cool and dry—like every other doctor I've ever met, all my life. I hope mine is, too. "Thanks so much for meeting with me."

"Aiyla Osman," she says. "And happy to. Anything for Sadie, really."

Sadie makes a flattered little noise and the two of them laugh like schoolgirls, which is apparently what they are to each other.

"We were roommates in undergrad," Sadie explains. "Trauma bonded over O-Chem."

"Oh *god*." Dr. Osman leans into the counter as a nurse passes through the hallway behind her, patient folder in one hand. "I wish I could tell twenty-year-old Aiyla she'd get through that class." She gestures around the waiting room. "That she'd be here, one day, doing this."

"Well, I knew it," Sadie says on a smile. "Even then."

Dr. Osman waves her off. "I thought you'd bring Silas." She peers around me, like he might just be coming in from the elevator bay. "Haven't seen that kid since he was, what? Fifteen?"

"Fifteen," Sadie agrees. "At the wedding. He's nineteen now—he'll be a sophomore at American in the fall. He's in the city, but with his friends today."

Dr. Osman shakes her head, her expression gone soft. "All

grown up, huh? Your first baby, practically. It's so great you wound up together in DC."

"Truly," Sadie says. "I'm already campaigning to get Lily out that way, too, and she's only thirteen."

Dr. Osman laughs, and Sadie gestures toward me. "Anyway, Audrey's going to Johns Hopkins in the fall, premed." I swallow, straighten my shoulders. "We're visiting a whole list of practitioners this summer so she can get a feel for different specialties."

"Are you seeing Dustin in Santa Fe?" Dr. Osman asks, still not looking at me. My skin's starting to feel prickly, on the perilous edge of breaking a sweat. On the opposite side of the country, Ethan starts classes at UPenn this afternoon. "Last I heard he's all set up with his own practice at that spa in the desert."

"We sure are," Sadie says, and I can tell she wants to keep talking about this. But, at long last, Dr. Osman catches sight of the clock and drops her hands onto the desk.

"Okay, I've got an appointment in an hour, so we should dive in." Her eyes meet mine, this woman who has everything I want, who's found her way to where I need to go. "Audrey, you ready?"

"I'm ready," I say. I've been standing here like a jangling third wheel, after all. I've been ready this whole entire time. This is the one thing about this summer that I feel ready for.

9

"Did she let you administer a vaccine?"

"What?" I squint through the café window, lift a seven-dollar latte to my lips. "No, Dad, that would've been super unethical."

He laughs, low and breathy. "That's what I remember about seeing the pediatrician—all the shots."

In our hour together, Dr. Osman told me about her patient load, introduced me to her full staff of nurses, talked me through the business of her business—insurance, billing, the logistics underpinning the practice. Sadie sat quietly through it, pressing for more detail only when I asked a question or expressed interest in something specific. It all felt simple and logical and true: a business built to do something helpful. It felt like Dr. Osman and Sadie and *science* existed on a different plane of reality from Camilla and *Letters to My Someday Daughter*. It felt like I could breathe for the first time since I left school.

"When's the last time you saw a doctor?" I ask Dad now.

"Mmmm . . ." He trails off and I picture his eyes turned skyward, trying to conjure the memory. "Probably the last time I went to the pediatrician."

I sigh, forcefully enough that he'll hear it through the phone. It's a constant point of contention; my dad hasn't been to the doctor in years. *Healthy as a horse*, he'll say, flexing at me with his hips angled sideways like a bodybuilder.

"I have you," he says. "My doctor daughter."

"Someday doctor daughter," I correct him, then recoil at my own choice of words. "I mean—"

"Someday daughter, indeed," he says, and my entire body tenses. I walked myself right into this one. "How's your mom doing, mouse?"

Dad is the only person in my life with the leeway to give me a nickname, especially one so cutesy as *mouse*. I earned it at five, when I mostly kept to myself but loved to tiptoe around backstage at Dad's shows, taking it all in. He's been in the music industry my whole life and worked as a tour manager for most of it, always on the road with his musicians. Hence my life with Camilla, the Summit School, Dad always out of the picture when I need him. But he'd called me his *little mouse*, all those years ago when I was living in LA and went to his local shows. The nickname stuck, along with nothing else from my life back then.

"How's my mother doing," I echo back to him. Stalling. "She's, you know. How she is."

"Hmm," Dad says. "She tells me you're avoiding her."

"Does she," I say, not quite as lightly as I intended. My parents' relationship is incomprehensible—they met at a concert and loved each other just long enough to have me, a flash-in-the-pan affair that was over before my first tooth came in. But all these years later they're on the phone twice a week, minimum. Making each other laugh harder than anyone else. Leaning on each other for advice, though their lives share no overlap that isn't named Audrey. Trading stories about me.

I was seven before I realized no one else in my class shared their mother's maiden name; we were making family trees, all grainy construction paper and gummed-up glue sticks. *You entered this world through my birth canal*, Camilla said when I asked her about it. I held up my tree like the evidence of a crime. *Not his.* So I was Audrey St. Vrain, my mother's daughter by name—instead of Audrey Ames, my father's. And he just let her have it.

Their respect for each other is a smooth-faced wall I'm always butting up against, no toeholds for me to grip on to and climb over. Even if I wanted to complain about Camilla to my dad, I couldn't. He loves me more than anything, I know. But, inexplicably, he loves her, too.

"She does," he says now. "I know you don't always see it, mouse, but she wants to spend time with you."

Doing what? I think. Is she going to quiz me on the terminology from today's biomedical ethics seminar at Penn? Is she going to comb through Ethan's notes for me, highlight the concepts I want to come back to later? Of course not. The only way for us to spend time together is for me to twist myself to fit where she wants me. To contort until I'm unrecognizable.

"For me," Dad says, when I still haven't responded. "If nothing else. Will you just try, for me?"

"Why does it matter?" I ask. A woman looks up from the table next to me, and I lower my voice. "Why does it matter to you how I get through this summer with her?"

"Because I love you," he says, and I have to close my eyes. It makes me squirmy, how quick he always is to say it, the open flow of his feelings. "And I want her to know you the way I do."

"I don't think she wants to," I say quietly.

The space between Camilla and me has calcified so solid over the years that it's nearly opaque. Any time I try to peer through, it obscures everything I know about myself. Back in Colorado, I knew exactly what was important to me. Exactly who I was. But when I come near my mother, I suddenly can't communicate any of those things—I feel myself folding up into her orbit like a circling star, overshadowed by her light like everybody else.

"She does, Audrey. Of course she does."

I take a sip of coffee and don't tell him what I'm thinking, which is that I want a mother who makes me feel the opposite of this. And that it hurts like a needle hitting bone to know I'll never have her.

"Besides," Dad says. "This isn't forever, mouse. You aren't stuck; it's just a summer."

"Right." I stare out the window, watch the café's potted hydrangeas waver in the wind. "It's just a summer."

10

They style the stage in San Francisco like a living room: woven rug, performatively cozy seating, lamps that trap us in a softly glowing circle. My mother sits next to me holding a mug of Saint-branded magnesium tea. I've sunk so deeply into this couch that I'm practically peering at the audience over my knees.

A stack of *Letters to My Someday Daughter* hardcovers sits on the coffee table between us and the moderator, their jackets proudly sporting a photo from my fourth birthday. In it, my cheeks are lit by birthday candles and I'm leaning face-first over a chocolate cake. Camilla smiles in the corner of the shot, her face looming larger than mine. I spend the first ten minutes of the show staring at my younger self, frozen there at four years old.

"The question isn't, *How much kindness do I deserve?*" Camilla is saying. "It's, *Where did I get the idea that kindness should be meted out?*" She looks at the moderator, lets her words land. "There is no bank. It's not a debit system." When her hand drifts over to me, brushing my kneecap, I fight the urge to flinch. "And when we upend our thought patterns—imagine that, instead of speaking to ourselves, we're speaking to someone we love like a daughter—kindness feels like a different type of currency entirely. It doesn't feel like a currency at all." She looks at me, and I force myself to smile. We started the entire evening with a slideshow of our relationship, a tense twenty minutes of questions about our mother-daughter bond that made me feel like I was gaslighting myself. *Of course it's empowering to have such a strong woman as my role model. Of course I'm grateful to have a mother who teaches me self-care.*

"There is no kindness you wouldn't extend to your child," Camilla says. "There should be no kindness you won't extend to yourself."

Applause. I think of Liam from the doctor's office, his little bicep thrust toward me in the waiting room. Of the calm I felt standing in Dr. Osman's supply closet, surrounded by boxes of nitrile gloves and hypodermic needles. How all that made perfect sense, and how Camilla sounds like she's speaking in tongues.

"That's so interesting," the moderator says. She's a psychology student at UCSF and won some contest to be here, doing this. She's misty-eyed at her prize, responding to everything Camilla says with the kind of awe usually reserved for marriage proposals and the northern lights. "We do think of it that way, don't we? Like we'll be sacrificing something else—going into some kind of red—if we go too easy on ourselves."

My mother nods deeply. "It's such a hard thing, to go easy. There's a reason every Inner Saint retreat begins with what we call *The Great Unclenching*." She spreads her fingers in front of her and demonstrates drawing a deep breath. She speaks again on the exhale: "An entire day dedicated to letting go. Going easy."

I have no idea what to look at. Magnolia told me during the insufferable hour we spent preparing for this that I couldn't look at my hands, that I couldn't make eye contact with the audience, that I couldn't stare off into space. But I absolutely can't look at Camilla while she embarrasses us both like this. So as the moderator prattles on, my eyes rove across the stage—to the giant poster-board sign with both our faces on it, to the intricate water carafe set on a glass table for no discernible reason, to the X taped to the floor for the book signing line that'll drain what little remains of my sanity.

And, in the shadowy folds of the stage curtains, to Magnolia—holding a clipboard and watching me like a hawk. I can just see Silas behind her, video camera propped on a tripod in front of him. He's studying its little screen, half his face obscured, but when he catches me watching him, his lips split crookedly into a smile.

"And with that, we'll take some questions from the audience."

The house lights go up, and I blink into the sudden sea of faces staring back at us. Women, almost entirely, holding their copies of *Letters* and far too many crumpled tissues. Who's crying? Why is anybody crying?

"In the blue dress," I hear my mother say, and register that she's stood up next to me, that she's holding a microphone. "With the baby."

A woman in the front row points to herself, eyebrows raised. She's holding what looks like a newborn, half her chest covered in a duck-patterned blanket.

"Yes," Camilla says. "You, mama."

My mind goes full Pinterest board: *Mama bear. Mama bird. You got this, mama.*

"Hi," the woman says. She stands slowly, like she's trying not to alert her baby to the fact that they're on the move. "I mean, thank you, first. Thank you for being here."

My mother reaches down to rest her hand on my shoulder, and I sit up taller. It's showtime, apparently.

"This is my someday daughter," the woman says, turning a little so we can see the side of her baby's face. "And she's already changed everything for me, you know."

"I do," Camilla says, and my whole body clenches. Maybe I could use a quick *Great Unclenching* myself, whatever the hell that means.

The woman continues: "I might be a little different from the other gals here, because I didn't read your book for the first time until a couple years ago. When I saw the Sex Summit story."

I'm not sure if a hush actually falls over the audience or if my entire brain just fuzzes out. But the world goes quiet—like I'm trapped inside a cotton ball, like I'm immobilized and mute. Camilla's hand doesn't move from my shoulder.

"That story just—well, it *moved* me," the woman says. "Seeing that bond between you and Audrey; your openness and intimacy. It's what I want to create with my daughter. And I was hoping you might be able to tell us more about that weekend and what it meant for you—especially for you, Audrey."

Silence. The woman and I stare at each other. My throat feels like it's stuffed with pipe cleaners, somehow both furry and sharp.

"What it meant for me," I repeat. All five of my mother's fingertips press into my shoulder. I glance at Magnolia, whose eyes are wide and afraid. No one here—not a single person in this entire auditorium—can ever know what that weekend meant for me.

11

The media called it the Sex Summit. They wasted no time giving it a cute nickname, a moniker so charming it felt ghoulish. There was nothing cute about that weekend, about the way everything went down—but the photos leaked to the press (by who? My money's on Magnolia) were irresistible.

Picture it: a standard-issue dormitory hallway, its concrete-brick walls, its scuffed laminate floors. Each side lined in sixteen-year-old girls, most of them wearing pajamas. Hair in topknots, makeup headbands slipped over foreheads, fuzzy slippers jutting into the aisle. And at the end of the hall, just outside the door to my room: Camilla St. Vrain, celebrity psychotherapist turned wellness empress, holding an oversized poster diagramming female sexual anatomy.

The Summit School wasn't religious anymore, but it had been. There were still a few tortoises on the school board, bow-tied old men who kept sex ed out of our classrooms. My mother was fresh off a talk show appearance that she'd ended by admitting to wearing a rose quartz yoni egg for the entirety of the interview—rose quartz, she informed everyone, because it opens the heart chakra to self-love. Saint had started selling "love and intimacy" products six months before. The yoni egg stunt cemented her status as a guru of sexual pleasure and well-being.

So I shouldn't have been surprised, I guess, that when she showed up on my dorm hall in the spring of my sophomore year, people had questions. Enough of the girls on my hall cornered her to ask for advice that she took matters into her own perfectly manicured hands. I stumbled out of bed, bleary-eyed from a starved and sleepless week, to find her posted up like that with the diagram. Talking about the clitoris like it was a word we normally threw around with casual abandon.

The school was furious. There were letters sent to parents, meetings with the headmaster, assumptions that I'd asked for this. At one point I thought I'd be expelled, but when the media caught wind of the story, the Summit School came under so much fire for their arcane lack of sexual education—in a liberal city in a blue state, no less—that they had no choice but to let me stay.

Camilla emerged looking like a hero. *Letters to My Someday Daughter* hit the bestseller list again for the first time in years. The narrative was clear: Camilla St. Vrain, liberated feminist icon, swooped in to save her daughter and all her daughter's friends from conservative sexual repression. Camilla St. Vrain thought that, if you were going to be having sex at sixteen, you should definitely be having orgasms. Not only that, she'd tell you how to make it happen.

Could Audrey St. Vrain possibly have a cooler mom?

No one thought to ask the only question actually worth asking, which was why had Camilla St. Vrain showed up at the Summit School in the first place, smack-dab in the middle of the semester?

It wasn't because I wanted a sexual education from her, I'll tell you that much. The answer was simpler and worse: I'd become a problem nobody knew how to solve.

By the time I was sixteen I'd lived at the Summit School for five years—it was more of a home to me than anyplace had ever been. While my role in Camilla's life had always felt complex, my role at school was simple: I was the smartest. I didn't score below a 98 on an assignment from the moment I set foot on Colorado soil. That school was my home and my family and my identity; somewhere I could rise. Then I got to second-semester chemistry, and everything changed.

The coursework was simple: the periodic table, conversions, atomic electron configurations. Then spring rolled around and suddenly we had labs. Hands-on. Science in practice instead of in theory. In the quiet of my dorm and the familiar rooms of my own mind, it all made perfect sense. I could walk through each part of the lab in advance, knowing exactly how to perform its reactions. And then I'd set foot in Mrs. Barclay's classroom, lean over the black lab counter, and become someone else entirely. My fear of getting it wrong ate me alive from the inside, hollowing me until my observations were off, until my reactions unfolded incorrectly, until my pipetting hand was dangerously unsteady. I felt sweaty and conspicuous, like each time I made a mistake I grew three inches until I took up the entire room, until all anyone could see was the enormity of my failure.

It was the first time I'd needed to apply knowledge in the physical world, and the pressure of not messing it up ensured that I did, every single time. How the hell was I going to be a doctor, I berated myself, if I couldn't excel at a tenth-grade chemistry lab?

My lab grade that semester was like a downward staircase: every assignment took me further into the dark and shameful basement of myself. The only saving grace was that 70 percent of our chemistry grade came from written work and exams. Only 30 percent of me was drowning. But then Mrs. Barclay assigned lab demonstrations for our midterms—my absolute nightmare. I'd have to stand in front of my entire class and fail in real time. No one would be focused on their own reactions; they'd all be focused on mine, and I'd have to admit what a fraud I'd turned out to be.

The panic came on slowly—nagging headaches and aching joints—and then, in the days leading up to the midterm, all at once. Two days before I was scheduled for my lab demo, I stopped getting out of bed. It wasn't a choice; it was a paralysis. A curtain falling, a twisted root growing from the base of my brain stem and binding me to my bed frame. It's not even that I was sleeping—I couldn't rest, couldn't think, couldn't eat. I could only sit still and try to swallow the endless wail that had taken over every part of me. My body was a wince; I was made of fear and failure.

I missed the midterm, obviously. I missed three days of classes before Fallon finally called my mother. I remember barely anything from that week, but I do remember the way her voice sounded, like she knew she was betraying me. *I'm so sorry, Audrey,* when I looked at her as Camilla walked unannounced into our room. *I didn't know what else to do.*

My mother got me to the counseling center, where a bespectacled therapist asked in a humiliatingly sympathetic voice if I'd ever talked to anyone about my anxiety before. But I wasn't anxious; I was possessed. Something had stolen into me, but after days of being paralyzed by it I'd developed the necessary antibodies. Now it was gone. I explained this to her.

"Audrey," she said, and I remember thinking how strange it was for her to use my name, for us to know one another at all. "Why do you think you chose that word? 'Possessed'?"

I blinked at her. Why did anyone choose any word? Words were just words, empty vessels. In my silence, she kept on—eyes gentle but unwavering on mine.

"I wonder if it's to create distance," she said. "To separate yourself from this feeling—to other it, instead of accepting it as a part of yourself."

I stood, then. Because she didn't understand; she wasn't listening to me. This entire experience had been *other*. It wasn't part of me; it was something happening to me that I would never allow to happen again. As I walked toward the door she recommended that I come back to see her and I did not.

Camilla coordinated with the school and Mrs. Barclay so that I could make up my midterm with a written assignment. She didn't address how she'd found me, or what I'd done. When I finally fell asleep after a week of eye-clawing insomnia, she posted up in the common room at the end of my dorm hallway and taught every girl I lived with about consent and pleasure.

And that became the story of her visit. That became the Sex Summit. That became a cornerstone in the public lore of our relationship; the infamous Colorado weekend Camilla spent with her *someday daughter*. She leaned right into all of it, playing it up as the wackiest time of our lives, when in reality I'd never been so scared.

In the span of just a few days, the world had come to know me as someone in tune with herself, someone who could talk openly about sex, someone absolutely comfortable being emotional with her mother. The few discerning people who asked why I wasn't actually in any of the photos from that weekend were brushed off like water from a duck's back. *Audrey doesn't like to be photographed*, Camilla said, instead of telling the truth. *And I, of course, respect her right to privacy.* In reality I had been trapped, alone, inside myself. But we both played into what the world thought me to be after that.

It was clear that what I'd done was something to be covered up. A shame too terrible to name. Camilla thought that there was something wrong with me, and we would hide it. I knew then that as long as I was the best—as long as I was smart and successful and well-adjusted—there would never be a moment like this again.

I doubled down on school, on college research, on all of it. I signed up for the Summit School's student EMT program the minute I turned eighteen. I bandaged cooking burns and stabilized broken ankles and wrung every fear of performing out of my body. I proved to myself that I was, after all, the person I knew myself to be.

Camilla and I never spoke of that weekend again.

12

how badly do we feel about kidnapping on a scale
from one to ten

Fallon sends the text as we're walking into the hotel lobby after the
show, and a selfie pings through right behind it. It's early morning
where she is. She's grinning in the photo with her cheek pressed
against a little girl's; they both have mango rind over their teeth,
so their smiles are mottled red and orange. The background's all
rust-colored sand and baobab trees, pale morning sun.

because this child is the best friend i've ever had no
offense to you

That child has parents!! I send back, and the typing bubble
appears immediately.

maybe *they'd* adopt *me* then? would you
visit me in uganda?

I'll literally come right now.

that bad, huh? food poisoning again?

Something like that.

Camilla spared me from responding to the Sex Summit lady; her laugh was charming as twinkle lights as she told the audience how embarrassing it is for me to talk about intimacy in front of my mother. "Just look at her blushing," she said, though what was happening with my face felt more like arson than a blush.

"That weekend was really about bodily autonomy," Camilla went on. "Our teenagers deserve to know themselves, to understand their bodies and their pleasure. As mothers we can make those things taboo, or we can face the facts: our babies are going to have sex. I know, I know!" Laughs and shouts of mock horror, Camilla's conspiratorial little smile. "It might not be today, it might not be tomorrow, but it's going to happen someday. And we're all better off when we create safe spaces for them to talk about it, instead of shrouding the topic in fear."

And I just sat there, trapped. Unable to run away this time, as she treated me like the subject of a lesson plan rather than a live human being.

The rest of the show had been softball questions: Did Camilla have any new books planned? (never say never!); if you could only make it to one of Saint's quarterly retreats, which one was best? (Aspen in October); did I plan to follow in my mother's footsteps and pursue a counseling degree? (no). Then there was the endless signing line, my scribbled name on the title page of *Letters to My Someday Daughter* alongside my mother's. It was nearly ten when we left the theater.

ok well you know you can tell me, Fallon says now. even if it's pukey

I know. I send her a white heart emoji, but the truth is I don't want to get into it. I know both of us remember what actually went down during the Sex Summit all too well, but it's not something we talk about. My embarrassment lives inside me like a sleeping beast; if I don't look at it, don't wake it up, don't remind it of its hunger, I can keep it at bay. But talking about what happened back then—what I put her through, and the spectacular depth of my failure—wakes it right up. Gnashing and feral and ready to devour me.

also we had inflight wifi, she sends, and I googled dr. stone on the way over here. did you know the lab she works in is the only one in the US dedicated to endo research? know we were *not* about cam's plans for you this summer but that lady is a certified badass

Of course I know. I spent the week before committing to this tour searching for Sadie Stone like a truffle pig. I sniffed her out everywhere she existed to be sniffed out. I read her paper in the *New England Journal of Medicine* about her lab's first-of-its-kind research to find a long-term therapy for endometriosis. I read all her reviews on American University's RateMyProfessor page. I even watched a YouTube video of her crossing the stage at her undergrad graduation. It appeared to have been uploaded by her dad and had seven total views.

Sadie Stone *is* a certified badass. And when she files into the lobby behind us, casting a wave and a *good night* over one shoulder, I realize that she has a copy of *Letters to My Someday Daughter* tucked under her arm. It's one of the new hardcovers, wrapped in that photo of Camilla and me. Why would she, a credible scientist, ever want to read something like *Letters*?

"Hey, we're going to the Haight."

I blink away from Sadie to find Mick standing right in front of me, hand stretched out like he was about to jostle my arm to get my attention. He lets it fall to his side.

"Walk around, maybe grab some drinks." He jerks a thumb toward Silas and Cleo, who are standing a few feet behind him playing a complicated hand-clapping game that looks like it's meant for third graders at summer camp. Silas messes it up, laughing loudly, and Cleo bops him on the side of the head. "You wanna join?"

He's watching me expectantly, all olive skin and dark eyebrows, black hair slicked back. For just a moment I let myself imagine it: walking unfamiliar streets in a city I've never been to, the evening cool and dark, taking a few hours' vacation from my life into theirs. But Ethan stayed up so I could call him about today's Penn lecture. None of us are even twenty-one. And, of course, the plainest truth of the matter: I don't do things like this.

"No," I say. I draw a breath, tuck my phone back into my pocket. "I have some work I need to do."

"Work?" Mick says, halfway to laughter. "On a Friday night in June?"

Silas and Cleo look over at us, drawn by his laugh.

"Yes," I say, and even I can hear how defensive it sounds. "I'm not going to waste my summer."

"Waste it?" Cleo echoes, her voice rising in the stone-floored lobby. She takes a step closer to us; her eyeliner is neon, painted in flares around her eyelids. Everything about her is sharp and crackling. "By having some fun?"

"Cleo." Silas nudges her elbow, glancing at me and then away. "If she doesn't want to come, she doesn't want to come. It'll be what it'll be."

"I'm just saying," Cleo says. "Shame to spend your last childhood summer studying."

But that's not what this is—not really. I can't remember the last time I felt like a child.

"Come on, Mick." Cleo wraps one green-nailed hand around his wrist and tugs. "You tried."

Mick lifts a hand in my direction as she shepherds him into the night. When Silas makes to follow them, he glances up at me, just briefly, before they're gone.

13

I watch my reflection the whole way up to my hotel room, my face distorted in the elevator's polished metal doors. I feel more like that Audrey than this flesh-and-bone one: blurred out, misshapen, being carried upward by forces beyond my control.

Can I call?

Ethan, prompt as a stopwatch. It's ten thirty on the dot, our scheduled video call time even though it's one thirty in the morning where he is. He sleeps less than anyone I know and works twice as hard in his waking hours.

Let me just get to my computer, I send. The elevator pings open and I pad down the silent hallway, key into my room. It's dark and empty, just my black suitcase waiting for me at the foot of the bed. Camilla offered to share rooms this summer, like maybe I was still six and afraid to be alone. But I grew into my solitude long ago—its reliability, the way no surprises waited for me there. Still, the room strikes me immediately as sad. I open my laptop so I don't have to think about why.

"Nice dress," Ethan says when he appears on the screen.

I glance down at myself: pale jeans and a white blouse, all

pleats and frills. Its shoulders are so ruffled I look like I'm drowning in them.

"It's a shirt." I try to smooth down the ruffles and watch them bounce right back into place on-screen. "Magnolia picked all these clothes that make me look like I'm going to my first communion or something."

"I think you look nice," Ethan says. He's in a dimly lit dorm room, face cast pale blue by his computer. "Different."

Different, certainly. I draw a breath. "Anyway, how was today?"

"Today," Ethan says, and dips his head to rifle through a notebook. "Today was . . . *ethical.*" He glances up. "You have the textbook, right? Page thirty-four is a good place to start. The biomedical ethics professor is this man Oscar Velasquez, he used to be the head of—oh, hey, wait."

Our eyes meet through the screen and for a moment I think I know what's coming: *How was the show? How are you holding up? Are you going to be okay all summer when you feel this alone?*

But Ethan says, "Did you submit your application for the Hopkins Hospital shadowing position?"

And it's a relief, really. To not have to talk about it. I nod at him and swallow it all down: the woman in the crowd who dredged up my worst memory without knowing, the fraudulent sheen Camilla's shellacked over my entire life, the desperate way I wish I were there instead of here.

"I did," I tell him. I submitted it yesterday, my plans with Sadie mapped out city by city like the best version of what this summer's supposed to be. The version that doesn't feel at all, so far, like what it actually is. "All set."

There's a whoop outside my door, distinctly Silas, and for a split second I think the interns have come back for me. But then I hear Cleo, farther away like she's waiting by the elevator: "Hurry up, dumbass!" And Silas's singsong reply: "I just forgot her bedtime meds! I'll be so quick."

The door next to mine opens and thuds shut. If I hadn't heard it at the airport I wouldn't recognize Silas's Puddles voice, but it comes unquestionably toward me through the wall that separates us.

"Audrey?"

I turn back to Ethan, blinking.

"When will you hear back?"

"Oh." I pull up the email from Hopkins, though I know the date by heart. "July sixteenth. About a month."

"You'll get it," he says, and I smile. "Of course you will." He slides his textbook toward him so I can see its bottom corner on the desk. "Okay, so page thirty-four . . ."

It's nearly midnight when Ethan finishes walking me through the lecture. He yawns, wide and wild as a lion cub, and it makes me want to crawl into the screen to get to him. Our visit in Miami isn't close enough—still six weeks and as many cities away. *I'm going to get some sleep*, he says. *I love you*, he doesn't. But I know this is how Ethan loves me: staying up until three a.m. so I don't feel like I'm missing out. Bookending my horrible day with steadfast reminders of my real life. His familiar, yawning face.

But then he's gone, and my screen goes black, and there I am again. Reflected back at myself. I blink and shut the computer.

When I slide it into my backpack, I feel a soft rectangle at the bottom of the bag. I pull out the used copy of *Letters* I bought at the Denver airport and for a moment we just stare at each other, quiet. The AC kicks on in the corner of the room.

To her, the book's dedication says. Two words my mother always claims to have written for me, though I didn't exist for seven more years after she wrote them. *But I've always known you*, she'll say, *in a way*.

I take the tattered book into bed, pushing back the starchy sheets and sinking into the pile of pillows. My shoulder ruffles shimmy up around my face and I shove them back down.

I flip to page one and wonder, briefly, if Sadie Stone is reading these same pages in this same moment in her room down the hall. Then I resign myself to it. It's not like this is anything new for me, like I don't always find myself here.

Reading the opening pages of *Letters to My Someday Daughter* is like reciting a nursery rhyme I learned as a child. That's how well I know it, like it developed as part of me and grew with my brain. I've read the book too many times to count: sometimes when I'm spiteful, sometimes when I'm sad, sometimes just to feel like I maybe understand my mother.

I have a lot of bad habits when it comes to her, bred from something dark and masochistic inside me. The airport bookstores, the rereadings, the therapy reviews.

Camilla hasn't been a practicing psychotherapist since a few years after *Letters* was published, when the fame and the money took her away from treatment. But the internet holds the proof. There's a collection of patient reviews from a now-defunct website that I have saved in a folder on my desktop labeled *First Semester Syllabi*. I pull it up when I feel my worst, even though it only ever pushes me lower.

I glance up from the book, eye the edge of my laptop across the room. I could pull it up now, even. No one would know to stop me.

There are a dozen reviews waiting for me in that folder. Maybe five that actually say much of anything. But I have a favorite: Bobbi from Silver Lake.

I know this seems crazy to say, she'd written. I can imagine her voice exactly: bubbly and sincere, Bobbi with an *i*. *But Camilla's like the mother I always wished I had.*

SANTA FE

14

I thought Camilla would grant a pause on Weekly Flow this summer, considering we're spending all our waking moments together, but I was wrong.

What's happening on the hotel rooftop honestly looks like some kind of cult. The mornings in Santa Fe are clear and crisp, 0 percent humidity and not too hot while the sun's still low in the sky. We're staying in a hotel right on the plaza and Camilla has the entire rooftop rented out—between potted cacti in tiled planters and pergolas webbed with string lights, the space is absolutely crawling with Saint-branded paraphernalia.

Lilac yoga mats spaced at perfectly even intervals. Foam blocks set just so at the top of each mat. Rolled towels and crystal-at-the-bottom water bottles in every mat's upper right corner.

I am, intentionally, the last one to arrive. Sadie and the interns have claimed all the mats in the second of two rows, which leaves my mother and Magnolia at the front—and the only available mat is the one right next to Camilla. She waves me over and I quickly count off four fingers before crossing the terrace.

"Morning, honey!" she calls, light and breezy as a song. "Saved you the best seat in the house."

I force a smile as Mick says, "I think Puddles has the best seat."

She's curled into a round, fuzzy dog bed at the edge of the terrace—completely shaded and already snoring. Beyond her, New Mexico spreads hilly and red under a spotless blue sky.

"How'd you land on the name?" Mags asks. I look over at her as I lower myself onto my mat. She's wearing Saint gear from head to toe and has her meticulously highlighted hair swept into a ponytail. "It suits her."

"She *is* kind of melty," Cleo says, pulling at her cheeks to mimic Puddles's bountiful wrinkles. "She came with it, right, Si?"

Silas has his legs stretched out in front of him, big hands wrapped around his feet. He's wearing gym shorts and a faded *American University Film & Media* T-shirt, that same *GG's Gardenshare* baseball cap.

"She did," he says, eyes on Puddles. "How could I change it? Look her at face."

"One big puddle," Cleo agrees. "It's apt."

"Speaking of apt names," Mick says, and Cleo groans so loudly Puddles cracks an eye open.

"Don't start, Mick." Cleo tips her whole head back. "We *know*."

"Audrey doesn't," Mick says defensively, gesturing at me. "Neither do Ms. St. Vrain and Magnolia."

"Mick's last name is Selinofoto—" Silas starts, and Mick shoves him in the shoulder.

"Steal my thunder!"

"—which means 'moonlight.'"

Mick grins wide as the horizon, raising his eyebrows at me. "Huh?" He gestures broadly with both arms. "Not bad, right?"

"I'm truly stunned this hasn't already come up," Cleo says,

adjusting her neon-yellow headband. "It's the first thing he tells any attractive person. Ever. Every time."

Mick and I flush in unison, and I get busy unrolling my yoga towel. For what, I don't know. What are yoga towels supposed to be used for?

"*Audrey* means 'noble strength,'" Camilla says, and I stop towel-fluffing to look up at her. She's sitting cross-legged on the center of her mat, her shoulders set straight. I can see the freckles on them from here, mirrors of my own. "Apt, too, I think."

The smile she gives me is small and quiet. It feels distinctly like an olive branch, though I have no idea what I'm supposed to take away from her pronouncing my noble strength in front of the whole group. She saw my strength fail, and she covered it up, and she covered it up again during the show in San Francisco. She opens her mouth to say something else, but Silas beats her to it.

"My mom chose my name for its meaning, too." Sadie is watching him, her expression a mix of sympathy and pride. I think of what he said at LAX—*Sadie's my bonus mom*—and the way Dr. Osman talked about him, like he was Sadie's own kid. "It means 'forest.'"

"I didn't know that," Cleo says, extending an arm to brush his knee with her fingers. They smile at each other, something so intimate passing between them that I have to look away. "Mine's short for Clementine, but I'm pretty sure my parents just like the fruit."

"Oh, I love clementines," Magnolia says, the answer to a question I'm sure everyone was dying to ask. "So much more accessible than an orange."

"So much more accessible," my mother agrees, in a tone that

means *we're going to move on now.* "Is everyone ready to breathe into their body?"

I hear Cleo's whispered voice, watch her shadow move into Silas's on the pale stone terrace. "So much more accessible," she says, but if Silas laughs, I don't hear it.

"Let's close our eyes," my mother says, and as everyone else follows her command I leave mine open. When Silas rests his palms on his knees, Puddles waddles out of her bed and moseys up to the front of his mat, helping herself to the foam block and propping her chin on it like it's a pillow. She collapses to the ground with a grunt, and Silas opens his eyes. He smiles down at her and then, like he can feel me watching, looks up at me.

"Breathe in through your nose," Camilla says, and we keep looking at each other. "Out through your mouth."

Silas smiles. It's crooked and goofy, everything about him like a gasket that fits just a little too loose.

"Let's find our centers," she continues, and he points to his stomach. Then he points to Puddles's. "Breathe deeply, letting your belly expand with every inhale."

We're still looking at each other—the only living things on this rooftop with our eyes open—when my mother says, "Let's center ourselves before tonight's show. Let's become grounded in our bodies so we don't feel the urge to flee, or to clam up when the moment calls for our presence."

I press my eyes shut, cheeks flaming. She's calling me out, barely any coding to it, right here in front of everyone. I can't believe her—except that of course I can. This is the story of our whole entire relationship: there is the outward language, and there is the subtext.

I know Silas is still watching me, but I keep my eyelids pressed shut and hope the darkness behind them will swallow me alive.

"Let's honor our own wholeness," my mother says. And one last drive of the knife: "Let's remember who's relying on us to show up tonight, just as we are."

So I show up as I am. And I am raging.

Because when Camilla says "as we are," she means: Camilla St. Vrain, beloved wellness guru, and her doting, openhearted, here-for-the-psychobabble daughter. She means: let's show the world how perfect it is, up here where we sit. She means: let's preach about self-love when we can't even be honest about the broken way we love each other.

But that's not as we are. We are as unknown to each other as two people can be. I know the freckles on my mother's shoulders and the blue of her eyes and all the parts of her that are mine. But I don't know what that book dedication means—*To her*—and I don't know why she brought me here.

There was no *her* named Audrey back then. There is no part of me she knows well enough to speak to unless it's in a social media caption. I realize, sitting under the stage lights in yet another floral dress, that I didn't say a single word to anyone during this morning's yoga session. That I've let all of this happen to me; that I've been letting Camilla just *happen* to me for my entire life.

"Audrey," the moderator says. We're at a packed theater dripping in Spanish tile. It's the most beautiful space I've ever been in, and the last place that deserves my anger. But it's where I am. As I am. "What's it been like for you to be a part of the *Letters* tour so far? To join this movement publicly for the first time?"

I look at Camilla before I say it, think of her big inhale in her Saint-logo'd yoga outfit, imagine how it felt walking out of my dorm room sophomore year to find her in that hallway, turning the worst time of my life into a publicity stunt. I look back at the moderator. I show up as we are.

"It's been absolutely horrible."

The truth is like a free fall: for a moment there's nothing to hold on to, just the euphoric rush before the concrete rises up. Saying it out loud feels like releasing a dam in my chest. Everything rushes out, wrathful, a relief.

Behind the moderator's astonished expression I see Silas at the edge of the stage, camera in front of him. He ducks out from behind it to look at me, his lips parted in surprise. Cleo and Mick stand in the half-dark just past him, but I don't have time to clock their reactions before my mother's hand falls to my wrist. Her laugh is like wind chimes, warning of a coming storm.

"Oh, Audrey, honestly." She smiles at the moderator, at her adoring fans. "She doesn't mean that. She means—"

"I do mean that."

We look at each other, and it's like I'm watching her scramble, play catch-up, figure out how to fix me.

In the held-breath pause, I keep talking. "I had plans for this summer, but instead I'm 'joining this movement publicly.'"

"The public piece is hard," my mother says slowly, her eyes still on mine. I watch the shift: something in what I've said has given her an idea, and she's turning this around. She faces the moderator.

"There's a big difference between living a private life and suddenly feeling like a public figure. We're human, too." Her hand is still on my wrist, and she squeezes it. "This is Audrey's first experience with the blurring of that line, the careful tightrope walk of a public life when we are all inherently private people."

This isn't my first experience—it's not even close to my first experience. My first experience happened before I could form memories, when my baby picture racked up over a million likes on her social profiles. My second was a day after that. All my others in all the years that followed. My whole life has been a careful tightrope walk that I'm one swift breeze from toppling off of.

But Camilla built the tightrope herself, and nothing I can do, it's clear, is enough to knock her off-balance. She's already running at full steam, regaling her audience with a psychotherapeutic exploration of what it means for us to have public and private personas. She's already buried me in my one attempt to gasp for air.

When my eyes drift to Silas, he's back behind his camera. But he lifts his free hand and points to his stomach. *Let's find our centers.* I close my eyes, and I count my fingers, and I do.

15

Sadie saves me the next morning, her knock at the door of my hotel room like the response to an SOS I never sent.

"Yes?" Magnolia calls. She and Camilla are sitting on the bed across from mine, side by side like they've been my entire life.

"It's Sadie." Her voice is muffled by the door. "Audrey and I need to leave for our Desert Winds appointment."

Desert Winds: the mental health rehabilitation facility whose website makes it look more like a spa than a treatment center. Not at the top of my list, but I'll take any excuse to get away from Camilla.

When Magnolia rises to open the door, my mother looks at me.

"I just don't understand why you'd bring it up that way in public," she says. We've been circling this drain for the last thirty minutes—her and Magnolia's Big Intervention after I took my own rideshare back to the hotel last night and hid from them in my room. I was supposed to video chat with Ethan, but I told him I wasn't feeling well and lay in bed with all the lights on instead. Dad has texted twice and called me three times, but I still haven't responded. "If you're upset, Audrey, you know you can always tell me."

She says this like it's a given. *You know this.* But I've tried to tell her, in all the ways I know how: turning down the tour in the first place, running off the stage in LA, turning down the tour a second time. I've told her, she just isn't listening. She doesn't listen unless we're in public—unless the rest of the world is listening, too.

But she won't understand that, so I stay silent.

"What can I do?" she asks as Sadie enters the room behind her. My mother doesn't move her gaze from mine. "I can't force you to want to be here, Audrey. It has to come from you. But tell me how to help."

The truth is, I don't know how to fix it. I don't know what the answer is, or that she'd hear me if I told her. I stand from the bed, smoothing my shirt. "I have to go," I say. When she nods, she looks as close to defeated as I've ever seen her.

"I hope we can talk more when you get back," she says, but I don't want to talk more, so I don't answer. When I look up at Sadie, she's watching Camilla, something preoccupied and far-away in the set of her face.

"Are you ready?" I ask, and she nearly jumps.

"Yes." She clears her throat. "Yes, yes. Let's go."

I hear the creak of the bed frame as we walk away, Magnolia sitting back down next to my mother. Their low, murmuring voices. Plotting how to iron me out, I'm sure. What shape to smooth me into next.

"Are you okay?" Sadie asks when I close the car door behind me. It's chilly in the hotel's covered garage, the desert sun not high enough yet to bake us. I'm looking down at my phone, at Ethan's texts from early this morning.

Feeling any better today?

Had a hard night, I'd responded. But a little.

Think you'll be up to talking later? Today's the
first microbio unit and we still have that last ethics
lecture.

I haven't answered him yet. The way I want Ethan feels primal
and a little embarrassing: I want to hear his voice up close. I want
to be in his single dorm room's twin XL bed, curled together so
tightly in the narrow space that my elbow's pressed to the wall. I
want to look at him and see myself reflected back.

The Audrey who Ethan knows isn't the one creating a scene in
public. She isn't the one letting her ridiculous mother make her
feel so lost. I want the version of myself Ethan knows—the one I
am when we're together in person, the one who's felt impossible
to find this summer. Video chat isn't enough, but it's all we have.

"Audrey?"

I look up, find Sadie watching me. She has both hands on the
wheel, her hair loose around her shoulders. There's a thin gold wedding band on her left hand—she has someone, too, somewhere else.

"What happened last night?" she asks when I still haven't
spoken. "I noticed you seemed nervous during the Sex Summit
conversation in San Francisco, and then this."

I feel a hot flare of shame. This isn't what I want her to be
noticing—the places I'm lacking, the mess of myself my mother
makes me. I want to keep Sadie where I need her: in the silo of
our visits, on the careful path that bends away from this disastrous
summer toward my future.

"Nothing that'll affect me today," I say, pulling on my seat belt. "I promise."

She drops her hands from the wheel and leans back in her seat. The car is still off. "That's not why I'm asking."

I stare at her. "Then why are you asking?"

Her eyebrows twitch together. "Because I want to make sure you're okay."

A pause. Beyond Sadie I can see out to the plaza, where artisans are setting up their booths in the morning sun. New Mexico feels like Mars, like another planet entirely—the perfect home, I guess, for this alien version of me.

"I'm okay," I say finally. Sadie is my mentor—my tutor, my guide through the one part of my life that still makes sense. Camilla brought her here, but beyond that they have nothing to do with one another.

For a moment Sadie just looks at me. Her eyes are pale brown and nearly blue at the centers, seeming to change even as I'm watching. Then she blinks, and maneuvers in the driver's seat to pull her phone out of her blazer pocket. She holds it up to me, photo illuminated on her lock screen: the slivered edges of two women's grinning faces, a laughing toddler smashed between them.

"Elliott," Sadie says, pointing to the kid. "And my wife, Cora."

I eye her, waiting for the rest. When she doesn't say anything else, I ask, "Why are you showing me this?"

Sadie exhales on half a laugh. "Because I have a family, too. I know it's complicated sometimes. And we can talk about it, if you want to."

I blink. Look forward through the windshield. "Thank you, but I'm good."

"Okay," Sadie says, carefully neutral. She turns the key in the ignition. "But I want you to feel comfortable around me. It's a standing offer, if you change your mind."

We roll out of the garage into the desert sun. I don't tell her that I'm not really the type to change my mind.

16

Desert Winds rises from a flat red mesa like the only human dwelling on Mars. It's surrounded by scrub grass and low, crawling cacti—all smooth adobe and wooden beams, turquoise window frames pressed into its face like jewels. The double front doors are pushed open to let in the cool morning, and a man in white linen stands waiting for us there.

"Sadie-May," he says, smiling broadly as we approach. "Aren't y'all a sight for sore eyes."

His accent is deeply southern—his face, too: blond hair and beach-tanned skin, like he grew up under the sun and never came inside.

"Hey, Dustin," Sadie says, accepting the hug he offers. "It's beautiful out here."

"Not too bad, right?" He glances inside, then turns his blue eyes on me. He's maybe forty, the faintest hints of silver at his temples. "You must be Miss Audrey."

"Sure am," I confirm, offering a hand. "Thanks so much for doing this."

"Thank *you*," Dustin says. "We've got quite a few Camilla St. Vrain fans in here. Eager to meet you."

It takes everything I have not to roll my eyes.

"Dustin and I met at a conference a few years ago," Sadie says, pulling off her sunglasses and folding them into a case. "We were on a panel with Aiyla—Dr. Osman. Dustin's the lead psychiatrist here at Desert Winds, but until recently he was in a private practice outside Savannah."

"Hard to believe," Dustin says. He lets out a gust of air. "Already feels like I've been at Desert Winds my whole life. This place kind of has a way of making the rest of the world fade away. Which is the point, of course, for the patients we treat." He gestures through the open door. "Why don't y'all come in? We've got a group just started I'd love to introduce you to, and then we can head to my office for some Qs and As."

Sadie waves me ahead of her and I step inside, where the lobby is all terra-cotta tiles and sun striping in from the windows. Dustin's right: the space is so beautiful, so ethereal, that the rest of the world seems faraway and almost irrelevant. Nothing bad, it feels, could happen in a place like this. He leads us to a lounge area with French doors overlooking a pool, where eight people are grouped on white couches in front of a massive fireplace.

". . . but I know it's my trauma speaking," one woman is saying. She's wrapped in a gauzy turquoise sweater, bare feet tucked under her. "It's like I'm split, the part of me that knows the right way and the part of me that's still stuck back there, when—"

She breaks off as we step into the room, and all eight sets of eyes fall on me.

"Audrey St. Vrain," another woman says. A smile spreads across her face, and I manage one in return. "Oh my goodness, we were just talking about your mother a minute ago."

"'If we believe other people deserve kindness from us, logic follows that we deserve kindness,'" turquoise-sweater woman says. "'Because we, too, are somebody's 'other people.' That quote changed my life."

I know it, of course. Chapter three of *Letters to My Someday Daughter*.

"Mine is 'Be your own safest place,'" a man says, seated right in front of the fire. "I have that one on a sticky note on my mirror."

They're looking at me like I wrote those things myself. Like they came from me by association, or like I at least know the woman who wrote them well enough to serve as a conduit. I slide one arm behind my back, count my fingers in silence where nobody can see.

"What's it like," a third woman asks, her voice soft with wonder, "to live with her?"

I feel Sadie turn to look at me, feel the eyes of every single person in the room. Always, my life cast through the lens of who I am to Camilla. And always, no idea how to explain who I am to her—because I've never been able to tell.

"I don't live with her" is the only answer I can think of.

What I want to say: *I'm not here to talk about her. This was supposed to be the one part of this summer that's not about her.*

What I actually say: "But I'm really glad she's helped you all so much."

Later, on the quiet drive home, Sadie finally breaks the silence. "That was generous of you."

"What was?" I'm looking out the window, watching New Mexico career past. It's like Colorado but wilder, redder, less mine. I'm thinking about the ICU shadowing position at Hopkins Hospital this fall, imagining that version of Audrey just two and a half months from now. The hospital badge clipped to my blazer, the notepad in my hand, all the tangible things for me to learn. I'm thinking about how much I'm going to matter there. Not because of my mother—because of myself.

"What you said to them," Sadie goes on. "About how you're glad Camilla's helped them heal." I finally turn to look at her—her window's down and the wind is whipping her hair around her face. She glances at me through the tornado of it. "I can tell that's not how you feel, and you didn't need to say it. But you did."

I don't know how to respond, so I just nod. I'm still looking out the window, five full minutes later, when she speaks again.

"I don't know what's happened between you," Sadie says. "But for what it's worth, Audrey, it sounded to me like she was trying this morning." I look at her, and our eyes connect under the incandescent midday sun. "And it was you pushing her away."

17

When we get back to the hotel, the interns are clustered out front with Camilla and Mags, peering through the window of one of the plaza's art galleries. Silas is gesticulating wildly, his long arms practically grazing the glass as he points out something inside. Puddles sits panting at his ankles and everyone's listening to him—even my mother.

I haven't said anything to Sadie since she speared me with her *for what it's worth* observation in the car, so when she leaves the parking garage in the group's direction, my first instinct is to head the opposite way. But then my phone buzzes, and when I look down it's Ethan again.

> Are we going to talk? Starting to feel like you don't want to go through the lecture together. I'm going to the library, but if you end up wanting to talk, maybe tomorrow.

I squeeze my phone until its hard corners bite into my bones. Sadie's voice echoes: *it was you pushing her away.* And now—Ethan, too. Maybe I'm a mess of my own making, after all.

The week before I left for California, Ethan and I stayed in the Summit School's library reading room until two o'clock in the morning. He had a calculus final at ten a.m.; I had an essay due at noon. The reading room was my favorite place on campus—its heavy oak tables spanned the room's full width and reminded me of renaissance banquets, grand dining rooms in stone-hewn castles. The ceilings were cavernous and wood-beamed, so whispers rose upward before floating back down like dandelion filaments. Every wall was lined in bookshelves save for the two at the front of the room, where glass-doored display cabinets towered from floor to ceiling, stacked with marble busts and peeling globes and other relics from the history department. Everywhere you looked in that room, there was something old and beautiful—something that had persevered.

It was just Ethan and me left that night. Side by side in soft-cushioned seats at the very last table in the room. We liked this table because you could see the whole reading room from its vantage point, feel the vastness of it. I was half-delirious at the hour but so far past tired I'd rounded a corner into something else entirely—something soft and romantic that didn't live inside me the same way in daylight.

"Ethan," I'd whispered, passing my hand over the table to touch his. "I'll miss you."

He blinked up at me from his calculus textbook, the torchiere lights casting the shadows of his glasses onto his cheeks. "When?"

"This summer," I said, angling my body into his. Ethan's arm slipped off the table and over my knees, his warm palm framing the outer curve of my thigh. "Next year. The whole time."

He dropped his chin to kiss me, that familiar press of his lips.

It was always a little shorter than I wanted it to be; I could have fallen into Ethan until I found the impossible bottom of him, a limit that didn't exist. But he was as careful and as studied and as thorough with me as he was with everything else. There was no falling at all for Ethan. He loved me in his own controlled way. If we were going to sleep together—anything other than the clothed tangle of limbs in his dorm room the few times I managed to sneak in—we'd plan for it. And we hadn't planned for it.

I wanted more. And I'd thought that maybe this summer, together at Penn, I'd get it. That those months would make us different; bring us to a kind of closeness that wasn't so controlled. Ethan and I would be all each other had there—surely, with so much time together, he'd turn toward me in all the ways I was too afraid to ask for.

"We'll go through every Penn lesson together," Ethan murmured, his mouth just an inch from mine. "You'll tell me about every doctor you visit with Dr. Stone." He kissed me again, and this time I lifted a hand to his face to hold him there. I was just starting to go tingly, unrooting, when he pulled back.

"We'll talk every day," he said. There was some part of me that knew, even then, with his warm hands on my body in my favorite place in the entire world. Something quiet but true, telling me that without Penn—without the summer we'd planned—things wouldn't be this exact way ever again. "You won't have to miss me at all."

"It's more about saturation," Silas says as I reluctantly join the group in front of the art gallery. I don't want to be around Camilla, around Sadie defending Camilla, around Silas and Cleo and Mick having their Great Adventurous Summer while I muddle stumbling and rejected through mine. But I *really* don't want to sit alone in my hotel room for the rest of the day knowing Ethan's mad at me. I texted him back right away—I do want to go through the lecture—but he must've already left for the library, because he hasn't responded. "See how the turquoise here plays off the richness of this red?"

Silas sweeps a hand over the glass covering a painting inside the window, a horse that appears to be levitating in an aquamarine sky.

"How do you know all this?" my mother asks, looking at him admiringly. She's wearing a pale pink dress, its fabric waffly and light.

"Well, that last part's just the color wheel," he says. He adjusts his green baseball cap, *GG's Gardenshare*. "Pretty basic, really. Like most of my working knowledge."

"Very modest for someone so talented," Camilla says, reaching out to nudge his elbow. From the sidewalk, Puddles looks skyward to watch the movement of her arm. "I'm going to take a closer look inside." She turns to scan the group. "Anyone interested in joining? Oh—Audrey, honey. I didn't realize you were back."

Everyone turns to look at me as Cleo says, "We were going to head to Taos for the afternoon, actually. Unless you need anything, Camilla?"

"Nothing I can think of," my mother says, turning to Magnolia. "Mags?"

"Feel free." Magnolia adjusts the purse on her shoulder. "Let's just make sure we get those show posts up before this evening, yes?"

"Sure thing." Mick holds up his phone, wiggling it a little. "I've got 'em all cued up and scheduled for three o'clock."

"Audrey?" my mother says again, her eyes zeroed in on me across the group. "Will you join us?"

"Or you can come to Taos," Silas says. I glance at Camilla—I can tell she's surprised he's contradicting her, but something about him has her charmed. She doesn't say anything; they both just watch me, waiting for me to decide.

It sounded to me like she was trying, Sadie had said. But I've done my trying, just by being here this summer. And look how far it's gotten us.

"Sure." I glance at Silas, seal my fate. "I'll come to Taos."

18

"Remind me how you two know each other?" I slide into the front seat of the rental car as Silas shoots a goodbye wave toward Sadie. He invited her to join us, but she said something about needing to call Cora.

"Sadie?" Silas asks, ducking in next to me. He's been cradling Puddles like a fat football under one arm, but now he holds her out toward me—tongue lolling from her mouth, droplets of slobber hitting the driver's seat with every pant.

"Surprise," Cleo chimes from the back. "We have a furry hitch-hiker."

"I hate surprises," I mutter, just as Silas says, "Can you hold her while I drive?"

We stare at each other over the center console. "Absolutely not."

"Oh, come on." He jiggles her so her back paws sway over the seat. "Can we try? She's a wonderful road trip companion."

"How long is this drive?" I ask, eyeing Puddles. Her breath is hot and smelly, wafting at me with every exhale. I imagine my blouse slick with slobber.

"Ninety minutes," Mick offers from the back seat, and I hold up both hands.

"It's a no."

"Give her to me," Cleo says, sticking her hands between the front two seats. She wiggles her fingers, sharp green nails flashing. When Silas eases Puddles off to her, Cleo looks at me through her long eyelashes—glittering with glued-on rhinestones. "She's a pug, not a piece of poop."

"I didn't say she was—"

"You're treating her like one," Cleo says, settling the loaf that is Puddles into her lap. "She has feelings, you know."

"The summer is young," Silas says before I can respond, finally dropping into the driver's seat and shutting his door. "We have time to make a dog person out of Audrey yet."

"Everyone's a dog person once they meet the right dog," Mick says. He reaches forward to squeeze my shoulders and I slide down in my seat, feeling acutely like I made the wrong choice in coming here. "Puddles is definitely the right dog."

"Anyway," Silas says. I watch his eyes flick up, check on Puddles in the rearview, before he taps the blinker and eases us onto the road. "Sadie was my math tutor. Does that answer your question?"

I look at the side of his face, half-hidden behind dark sunglasses and that baseball cap. Silas called Sadie his *bonus mom*, so . . . "No?"

He smiles crookedly, casting a glance my way. "My dad hired her to help me after my mom died. My grades were terrible, along with everything else about me."

I turn away from him instinctually, tensing at the honesty of this admission. We don't even know each other.

"Sadie was at the University of Michigan then," Silas says. He punches on the radio, and something acoustic fills the car. "In Ann Arbor. At first she was just helping me with algebra, but then she kind of stuck around to help me with everything else. Lily, too—my sister." I hazard a glance in his direction but he's staring straight ahead, eyes on the road and one hand on the wheel. The other drums his knee, casual, like this is the easiest thing in the world to talk about. "Our dad was having a hard time—Lily was seven and I was thirteen and Sadie kind of saved us, I don't know. She took a job at American right before my senior year and I didn't really know where to go for college so I went there." He slows for a stoplight and looks over at me, and I'm grateful for the sunglasses between us. "My dad had no idea what to do with us after my mom died. And Sadie just became our family."

What happened to your mom? It's right there at the back of my throat, waiting to be asked. But I can't make myself say it, and as music fills the space between us, Silas looks at me again. He laughs, shaking his head a little.

"What?" I say.

"You know that term *resting bitch face?*" I frown, bracing for the insult. "You have resting mathematician face." His eyes flick to mine before falling back to the road. "Like you're always trying to figure something out."

"Probably how she wound up in this car with you two idiots," Cleo says, but there's something unquestionably affectionate about it. From the corner of my eye, I see her reach forward to tickle her fingernails along the back of Silas's neck.

The plaza in Taos is a scaled-down version of the one in Santa Fe, an unshaded park surrounded on all sides by tourist shops. The park is bare and hot, its few trees doing little to provide relief from the afternoon sun. I watch Puddles totter into the grass and squat to pee for the third time since we left the car.

"So," Cleo says. She's holding Puddles's leash while Mick and Silas buy us ice cream, and her eyes flick to mine behind her square yellow sunglasses. "That was kind of gnarly last night."

The show is the last thing I want to talk about—especially with Cleo, who seems to hate me. The Polaroid camera dangling from her neck sways precariously as Puddles tugs her farther into the grass.

"If I called out my mom like that in public, she'd evaporate me. Like, ream me so intensely I'd simply vaporize." She cocks an eyebrow at me. "My mom's not Camilla St. Vrain, though."

"Lucky you," I mutter, and Cleo studies my face.

"Why do you hate her so much?"

"I don't hate her," I say, though it feels more like an automatic response than one I've actually considered. "It's more complicated than that."

"I mean, sure," Cleo says. "She's your mom. That shit's always complicated."

"What's complicated?" Mick asks, stepping up beside us and extending a mint-chip ice cream cone in my direction. Silas hands one to Cleo, something rainbow swirled and exactly as colorful as she is. She trades him for Puddles's leash and I wonder, not for the first time, what exists there between them.

"Motherhood," Cleo says, licking at her ice cream. We drift across the plaza toward a line of low-slung tourist shops. "Being a daughter."

"Mmm," Mick says sagely, like this is enough of an answer all on its own. "So we're talking about the show."

I wince—part brain freeze from my ice cream, part humiliation. Clearly, they've all talked about it without me.

"I thought it was kind of funny," Mick says, shrugging. "That lady's so *peace and love* all the time it honestly freaks me out. 'Absolutely horrible' is a little intense, but—"

"But you chose to be here," I say, and all three of them turn to look at me. Like they're surprised: *she speaks*. "I didn't choose this. She's always choosing for me."

There's a beat of silence before Cleo says simply, "That sucks."

"But you're almost in college," Mick says, chocolate ice cream on his chin. "She won't be able to tell you what to do once you're gone."

"I've *been* gone," I tell them. "She sent me to boarding school in sixth grade."

Silas stops, turning back to look at me. "You've been away from home since *sixth* grade? What is that, like eleven years old?"

I nod, surprised by his surprise. With all of us stopped, Puddles shuffles toward me and starts licking my ankle. I move it swiftly out of her way.

"How often do you see your parents?" Silas asks, and behind his shoulder Cleo drags Mick toward one of the shop windows to point something out to him.

I think about it, running through the last calendar year. "Twice a year, maybe? My dad tries to visit, and I usually see Camilla at the holidays."

"Summers?" Silas asks, taking a step closer to me.

"Camp." Ice cream drips onto my hand, and I lift it to my mouth to lick it off. "Or summer sessions at school."

Silas's gaze lingers on the back of my hand before coming up to mine. "That's lonely," he says.

The words move through me like ice. I feel cold, suddenly, and exposed. I feel eleven years old, gulping back tears at the Summit School while my mother flies home to launch her lifestyle brand.

"It's what I'm used to," I say. Mick and Cleo have disappeared into the store, so I step over to a bench and sit down. I don't look at Silas as he follows, parking Puddles between his feet. I'm worried that if we make eye contact, he'll see through this version of me into that younger one, scared and alone. "And it's good to get ahead in my coursework."

"Right," Silas says, running a hand over Puddles's head. She's panting hard, her tongue so long I can't quite believe it fits in her mouth. Silas going quiet makes me want to keep talking—to fill this weird, sympathetic silence between us.

"What does it mean?" I ask, and he looks up at me. I point to his hat. "*GG's Gardenshare*?"

"Oh." He smiles, adjusting it on his head. "My grandma runs this gardenshare program—like a CSA, but it's just stuff from her garden. My cousins and I would help her out with the deliveries when we visited on summer breaks growing up. She makes us all call her GG because she thinks *grandma* makes her sound old." I imagine a swarm of children moving between rows of vegetables; grandparents in overalls watching them from a back porch. It could be a fantasy, it's so unfamiliar to me. My parents are both only children; I have one grandfather on my dad's side, in a south Texas town we never visit. My mom's parents died when she was twenty. "She lives in the mountains about an hour from Denver, little town called Switchback Ridge." Silas looks up at me, sun in his eyes. "I'll visit her in a couple weeks when we're in Colorado. You should come."

What?

"I get it now, you know."

I blink at him, holding my ice cream like a shield. "Get what?"

"At the show in LA, that back alley. The centering practice." He holds up his fingers and taps his thumb to each one in turn, the first time I've ever seen someone reflect my habit back at me. "You're centering yourself."

I picture him yesterday morning, eyes on mine in the pale morning light on the rooftop. Backstage at the show last night, reminding me with one quiet gesture of all the calm I contain. I want to push back—I want him not to be able to read me like this. But it comes out all on its own, one quiet word. "Yeah."

He nods, looking down at Puddles. A few strands of hair fall loose from the *GG's Gardenshare* cap and brush his cheek, hide him from me. "Did she teach you that?"

"No," I say. I picked it up during my first and only counseling session at the Summit School. *When you start to feel ungrounded,* the therapist had told me, *find something concrete to focus on. Like noticing the colors around you. Or eating a piece of candy.*

Colors were a shade too subjective—cast through the unreliable filters of our eyes, the time of the day, the slant of the light. And how often did I have candy on me? But I always had my same hands. My ten fingers.

I don't tell Silas any of this. I say, "That one I learned on my own."

19

My father is preternaturally loud. His inside voice can only be classified as a shout; his outside voice is so deep and booming it sounds like it's coming from the earth's core—like a seismic, apocalyptic event orchestrated with the express purpose of blowing out all of humanity's eardrums at once.

When he bellows, *"Mouse!"* at me from the front porch of Patsey's, all three people within a twenty-foot radius flinch. I motion at him to lower the volume, pushing my hands up and down through Austin's soupily humid air. We've been in Texas for two days and the Colorado girl in me is still having trouble breathing.

"Please don't scream," I say as he hops the two steps off the porch toward me and lifts me clear off the ground. When he spins me around, he shouts right in my ear: "Sorry!"

I wince, and he sets me back on the sidewalk. "Are you taller?"

I look down at myself: tank top, flip-flops, denim shorts with my phone shoved in one pocket. Two unanswered, outgoing calls to Ethan sitting in its log. "No?"

"You look taller," Dad says, holding me at arm's length with both hands on my shoulders. He's in his customary band T-shirt and jeans, gold aviators he's had my whole life. "Maybe I'm shrinking in my old age."

Maybe if you saw me more, you'd remember how tall I am. But I don't say it, just swipe a hand over the top of his head. His hair is the same dark brown as mine. "Doubt it."

"Where's your mother?"

I feel myself frown, my whole face pinching with it. Dad landed in Austin this morning for a show along the tour he's managing this summer—we have exactly three hours of overlap in our schedules. Three hours that we discussed *explicitly* would be Camilla-free.

"She wasn't—" A white town car slides up to the curb right beside me, its back passenger door clicking open. My mother's ankle juts out of it, and I watch her leather Hermès sandal make contact with the sidewalk. "—invited."

"I invited her," Dad says. "And really, mouse, you forced my hand by ignoring all my calls."

"I didn't—" I splutter, but he's already hugging Camilla, and the rest of my sentence disappears into the commotion of them reaching over me to get to each other.

He eyes me over her shoulder. "You did."

God *damn* it. I look back toward South Congress, the twenty-minute walk I took to get here from our hotel. Of course Camilla drove. Of course my dad would ambush me like this. Of *course* I can't get out of it now.

I've spent the days since Taos holed up in my hotel room, catching up on the Penn readings and course notes Ethan's sent. But we haven't talked through anything but email; every time I've tried to get ahold of him, he's sent me straight to voicemail.

"Hi, honey," Camilla says, finally letting go of Dad and turning to face me. I sat with Sadie and the interns again on the flight from New Mexico, and to be honest I haven't seen her up close in a few days. Avoiding, self-preserving, whatever you want to call it—we aren't really speaking. "Thanks for including me."

I can't quite tell if this is a dig or she's just that blithe, that used to the world reorienting itself around her.

"Ames?" the hostess calls, southern twang ringing over the front porch of this house-turned-restaurant. "Roger Ames, party of three?"

"Here!" Dad hollers, and before I realize what's happening, Camilla and I are looking at each other, our simultaneous eye rolls connecting behind his back. *So loud*, she mouths at me, and I jerk my gaze away before this can turn into A Moment.

Dad's rented out the private back room of the restaurant, a bricked-in space that looks like it was a sunporch in a past life. Half the eyes in the restaurant follow us through to our table, the other half jerking hastily our way as soon as someone points out my mother. I forget, when I'm away at school, what it's like to move through the world with the conspicuous obstacle of Camilla next to me.

"I'll send your server over right away," the hostess says, hesitating behind Camilla's shoulder like she's debating whether or not to say something. *Don't*, I think, and she doesn't, and we sit.

When the door to our room is firmly shut, Dad says, "My girls." He reaches over to squeeze both our shoulders, and I lift my menu to cover my face. "The apples of my eyeballs. Tell me everything."

This is for my benefit, I'm sure. Clearly Camilla has been tattling on me to Dad, or he wouldn't have staged this reunion-brunch-turned-intervention. But my mother just looks at me across the table, smiling patiently.

"Mouse?" Dad prompts, when neither of us have spoken.

"Can I at least order a coffee before the firing squad begins?"

"Hey, there's no firing squad here—"

"Roger, honestly," Camilla says, glancing toward the glass panes in the door. A few people in the dining room are still staring. "Lower your voice."

Dad ducks his head, leaning closer to us over the table. His lowered voice is one decibel below the kind of projection you'd expect at an a cappella performance. "Of course you can order a coffee, Audrey. But we aren't a firing squad; we're your parents. We love you."

I look at him as he says it. I can feel Camilla watching me, but I can't bring myself to glance her way. She lets his *we* do the heavy lifting and keeps her mouth shut.

"Okay," I say slowly. "What do you want to know?"

"Are you having fun?" Dad says. The question is so off base I don't know how to *begin* answering it, but he keeps going. "Are you learning with Dr. Stone? Is something going on that you want to tell us about? Because you don't seem yourself."

He's right, something whispers inside me, reverberating with truth. I'm not myself—I haven't been myself. I don't know how to be myself, this far out of context.

"Good morning!" a bright voice chirps, the door to our room jangling open. A waiter in a waist apron steps inside and starts passing out water glasses, carefully looking at anything but Camilla. There are three types of people in public: those who have no idea who she is, those who know exactly who she is and slobber all over her, and those like this guy. Who clearly knows who she is and is going to do everything in his power not to act like it. My favorite type. "Can I start y'all with anything to drink? Coffee, tea? Mimosas?"

"Mimosa?" Dad asks, pointing at Camilla. She shakes her head, smiling up at the waiter. "Chamomile tea for me, please. Lemon wedge and honey on the side, if you have it."

"We sure do," he says, taking notes on a little pad. "Mimosa for you, sir?"

"Why not?" Dad booms, and I order my coffee, and the guy leaves. Both my parents swivel to look at me, and I feel heat rise to my cheeks.

"Honey?" Camilla prompts softly, like she's trying to compensate for Dad's volume. She sounds so sincere I actually think, for a moment, that she's really going to try here. That my dad—too wordy and too loud but genuine down to his bones—might actually have brought out the good in her. But then she says: "Tell us why you said what you said in Santa Fe."

And that's what it's about; that's what it's always about. Me marring her public image, failing to fit into whatever box she's constructed for me on whatever given day. It doesn't matter to her that I don't seem myself. She doesn't know what I seem like when I'm myself.

My phone buzzes, half-wedged into my hipbone. I wrestle it out of my shorts' pocket and, seeing Ethan's name there after two days of resolute silence, unlock the screen. He's texted me twice: one photo, one message beneath it. The message is just three words: Who is this? And the photo is of a social post with nearly three hundred thousand likes, a candid shot of Silas and me. Silas and me. *Silas and me*, on a gossip magazine's feed.

ST. VRAIN STRIKES OUT, the overlay says. Beneath it: Silas leaned forward with his elbows suspended on his knees, Puddles's leash knotted up in one hand. She's between his feet, tongue hanging to the side. And the photo, it's—shit. It's not that Silas is looking at me, because he isn't. It's not that we're touching, because there are two solid feet of space between us. We aren't even smiling. The problem is me—the way I'm looking at him, captured so clearly there in full color. Like Silas is a math problem that I haven't figured out yet; like he's the only thing I want to spend my time on until I've cracked it. I'm so absolutely focused on him.

It's a dishonest portrayal, of course. It's showing something that isn't there, a trick of timing. The photographer must have captured me in the exact, exact moment I was scrambling for something to change the subject after Silas told me how *lonely* my life seems.

"I have to go," I say, pushing back my chair.

"What?" Dad's wide eyes track me as I make for the door. "Audrey, sit back down, we aren't—"

"I'll be right back." Camilla is the last thing that registers before I leave the room, the way she looks at my dad, like: *See? She's impossible.*

I know I've made myself look like the problem. I know. But as I dial Ethan's number and push through the restaurant, phone lifted to my ear, I also know I can only put out one fire at a time.

"Audrey," he says by way of greeting. I step through the restaurant's front door, looking for somewhere quiet. I hang a left and beeline down the porch toward a pair of unoccupied rocking chairs.

"Ethan." I sit down so forcefully the chair whacks into the house. "How did you find that?"

There's a beat of silence. "Does it matter?"

"I, no—I mean, I guess not." Ethan's hardly on social media; someone must have showed it to him, which somehow makes it worse. "I just can't believe anyone would follow me, or even want that picture? It doesn't make any sense."

"It makes perfect sense," he says calmly. "You're the child of a celebrity. And it looks"—he hesitates, the word coming awkwardly like he's forcing it through a straw—"suggestive."

Oh, Ethan. Oh, Christ. "It's not," I say quickly. "Ethan, I barely know him."

"Who is he, Audrey?" He doesn't give me a chance to answer. "You cancel our last call, and then I barely hear from you—and here I am, thinking you're so busy with the tour, and with Dr. Stone, and then I find you on the internet eating ice cream with this person you've never even mentioned to me?" He draws a breath, and I press my eyes shut. "I'm sorry I haven't been returning your calls, but I didn't even know how to bring this up. It took some time to process."

"Ethan," I whisper. My chest feels like someone's taking a hammer to it from the inside, cracking each of my ribs in turn. How have I let everything get this bad, this fast? Who would I even have, if I didn't have Ethan? I want to transport us to Miami, where we'll be together in person—where nothing will feel this wrong. "He's nobody, I swear. He's just one of the interns."

"I thought you said the interns were annoying?"

"They *are* annoying," I say. "We have nothing in common. I didn't even want to be around them, but it was right after the show in Santa Fe, and I kind of tried something there and it didn't work out, and it made things really tense with my mom, and going on this road trip with the interns kind of got me out of doing something with her and I didn't feel like I had a choice; I shouldn't have slipped on the readings, it's just honestly been a lot, but I'm going to get it back together, I've read all of this week's lecture notes and I've been wanting to talk to you about them but I haven't—"

"Hey." Ethan's voice comes through the line, softly, like a hand pressed to a racing heart. "Audrey, slow down."

I suck in a rush of air, open my eyes. My dad is coming right at me down the porch, looking none too pleased.

"Ethan, I have to go, I'm so sorry, my dad is coming to get me—"

"Your dad is there?"

"Yeah, he met us in Austin and I kind of cut out of brunch to call you, but look, I'm sorry, okay?" I hold up a hand to my dad, who stops a few feet away and just stands there, watching me. "That picture isn't anything. That guy isn't anything. I'm sorry."

"Okay," he says. There's a pause; I think I can hear him breathing, but it might just be my own panicked inhales. "Can I call you later?"

"Yes," I say, relief moving down my body in a wave. *That's lonely*, Silas told me. But I'm not lonely; not with Ethan. "Yes, please."

"Okay," he says again. *I love you*, I want to say. A flickering impulse that feels maybe more like an olive branch than something I really feel in this moment, panic-stricken on an unfamiliar porch. But I don't say it, and Ethan says, "Okay," one more time, and I say, "Okay," and then we're hanging up.

"Okay?" Dad asks, eyeing me.

"Okay," I repeat, but I'm pretty sure neither of us is convinced. "Can we go back inside?"

I stare up at my father from the rocking chair. I feel rooted to it, leaden. "I really don't want to be around her right now."

Dad's eyebrows twitch together, and he lowers himself into the seat beside me. I hold up my phone, open to that photo of me and Silas, and watch his eyes track across it.

"I don't want this," I say. "I don't want to do this with her and deal with all of this." The anger rises in me like carbonation, fizzing frantically, looking for a way out. "She's using me, Dad. She's using me for her career bullshit, and it's snaking into my own life, and she doesn't even care that—"

"Audrey." It's so rare he calls me by my name that my mouth snaps shut. "Your mother loves you, and she's not trying to use you." He leans closer, eyes scanning mine. "And you know she can't control every action of the press, right?"

I squeeze the arms of the rocking chair. I shouldn't be surprised that he isn't on my side. "I wouldn't have to deal with the press at all if she hadn't brought me here."

He sighs heavily, reaching out to jiggle my arm. He's always cutting the tension this way—picking me up, jostling me, wrapping me in some big bear hug. It's easier for him, I think, than finding the words. "We'll see if Magnolia can help. But cut your mom some slack, all right? She's been through the ringer, too."

"Really," I say. "Like when?" I wave my phone at him. "I don't see the press actively dismantling *her* relationships."

"You deserve to be mad about this," Dad says. "All I'm asking is that you give your mom the benefit of the doubt every now and then, okay? You don't know everything about her."

I lean back, searching his familiar face. "What's that supposed to mean?"

"Nothing, mouse. Just that you assume the worst of her, and she doesn't always deserve it." He stands, reaching for my hand. I don't want to take it, but I do. "Come inside and eat your breakfast."

20

"Let's say the patient presents with sudden numbness on the left side only." Dr. Kowalski leans back on her heels, arms crossed. "What do you do first?"

Sadie and I are in the emergency department at Zilker Hospital, where her contact here in Austin—a pint-sized doctor named Maureen Kowalski—is giving me the third degree. Unlike the other visits, which have basically been lovefests for Sadie rounded out by offers of future rec letters for me, Dr. Kowalski doesn't seem to really care who Sadie is. She seems to care *much* less who I am.

But the leveling of her gaze, the paces she's putting me through, the double doors from the ambulance bay rushing open to wheel in someone who needs real help—this is the best thing I've been a part of all summer. This is where I make sense.

"The FAST assessment," I tell Dr. Kowalski. "The patient's having a stroke."

She eyes me. "Maybe. Good place to start. What about periumbilical pain that migrates to the right lower quadrant, accompanied by vomiting?"

I hesitate. "Kidney stones?"

"Appendicitis," she says curtly. "But good guess. Dr. Stone tells me you were a student EMT, so you were probably more likely to be dealing with a burst appendix than a kidney stone, at any rate, given the average patient's age in your line of work."

My line of work. Even after getting the question wrong, it sends a shiver of pride up my spine. Dr. Kowalski turns on her heel to lead us deeper into the ER, and Sadie falls into step beside me.

"Nicely done," she says quietly. She apologized as we drove to the hospital this morning, finally acknowledging what she'd said in the car back in Santa Fe. *It wasn't my place,* she said. *She's your mother, not mine.* And I just nodded, zipped it away. I hate that Camilla touched this part of the summer, that even there—driving to meet a doctor I'm desperate to impress—we were talking about her. But I shouldn't be surprised; Camilla is ruining everything. Including, if I'm not more careful, my relationship with Ethan.

"We'll wrap up in the ICU," Dr. Kowalski says now, leading us down a hallway tiled in scuffed laminate. "So you can get a feel for what it'll be like at Hopkins Hospital in the fall. That shadowing position will really set you up—one of the best in the country."

Don't I know it. When I start to lose my grip on reality—when Camilla slips a vacuum-sealed face mask under my hotel room door or emails me interview questions for some press piece—I imagine myself there. All the tactile things about it: a laminated badge with my face on it, the sturdy sneakers I'll buy, my chapped knuckles from so much handwashing.

"Tell me more about your EMT experience," Dr. Kowalski says, casting a backward glance in my direction as we push through the doors into the ICU. "What was typical for you? Broken bones?"

"Some," I say. "Only seniors are eligible, because you have to be eighteen. I did it for about six months and was on call two days a week, so it wasn't as in-depth as I'd have liked, but—"

"But probably a good thing," Sadie says, "that a campus full of teenagers didn't require frequent emergency care."

"True," I say. There were drunk moments at parties, girls on my dorm hall too scared of being expelled to call 911 knocking on my door instead. Two o'clock in the morning, turning someone sideways on the tiled floor of our communal bathroom so they wouldn't choke. A broken wrist in winter, straight-faced Alex Rao with tears in their eyes as they held their arm out toward me. But there was only one time I'd felt out of my depth—kneeling on the turf at a football game with Ty Ashton's head stabilized between my trembling hands. The unfocused way he was looking up at me and the slur of non-words he was trying to speak. How I imagined his brain through the thin bone under my fingers, precious and damaged. I sat with him until the ambulance arrived, and when they finally carried him off the field and our mountain-ringed football stadium erupted into cheers, I darted across campus and threw up behind a purple smoke bush next to the library.

But that was my secret, that moment. Like the Sex Summit—a flicker of weakness I could hold close and keep quiet. When I got back to my dorm that night Ethan was waiting for me, studying as Fallon played video games across the room.

"How was the game?" he'd asked, looking up as I came through the door.

"Concussion," I said, and Ethan's eyes widened.

"What grade?"

At least three, I knew. Ty had been unconscious when I got to him. I shook my head. "I don't—"

"Who?" Fallon asked, sitting up in bed. "Are they okay?"

I looked back and forth between them, both their faces open

with wanting—*tell me everything*. But for very different reasons, and when I slumped onto my bed next to Ethan, he was already googling *EMS concussion protocol*. Not to learn about it, because we'd studied it together to earn our places as student EMTs. He was looking it up to confirm what I'd done. He was checking my work.

I've been back from the hospital for fifteen minutes when a knock rackets against my hotel room door.

"Audrey!" Mick shouts from the hallway, tapping his knuckles jauntily against the wood. "We're going to the park!"

I glance at my bed: I have two Penn textbooks spread across it, my laptop open to Ethan's most recent lecture notes. An email half-drafted, thanking Dr. Kowalski for her time today. I'm not going to get caught eating ice cream by some slimy photographer again when I should be working.

I pull the door open, find all three of them standing there watching me expectantly. Four if you count Puddles, who's tucked under Silas's arm with her tongue poked between her lips.

"Hi," Silas says, smiling easily at me. He's wearing his hair loose and wild, all tumbling waves. I think of that photo, the way I was looking at him, and lift a hand self-consciously to my neck.

"Hi," I say, at none of them in particular. "I'm, um. Working."

Cleo rolls her eyes straight up at the ceiling. She's wearing a leopard-print minidress and black platform boots, hardly *park* attire last time I checked. "I told you this was futile," she says, reaching for both boys' wrists. "Let's go."

"*Futile?*" Mick repeats, raising his eyebrows at me. "Audrey, you gonna let her describe you that way?"

Silas grins at me over both their heads. "Can we try something?"

I narrow my eyes. "Depends what it is."

"Bring your work to the park," he says. "Get out of this hotel room. It's nice outside."

"It's ninety-two degrees and ninety-five percent humidity."

"Meteorologist Audrey St. Vrain," Mick says, walking backward as Cleo drags him away, "reporting live for NBC 7. The news is next."

I feel myself flush, and Silas huffs a laugh that makes Puddles's tail wag.

"Just come," he says, softer. Cleo and Mick are halfway to the elevator. "We won't disturb your studying at all. We'll be so quiet."

Puddles chooses that exact moment to let out a loud, wet burp. Silas covers her mouth with one big hand, eyes never leaving mine.

"Did you see the picture?"

I nearly look around to check who asked such a forward question, and then I realize that it was me.

"What picture?" Silas asks, at the same moment Cleo shouts for us from the elevator, one neon-manicured hand waving through its open doors. Silas looks back at me, taking a step in Cleo's direction. "Show me at the park?"

So that's how I wind up on a grassy slope along the Colorado River, trying to read a biology textbook with a hotel towel spread beneath me. We're in the shade of a big oak tree, but still—I'm hot as hell. Mick is in the river, shorts and T-shirt and all, his dark head bobbing in and out of the water. Cleo sits next to him on the bank, black boots parked beside her with her socks rolled up inside them. Her feet are in the water, and I watch Mick grab them and pretend to drag her in—she screams, and Puddles lunges out of Silas's lap toward them.

"Whoa, girl," he says, grabbing her two-handed around her rib cage. He's been reading next to me, some mystery novel with a worn cover and a big crease in the spine. "No water for you." He glances over at me. "She can't swim."

"Well," I say, not looking up from my book, "I guess we have one thing in common."

There's a pause, and suddenly Silas is right next to me, craned over with his whole face in my space. "You can't *swim*?"

I lean back, catching a whiff of him—salt sweat, the sunscreen I watched him rub into the back of his neck when we got here, something deeper and clean and good. I think of Fallon, reading to me from a paperback romance novel in our dorm room this spring: *He smells of sandalwood, of early summer mornings and hope.* The huge, characteristically Fallon snort she'd let out as she turned to me and said, *That's how you identify the love interest, Audrey. He smells like something insane. Human beings smell like BO or nothing.* Fallon loves romances: the tropes, the comfortable predictability, all those sandalwood-smelling men. *Ethan smells like pine trees*, I'd told her, and she'd gagged.

"Camilla never taught me," I say now, shifting on the towel to put more space between us. I don't need to be close enough to Silas to smell him, preferably ever again. "She was too busy, and then I went away to school."

He's watching me, open-mouthed. He scrambles for a couple different words, lips moving until he finally manages to whisper, "Wow."

"Cool," I say. "Thanks for making me feel like a specimen."

Silas laughs, adjusting Puddles in his lap. "Sorry. It's just hard for me to picture growing up without this." He spreads his hands in front of us. "Swimming in lakes and pools and smelling like chlorine all summer."

I look over at him, try to imagine him small. "Did she teach you to swim?"

His brows twitch together. "Sadie?"

I shake my head. "Your mom."

He hesitates, looking away from me, and I could strangle myself. What is *wrong* with me? "I'm sorry," I say quickly. "I shouldn't have—that was. It's not my place."

"No," he says, smiling softly, "it's okay. I'm just trying to remember—it was so long ago. It feels like something I've just always *known* how to do, if that makes sense." He rakes a hand through his hair, leaving it messy. "But yeah, I'm sure she did—my dad was always working, so it must have been her." We're quiet for a minute, watching Mick splash Cleo on the riverbank. And then he says, "I'm impressed that you have the stomach for it, going to an ICU like that."

We look at each other, textbook falling shut as I turn toward him. I'll lose my place, but I leave it. "What?"

"Sadie told me you were going to the ER this morning. Or the ICU—I'll be honest, I don't know the difference." He smiles. "But it's pretty badass, either way. I can't do hospitals after what happened."

I blink at him, trying to decide where to start. I don't think anyone has ever called me *badass* before. I didn't know Sadie and Silas were talking so much about our plans this summer. But what comes out is— "Was she sick?"

"Yeah." He runs a hand down Puddles's back. "For a while, so we spent a lot of time in and out of places like that." He looks up at me, draws a big breath. "Breast cancer. GG had it, too, but she's all right now."

My hand twitches on my lap, like I'm going to—what, *reach for him*? He glances at my fingers, like he saw it, too. "Silas," I say, swallowing hard. "I'm so sorry. That's terrible."

"It was," he says, one corner of his mouth lifting in a small way. "Thanks. It put me off hospitals as kind of a general rule, so I'm glad there are people like you. Still signing up to save the world."

"I don't know about saving the world," I say quietly, nudging my palm into the corner of my textbook's cover. "Hopefully a few people, though."

"A few would be enough," he says, and when I look at him it feels dangerous, like a great hole opening up. Something dark and unfamiliar to fall into. I blink, and Silas clears his throat, and over the sound of Cleo's laughter I hear him say, "Was there a picture you wanted to show me?"

"Oh." I reach for my bag, pulling out my phone and opening up the text thread with Ethan. I hold it out to Silas, that photo of us filling the screen.

I watch him study it, dark eyebrows knit together, one hand curved over the screen to shade it from the sun.

"This is what I'm talking about," he says finally. I brace myself, Ethan's words echoing in my head. *It looks . . . suggestive.* Silas holds the phone up so I can see it, pointing to me there. "Resting mathematician face." His mouth cracks into a grin and I swipe the phone out of his hand, burying it in my bag.

"It's not so bad," he says, leaning over to nudge my shoulder. "Kind of cute, if you're into that sort of thing."

I rub my arm where it made contact with his, try to get this conversation back on the rails. "It's invasive."

"The photo?" Silas says. "Or me calling you cute?"

Shit. Shitshit*shit*. "I—" When I finally look at him he's still smiling, but when he sees my face his lips flatten out, everything about his expression closing up.

"I'm sorry," he says, leaning out of my space. "I didn't mean to, um—"

And here's the thing. Here's the stupid, nonsensical thing. I don't want him to be sorry. I don't want him to feel bad. I don't want that so much I almost don't say what I say next—but I do. In the end, I do.

"It's just, my boyfriend sent it to me."

Silas's eyes move over mine, back and forth just once before he looks out over the river. "Ah," he says. One syllable, the smallest noise I've ever heard him make. "I'm sorry."

"There's nothing to be sorry—"

He turns back to me, smiling again. "At least they got a good photo of Puddles, right?" When he lifts her between us, bringing her nose to his, I see this for what it is. A pivot, the closing of a door.

And I don't know what to say, either—how we've wound up here—so I just reach out and smooth one hand over the top of her head. Warm from the sun. Softer than I expected.

She turns toward me, panting in a way that makes it look like she's smiling.

"They did," I say quietly. "At least there's that."

21

The Austin *Letters* show is at the university's auditorium, which means "backstage" is a classroom. Two classrooms, really—my mother with Mags in one, me with the interns in another. Mick is hunched over his phone in the corner of the room, replying to DMs on Camilla's accounts, mumbling to himself at regular intervals. Cleo's drawing on the massive chalkboard, standing on a maroon chair. And Silas—well. I'm actively trying not to be aware of what he's doing. (He's cross-legged on the floor in front of his video camera, fiddling with a memory card.)

Good luck tonight, Ethan has sent me. I'll call you after? I respond yes and add a heart emoji for good measure. We've been talking every day since he sent me the paparazzi photo—I'm back up to speed with the Penn coursework, and when I told him about visiting Dr. Kowalski with Sadie his eyes lit up over video chat, rapt and round and hungry for every detail. It was there, the Ethan I knew: fascinated by the same things that fascinate me. Eager to share all of it. I think of that flicker of doubt, back at breakfast with my dad—the soft whisper that stopped me from telling Ethan I loved him. As my phone pings with another text, I shove the memory away.

i made this, Fallon says, alongside a photo of a well—a metal spigot rising from a circular concrete pad. meet my firstborn child

They're beautiful, I reply. What was it like giving birth?

dirty, she says. and wet

That tracks, I send, and she says: how are you aud

I stare at the words, finding myself at a full-body loss for how to respond. How am I? I have no idea. Cleo calls for Silas across the room, and I watch him look up at her. His eyebrows arched, his hair tied into a messy bun, his standard show outfit: black jeans, black Henley, black Converse. So he blends into the background while he's filming, surely. Not so that he looks like a brooding artist, and definitely not so the green in his brown eyes becomes so bright by contrast that it's striking. Striking to someone else—not to me, when his gaze flickers in my direction before he crosses the room toward Cleo.

I'm losing my grip on reality, I could tell Fallon. But instead I just watch Cleo and Silas: the way she grabs his elbow once he's next to her, their heads level with her standing on the chair. She points up at the top of her drawing—an enormous dragon, its shingled scales formed into points. She hops down from the chair and Silas climbs onto it, reaching down for her chalk. With Cleo directing him from below, he extends a long arm upward and finishes the few lines at the top of the drawing she couldn't reach—the dragon's head, the steam billowing from its nostrils. They grin at each other and I look away, back down at my phone. This is none of my business. *None* of it.

"Audrey," Cleo calls, motioning me toward her. Her eye shadow's rainbow tonight, solid lines of color striping up toward her eyebrows. "Come here a sec."

Silas and I meet eyes, so briefly, before he ducks his chin and crosses the room back toward his camera. When I come to stand next to Cleo she hands me a piece of chalk. "Help me color in the scales? Every other, I think."

I can't remember the last time I drew something, but shading in the scales is weirdly soothing—every time I finish one it feels disproportionately fulfilling.

"Fun, right?" Cleo looks down at me from her perch on the chair, and I nod. "Can't believe I've got Audrey St. Vrain doing something *fun*." She holds up her fingers, faking a camera and snapping a photo of me. "This is one for the scrapbook."

I sigh harshly. "Am I really so horrible?"

"Yeah," Cleo says, but when I jerk back to look at her she smiles and nudges me with her knee. "You're, like, borderline horrible. How about that?"

"Great," I mutter, and she laughs.

"You're growing on me, though." I look up at Cleo, watch her swooping white lines of chalk across her dragon's torso. "Like a fungus." She glances down at me. "On all of us, I think."

I swallow, pressing my chalk into the board. I don't meet her eyes when I whisper, "Is there, um. Something? Between you and Silas."

She's quiet for so long that I finally have to look up at her. When I do, she bursts out laughing. "*Silas?*" She says it so loudly that when I risk a glance at him, he's looking over at us. When our eyes meet, he immediately looks back down at his camera. "No."

Cleo drops into the chair next to me and I crouch to fill in some of the dragon's leg scales, bringing our heads close together so she doesn't have to keep shouting.

"Silas and I made out at a party during O week in a *truly* disastrous frat house basement—like, I think this place has since been condemned. We both have black mold poisoning, probably." I don't want to picture it, but I do: tall, lanky Silas with his easy smile and his jangling laugh. Cleo in some colorful leather outfit and immaculate eyeliner, her obsidian hair cascading over one shoulder. Silas reaching toward her, smoothing it out of the way, leaning close to—

"It was the stupidest thing either of us have ever done," she says, snapping me out of it. *What* is my malfunction? "The next morning we ate stale bagels in the dining hall, hungover as all hell, and it was like—*oh*, you are my literal brother. We came from the same womb. Kissing Silas was like being one of those twins that eats the other one in utero. That's how fucked up it was."

I grimace, and she laughs. "Anyway, we wound up in the same media program and we've been friends ever since, but the kiss was an idiot move. College is wild." She looks at me. "You're gonna end up doing some weird shit you won't be able to explain later. You'll see."

I'm already doing some weird shit I can't explain *now*, but I don't say that.

"Why do you ask?" Cleo says, studying me a little more closely. "Did he say something?"

"No, I—"

"Audrey?" We both look toward the door, where Mags is standing with a clipboard in one hand. "You're up in five. Ready?"

I nod, and Cleo nudges me with an elbow. "Try not to dunk on your mom this time," she says, already turning back to her drawing. "It makes Mick's job way harder, handling all the social media shit afterward."

When Magnolia sees me coming she turns on her heel to leave, so I'm all alone in the classroom's doorway when Silas stops me.

"Hey, Audrey." I've never seen him nervous before, but when I turn toward him he's tucking loose hair behind his ear in a way that can only be described as *fidgety*. He takes a step closer to me, a careful distance between us, his voice low. "Look, I just wanted to—what I said yesterday, at the river."

Everything inside me wants to stop this before it starts. *It's fine!* I want to shout, right in his face. *Let's pretend it never happened. Let's not interrogate it too closely. Let's keep twenty feet between us at all times.* But I force myself to stay silent and let him speak.

"I'm sorry," he says, eyes meeting mine. "I didn't mean to make you uncomfortable. I'd never want to—" He inhales, stops himself. "I just, it won't happen again. I promise."

"Silas," I say, practically a whisper. Uncomfortable is exactly how I feel around him, but not because of anything he's done. It's because I don't recognize myself when Silas is nearby, because even here in this weird apologetic moment, something about him makes me feel calm. Centered. "Let's put it behind us. It's okay."

Okay isn't right. *Okay* isn't the way to describe this, the six weeks of travel still stretched ahead of us. I'm not okay with how it feels, standing here with him, my mind flickering to Ethan and back. So I take a step away, and then two.

"I have to go," I say, and Silas nods, and I go.

I'm floating during the show, distracted enough to let it carry me along like a river. They have an English professor moderating. When she asks me what it's like to know that I've inspired a generation of women to be kinder to themselves, I manage to smile and say, "Oh, my mom did that."

We're nearly to the end when the moderator says, "This tour is all about getting personal with Camilla and Audrey, her *someday daughter*." I'm looking at Silas, the dark curve of his shoulder in the shadows just past the stage. "And I'd like to dig into who you were, Camilla, when you wrote the book. What that headspace was like when you were, what, twenty-seven?"

"Oh, I wish it was just twenty-seven," my mother says, smiling graciously. "*Letters* is a hundred-and-twenty-page book that took me three years to get right. I started it when I was twenty-four."

The moderator's eyebrows rise, and I turn to look at Camilla. For my whole life, she's been the person she is now: *Letters to My Someday Daughter* a thing she created in the rearview, a catalyst for her identity as I know it. I try to picture her at twenty-four, picking away at a manuscript, and can't.

"Twenty-four?" the moderator repeats. She gestures at me. "That's practically Audrey's age."

I feel myself make a face; I won't be twenty-four for another six years. By the time I'm twenty-four I'll be halfway through medical school.

Camilla looks at me; I can tell she disagrees, too, but her words come out on a charmed, diplomatic laugh. "Twenty-four certainly feels closer to her reality than mine."

"So young," the moderator says, "to have this kind of wisdom."

"Well." My mother shifts a little in her seat, gestures toward the audience like she's inviting them in. "Life moves differently for all of us, regardless of age. The experiences that mold us come

120

at different times. I was young when I went through the hardest things, the ones that forced me to learn."

I think: *her parents dying*. She says, "Like my parents' deaths."

"Mmm," the moderator intones, casting her whole face into a portrait of sympathetic understanding. "A car crash, wasn't it?"

"It was," Camilla says. She's told me the story maybe twice in all my eighteen years—brief and bleak. A rainy day, a skid into a median, both her parents gone in a flash while she was in college all the way across the country.

The moderator leans closer to us. "And do you feel like that experience informed *Letters*?"

My mother draws a breath. It's subtle, the way she hedges—if you didn't know her, you'd miss it. It's in the twitch of one eyebrow. How her teeth just scrape the edge of her lower lip before she speaks. "Of course," she says. "Especially set into the context of the rest of my life then."

The moderator presses on, tacking into a discussion of grief. But I hear the not-lie, the careful choice of her words. The "context" she doesn't explain.

And I think of what my dad said, on that humid wraparound porch just a few days ago.

You don't know everything about her.

22

Mick is halfway through hefting my mother's enormous Louis Vuitton suitcase onto a luggage cart when Mags lets out a theatrical gasp that stops all of us in our tracks.

"*No*," she says, taking off her sunglasses to get a better look at the departures monitor. "Our flight's been rescheduled."

My mother exhales through her nose, a controlled show of frustration. She's wearing a wide-brimmed sun hat, salmon-colored with a white ribbon, and black circular sunglasses. If you didn't already know who she was, you wouldn't guess. Mags gave me a UT Austin baseball cap to wear at the airport—*just in case*—because that Taos paparazzi photo was only the beginning, and people have been noticing us everywhere. It's disorienting.

Camilla steps up next to Magnolia. "To when?"

"A full twenty-four hours," Mags says, sucking her teeth. "Tomorrow morning."

"When would we get in?" Sadie asks, moving closer to them. Mick sits down on my mother's suitcase, then quickly stands back up when she casts a sideways glance at him.

"Just after noon." Mags points up at the board. "Same as we would've today."

"Damn it," Sadie murmurs, pulling out her phone. "Audrey and I are supposed to be at our next appointment at nine tomorrow morning. It was the only time Dr. Bautista could meet with us in Chicago, I'll have to—"

"What's going on?" Cleo asks, sidling up beside me and hiking a tote bag higher onto her shoulder. Silas trails behind her with Puddles's carrier in one hand.

"Flight's pushed to tomorrow," I say, dread swallowing up the air in my lungs. A whole week in Chicago without a single doctor's visit, nothing to focus on but Camilla and my secondhand echo of the Penn program.

"Can you get us back into the hotel for another night?" my mother asks Magnolia, who immediately pulls out her phone.

"Sadie," I say, and she looks at me. "There's no way we can reschedule?"

"I'm so sorry, Audrey, he was really clear that his week was busy and I could only—"

"What if we drove?"

We all turn to Silas, who lowers Puddles to the floor and holds his phone out to Sadie. It's open to a map with a big blue line running north across it. *16 hours, 48 minutes*, it says.

"Si," Sadie says, "we'd get there at, like, three o'clock in the morning—"

"*Surprise road trip!*" Cleo shouts, and a few people standing in the terminal turn to look at her.

"I'll go rent a car?" Mick offers, grinning, his whole face lit with excitement.

"I'll rent the car." Sadie places a hand on his shoulder. "It's cheaper if you're over twenty-five. Audrey, are you in?"

I look at each of them in turn. This is happening too fast for me to process. "Guys, it's so far, and, I mean, this wasn't the plan—"

"This is the only way to *keep* the plan," Cleo says, quirking an eyebrow at me. I bite my lip, press my thumb to my pinky finger. Okay. Okay, okay.

"Okay," I make myself say, and all four of them look at me. "I'm in."

Camilla and Mags stay in Austin to take tomorrow's flight. Traversing the country in a Honda Odyssey minivan with four teenagers, one biology professor, and a very slobbery dog is not, apparently, my mother's speed. To be honest, I'm questioning whether it's mine.

"Okay, you're looking for I-35 north." Silas is in the passenger seat, Sadie driving, Puddles peeking at me over Silas's shoulder. Her tongue is hanging out, as usual, dripping saliva onto the collar of his T-shirt. "And we'll be on that, basically, until Dallas."

"What's our ETA?" Cleo asks from beside me. Mick is in the third row of seats, already sprawled horizontal across them though we're not even five minutes from the airport.

"Um." Silas hesitates before turning back to look at her. "Three fifteen a.m. With no stops."

Mick lets out a low whistle. "Hopefully no traffic."

Silas hums his agreement, turning back to face forward. "It'll be what it'll be."

Silence falls, and for some reason it takes a great effort to force the words from me, like the sincerity of them is catching in my throat. "Thank you," I say. "For doing this for me. I, um." Sadie's eyes rise to mine in the rearview. "I really appreciate it."

"You'll never see me turn down a road trip," Cleo says, sliding out of her sandals and pulling her bare feet under her. "So I, for one, did not do this for you."

"Similarly," Mick says, "I hate flying and much prefer land travel. Not for you."

"And I'm in it for Puddles," Silas says, rolling down his window. He holds on to her as her little paws grip the sill, her head poking out into the wind. "No thank-yous needed."

"Okay," I say, and Cleo reaches over to nudge me with a pack of Twizzlers. I take one out, stick it between my teeth, dig into my backpack for the Penn textbook. Feel a warmth that has absolutely nothing to do with Austin's oppressive humidity. And then I settle in for the long haul in this car full of people who are, decisively, not doing this for me.

23

We're an hour outside Little Rock, the sun just starting to dip, when Cleo swings a right off the highway.

"Whoa," Mick says. He's on navigation, riding shotgun with Puddles in his lap. Sadie sits next to me, and Silas is asleep in the back seat, one long arm thrown over his eyes. "Wrong turn, maestro. You're on 40 for another seventy miles."

"Don't question me, Michelangelo," Cleo says. She has her big yellow sunglasses on and is blowing bubble gum with loud smacks. "We're going to a point of interest."

"What point of interest?" Mick asks, at the same moment I say, "Is your full name Michelangelo?"

He laughs. "I wish. It's just Michael."

"Don't sell yourself short, *just* Michael," Cleo says. She hangs another right and suddenly we're on a gravel road, Arkansas spreading flat and arid around us. "You're Michael fucking Selinofoto. My moonlight baby."

"Where are we going?" Silas asks, his voice gravelly with sleep. When I look back he's stretching, T-shirt hiking up to expose a thin strip of his stomach, and I look quickly away. At anything, *anything* else. "Rest stop?"

"We are going," Cleo says patiently but emphatically, "to a point of interest."

"How far is it?" Sadie asks, glancing at her watch. "Just want to remind the group that our ETA is three thirty in the morning and some of us aren't as spry as others."

"You don't look a day past twenty," Silas says, and Sadie rolls her eyes.

"It's fifteen minutes away," Cleo says. "And it's going to be worth it, okay? So everyone calm the eff down."

"How'd you find it?" I ask, and she catches my eyes in the rearview.

"I googled it while you were studying the space-time continuum or whatever it is you're doing back there."

I glance at my lap, where the Penn textbook is open to a diagram of the four different types of glial cells. "It's biology," I say, and Cleo gags.

"Disgusting. Why?"

"I'm taking a course—" I catch myself, amending: "My boyfriend, Ethan, is taking a course at the University of Pennsylvania this summer. It's where I was supposed to be, instead of here."

"So you're *not* taking the course," Mick clarifies, turning in the front seat to look at me.

I clear my throat. "I mean, technically—"

"She's not taking the course," Cleo says loudly, spreading her hand over the center console to emphasize every word, "but she's reading the textbook back there like a freaking *librarian* instead of enjoying our great American landscape."

I glance out the window, flat farmland as far as the eye can see.

"I can still learn," I say, trying to keep the edge out of my words. "Even if I'm not there."

"Or you could just be here," Cleo says. "You know, *be* here. Instead of—"

"Cleo," Sadie says. Her voice is soft, but Cleo stops immediately. "Give it a rest."

I can't bring myself to meet anyone's eyes. I don't need Sadie to defend me; the way I'm choosing to spend my summer doesn't need defending at all. Cleo doesn't even know me. She has no idea—

"There," Cleo says. "The sign."

All four of us turn to look out the window as we pass a massive metal sign hand-painted with the words *Mailbox Station, USA*.

"'Mailbox Station'?" Mick rights himself in his seat, turning back to her. "I'm not sold so far, Clementine."

"Don't call me that," she says, pointing a finger at him. "And please hold your judgment until we're fully on the premises."

Cleo drives past a crop of dense trees, and when we round the corner we're suddenly in a postage stamp of a parking lot with hundreds of mailboxes spread out in front of us. They're all different colors, materials, eras. Our car is the only one in the lot, so Cleo pulls right up to the fence that separates the parking spaces from the field of mailboxes.

"Let's go," she says, throwing the van into park. "To Sadie's point, we don't have all day. Also, someone else is driving when we're done here."

We pile out of the van and Silas takes Puddles from Mick, hurrying ahead of us as she drags him over to a patch of grass. The rest of us cluster at the entrance of Mailbox Station, where a plastic box with a clear lid sits full of notepaper and envelopes. A golden plaque on its front reads *Take what you need so you can leave what you need*. And next to it, a sign with a lockbox attached: *Lovingly maintained by our amazing volunteers*. Mick digs in his pockets, dropping in a few quarters, and Cleo says, "Do they have a credit card reader or what?"

Mick snorts and drags her into the rows of mailboxes as Sadie pulls a ten out of her wallet and sticks it in the lockbox.

"Shall we?" She motions me ahead of her, so I step into the labyrinth and duck to look into a mailbox. Some of them have stacks of letters inside, some are empty, some house just one lonely note. They're all splashed with different handwriting:

For Max

To Adeline, wherever you are

To Daddy—miss you

I look around, breathing in the heat. There's something reverent about the air out here, moving through all these left-behind words.

"There are no addresses," I say, almost to myself.

"I think that's probably the point." Sadie looks over at me, a few mailboxes ahead. "Things you wish you'd be brave enough to say for real, you know? Or what you'd say to someone who can't hear it. Someone who's gone."

Mick and Cleo are far away now, peering into a set of retro red mailboxes side by side. I spot Silas by the parking lot, pulling a piece of paper out of the box with Puddles panting at his feet.

I look at Sadie and find her watching him, too. She smiles at me, and I wonder if we're thinking about the same thing: Silas, and what he'd say to someone who's gone.

"Elliott would love this," she tells me, resting her hands on her hips and turning in a circle to take it all in. "He's obsessed with the mail service, ever since we brought him home. We wait on the porch to say hi every single afternoon."

"Brought him home?" I ask.

Sadie looks at me, eyes hidden by the reflection off her sunglasses. "He was eighteen months old when we adopted him."

"How old is he now?"

"He was three in May," she says, smiling. "And wilder by the day."

I reach for the mailbox closest to me, lift its metal flag skyward and then tuck it back into place. "You miss him?"

"Oh, constantly," Sadie laughs. "It's like being hungry for your favorite food, but only the way your favorite restaurant makes it, and they're closed all week. So you eat something else, and it fills you up, but it's not the same."

Across the field from us, Silas is licking the seal of an envelope and pressing it carefully closed. I think of my first year at the Summit School, the few futile letters I mailed to my mother. They were assignments—we practiced narrative writing by drafting handwritten notes to our parents. The language arts teacher made a big show of passing around stamps, of collecting the envelopes and stacking them neatly in a box for transport to the post office. I sent Camilla long, rambly messages about my days: about my new roommate, Fallon, and the spaghetti in the dining hall, and the way fresh snow made everything unnaturally quiet. I imagined her reading the letters in her great, sloping yard, overlooking the ocean. Missing me. The responses came weeks, sometimes months, afterward—unsigned Hallmark cards, my name and school address inked in Magnolia's handwriting.

Silas starts across the field with Puddles and I look away from him, down at the grass. My cheeks burn with the memory: how desperately I'd reached out for my mother, and how transparently she didn't care.

"Hey, listen," Sadie says. I blink, looking up at her. "You did really great in Austin, with Dr. Kowalski." I fidget under the praise; all I've ever wanted is to impress people, but I never know how to behave when they tell me I've done it. "I was talking to Camilla about it, and we think you should share more about your work this summer, during your appearances with her. Let people get to know you for what you're so great at." She watches me, trying to gauge my reaction. "If that's something you'd be interested in."

"My mom thinks that?" It comes out of me without any processing at all; I speak the words in the same moment they occur to me. It doesn't make sense that my mother would want me to talk about this—my visits with doctors, my time with Sadie, the one part of this summer that's not about Camilla. And since when do she and Sadie talk about me, anyways?

"We both do," Sadie says slowly. She studies me for a beat, then adds, "At least consider it, okay? This tour is about both of you— you should get to share your experience, too, if it's something you want."

A butterfly flits past, and I watch the shudder of its wings in the thick July heat. It is something I want, isn't it? To be known for who I am, apart from her.

"Either way," Sadie says, starting to move back toward the car, "tomorrow will be great. Dr. Bautista was actually *my* physical therapist when I was doing my postdoc—he was on rotation in

Michigan and I swear he saved my back after so much nonstop standing in the lab. . . ."

I let the rest of her sentence melt into the shimmering heat, into all the other words swirling between us in this place. Separated from us by rows of metal flags and letters, Silas has stopped in front of a wood-paneled, white-painted mailbox. He looks down at the envelope in his hands, balanced in both palms like something precious and breakable. Puddles waits patiently in the grass, like even she knows to give him time. And then he slides the letter into the box and lifts the little red flag.

It's stupid—nonsensical and illogical and as unscientific as something can get. This entire place is built on feelings, no hard facts to it at all.

But still, I find myself hoping that they get the message. Whoever it is Silas is reaching out for.

Ethan calls me at nearly ten o'clock, when we're driving through the endless flatlands of southern Illinois. I've just finished my turn at the wheel and am hidden in the dark in the third row of seats, Silas driving with one hand pushed through his hair to prop his head against the windowsill. Cleo is curled in the passenger seat with Puddles in her lap, both of them snoring softly.

"Hey," I whisper, my voice as quiet as I can get it. But even still, even over the music wafting from the van's speakers, Silas looks up to catch my eye in the rearview. I look away first.

"Hey," Ethan says. He sounds wide awake, as ready to jump into the lecture notes as he always is. "You make it to Chicago?"

"Ah, not yet," I say, playing with the frayed hem of my shorts. "Our flight got pushed to tomorrow, so we're actually road-tripping up there so I can make it to this physical therapy meeting by morning."

"Road-tripping?" Ethan says. "Your mom?"

I breathe a laugh, leaning my head back against the seat. "Of course not. She's flying out tomorrow."

"So you're with Dr. Stone?"

"Dr. Stone," I repeat, feeling nervous for no reason. These are just the facts, just the people I'm spending my summer with. "And the interns."

"Sorry, who?" Ethan's voice goes crackly, and I sit up straighter.

"The interns?" I say, keeping my voice even. "Mick, and Cleo, and—"

"Audrey?" Static fuzz, and then nothing. I look down at my phone, *call failed*, zero bars in its upper right corner. I draw a steady breath, and Sadie's voice reaches toward me through the dark car.

"Everything all right?"

"Yeah," I say, dropping the useless phone into my bag. "No service out here."

In the shadows past Sadie and Mick, Puddles jumps down from Cleo's lap and makes her way toward me, picking through the backpacks and empty fast food bags on the floor. I'm staring at her, unsure what to do, when she leaps onto the back row of seats beside me. My legs are tucked underneath me, ankles splayed out to one side, and she curls into me before dropping onto her belly and resting her fuzzy chin on my foot.

We look at each other—her big, dark eyes pooling up the night and reflecting it back at me. When I glance toward the front of the van, Silas is watching us in the rearview, a small smile on his face.

He looks back at the road, and I look back at Puddles, and her eyes fall shut. A hot little breath puffs from her nose onto my ankle.

What the hell, I think. She's already sleeping. So I let her stay there, chin to foot, as my own eyes fall shut. And I sleep—the van lulling us through the quiet midwestern dark—the rest of the way to Chicago.

CHICAGO

24

Mom picks me up from Dr. Bautista's office in a town car, rolling up next to Sadie and me on the curb and lowering a tinted back window.

"Audrey, honey," she calls from inside. "Can you hop in? We're due in Winnetka in fifteen minutes. We'll be late as it is."

When I open the door she dips her chin, looking out at Sadie on the sidewalk. "Do you need a ride, Sadie? I can have Mags call you a car, she just got to the hotel."

"I'll take the L," Sadie says. I imagine the two of them without me, talking about my work this summer. They meet eyes through the lowered window, and when they smile at each other I wonder what else they've talked about when I'm not around. "Thanks, though."

"Well," Camilla says when I slide into the car. "How was the drive yesterday?"

I think of Cleo flitting through those rows of mailboxes in Arkansas, Mick passing around cartons of french fries at a rest stop in Missouri. Puddles asleep on my foot, and Silas watching us in the dark. "Long," I say finally.

"Do I look all right?"

I turn to her, watch as she runs a hand through her glossy hair. She's in white jeans and a pale-blue knit tank top—mascara and pink lip balm. She always looks perfect.

"Of course," I say, and she touches my knee.

"Came straight from the plane." She reaches into her purse as we wind up Lake Shore Drive. "Had to change in one of those hideous airport bathrooms. Here." I take the paper she's holding out to me, a list of discussion questions undoubtedly typed up by Mags and printed at the hotel before they left Austin. "The book club guide. I'm not expecting us to go through all of these—I know Preeti and she's not quite so formal as all that. But helpful to look over, nonetheless."

The paper is a nightmare—*When Camilla writes that "the permission to live as we want is our own to give," what does that mean to you?* And *What one message would you want your someday daughter to know? How can you apply that message in your own life?* And, worst of all, at the very bottom of the page: *Open forum for Audrey questions—what has it meant to her to experience this kind of radical self-love at home, how has this emotional openness shaped her relationship with Camilla, etc.*

I swallow, turn to watch Lake Michigan hurtle past. *Radical.*

The house in Winnetka is gated, its plot so wooded you can't see even a hint of the house from the road. The driver checks in at the radio box, announces my mother's presence, and we're buzzed in. I shouldn't be surprised anymore by the company Camilla keeps, but still—my mouth falls open as we roll up the driveway. A colossal stone mansion, crawling with carefully groomed ivy. Flower boxes in every window, frothy with huge white blooms. And a three-story arched window at the front of the house, giving us a clear view through its airy living room to the churning blue of Lake Michigan beyond it.

"Stunning," my mother says. "Preeti's always had such good taste."

"Who is this person?" I ask as we step onto the smooth driveway.

"One of Saint's early investors," Camilla says. "She comes from tech and had the good fortune of a software buyout in the early aughts; now she runs a capital firm from the city. Two young daughters," she adds, looking at me as she reaches to ring the doorbell. "And a great interest in meeting you."

I feel myself bristle and consciously lower my shoulders, trying not to stare through the window in the door as Preeti appears and heads toward us.

"Camilla," she says, hugging her the moment she opens the door. Her accent is lyrical, turning my mother's name into music. "And you must be Audrey."

"Nice to meet you," I say, taking the hand she offers. Preeti looks about forty, a sage-colored linen dress hanging from her slim shoulders.

"Please, please, come in." She waves us onto the wide wooden floorboards of her entryway, then into an airy living room where six women sit on couches with champagne glasses in hand. It is . . . one o'clock in the afternoon. Everyone gasps when Camilla walks in, a whole chorus of breathy preening. I don't know where to look as my mother meets each woman in turn, so I step over to the window and look out at the lake instead: it's sunlit and big as the ocean, endless from here.

"And my daughter," Camilla says, my cue to turn around. "Audrey."

Their collective *hellooooo* turns into a hum, a harmonious croon.

"Sit next to me, sweetie," one woman says, patting the couch. I manage a smile and tuck myself in beside her—the whole room smells like perfume, like huffing an expensive candle.

"How's it *been*?" another woman asks, directly across from me. "This summer, so far?"

I glance at Camilla, know that we're both thinking about the last time I answered this question. *It's been absolutely horrible.* I open my mouth, but my mother beats me to it.

"Tell them about your work with Dr. Stone," she says. Sadie prepared me for this, and even still—I'm so surprised that the words have to sink in slowly, one by one by one. "Just this morning Audrey was visiting a physical therapy practice downtown, but that's only a small part of her independent study." She meets my eyes. "Go ahead, honey."

I make some kind of stuttering, unhinged noise—like a car that needs to grumble along a bit before the engine catches. And then I'm telling them about Sadie, about her research, about everyone we've seen and will see.

I hadn't been expecting a whole metric ton from Dr. Bautista's practice, to be honest—physical therapists are technically doctors, but a DPT degree only takes three years. Not exactly the same as the path ahead of me after undergrad: four years of med school plus three years of residency (at minimum, minimum, minimum). Plus, no MCAT. But Sadie spoke highly of him, which is no small thing. And we *did* drive seventeen hours to be there.

I certainly wasn't expecting Dr. Bautista's state-of-the-art, sun-filled facility overlooking the river in downtown Chicago. The name he'd made for himself as the leading authority in postparalysis rehabilitation. The leather binder he let me flip through on his desk, thank-you notes from his greatest success stories captured there behind plastic.

And, most of all, I wasn't expecting the way he'd smiled at Sadie when he walked me out after the tour—when she was waiting for us in the lobby, copy of *Letters* open in her lap. The way he'd said, "Still reading that book, huh?" Like he'd seen her do it before, all those years ago in Michigan. Or how she'd clicked her pen and snapped the book shut—like she'd been taking notes inside it that she didn't want us to see.

I had my own habits when it came to that book, my own secret reads. But I couldn't, for the life of me, figure out why Sadie would. I wanted to know what she was writing there, but I couldn't bring myself to ask.

"It's been incredible," I say now, pushing down the memory to focus on what's in front of me. "To see all these different practice areas, and to do it with a scientist I respect so much." I glance at my mother and find, to my surprise, that she's watching me as intently as everyone else. Like she actually wants to hear about this. "I'm in the application process for a shadowing position at the Johns Hopkins Hospital ICU this fall—they only take one premed student, but what I'm seeing this summer has been so valuable. I can't, um." I hesitate, realize I've been talking everyone's ears off. The first time, since joining this tour, that I haven't had to dredge words up against their will. "I can't wait to be there."

"Wow," the woman next to me says. "What an impressive young woman you are."

I flush, glancing at Camilla. And she doesn't do what she normally does—swoop in, take credit, turn the conversation back to herself. She just smiles at me. She just lets me fill up this space all on my own.

25

Thursday is the Fourth of July, and Cleo's eye makeup knows it. She has blue stars dotting the lids of both eyes, red lines swooping along her lashes and flaring up toward her eyebrows.

"America has some considerable shit to answer for," she says, closing a hand around my wrist and dragging me toward a funnel cake stand at the very tip of Navy Pier. "But lord knows I can't pass up a firework."

"You do this a lot," I say, breathing in the sugar-sweet night air.

"Do what?"

I hold up my arm, still gripped in her small but mighty hand. "Yank people around."

"Woof." She drops my wrist. "Sorry. Don't mean to—it's just, I'm usually going in the right direction."

"What about the time," Mick says, him and Silas stepping into line behind us, "that you got us so lost in Arlington we were forty minutes late to dinner with my grandparents during family weekend?"

"You can't get lost in Arlington," Cleo says, staring up at the menu. "You just use the Lincoln Memorial like the North Star."

"That's just . . . not true," Mick says. "At all."

Cleo looks back at him. "Should I get apple pie topping or cinnamon sugar?"

"Why not both?" Silas asks.

"Oh," Cleo gasps, widening her eyes at him. "*Oh*, I love you. Yes." Then she adds, "Not in the romantic sense," and glances at me in a way that I thoroughly do not enjoy.

"What are you getting, Audrey?" Mick asks, drumming his fingers on one bicep, his arms crossed as he stares up at the menu.

"Classic powdered sugar," I say, and Cleo groans.

"You would. I bet your favorite doughnut flavor's plain glazed, too."

It . . . is. "Because it's the best one."

"Well, I'm getting rainbow sprinkles," Mick says.

Silas eyes him. "I don't think that's an option."

But Mick points over his shoulder, where a six-year-old in pigtails holds a funnel cake smothered in sprinkles.

"That's for kids," Cleo says, just as they call her up to order.

"Which is what I am," Mick tells her solemnly, "at heart."

"You?" I ask, glancing up at Silas. He's wearing khaki shorts and a white short-sleeved button-down over a T-shirt. Those same abominable hiking sandals from the plane in Los Angeles. His hair's a little wet, like he showered before coming here.

"Oh, caramel sauce for sure." He combs a hand through his curls, trying to tame them at the nape of his neck. "Lily would kill me if I got anything else—my sister."

I remember, but I don't tell him that.

"She's super into all those baking shows," he says as we step forward in line. "Taught herself to make the perfect caramel sauce last summer before I left for school. Now she wants me to order it out at every opportunity so I can report back how much better hers is."

"She wouldn't know, though, if you got something else."

He looks at me, narrowing his eyes in a good-natured way. "Are you trying to rob my thirteen-year-old sister of a moment of glory, Audrey?"

I hold up my hands, a peace offering. "I'm just saying you should get what you want."

His eyes linger on mine for just a moment, something inscrutable flickering across them, before he looks away. "It is what I want now," he says. "She's got me trained like one of Pavlov's hounds."

"What can I get you?" the funnel cake guy calls out to us, and Silas motions me ahead of him. He's been true to his word, to what he said back in that classroom in Austin: the way Silas acts around me is easy and friendly and perfectly polite. Not a word or a glance out of place. The problem isn't Silas, it's me. It's me, stepping around him and imagining what it might be like for his hand to reach out as I do it. To graze the small of my back.

"Let us have a bite," Mick says, crowding my space as soon as I turn away from the window with my funnel cake. He holds his own besprinkled cake to the side while reaching for mine and ripping off a piece.

"Hey!" I say, in the same moment that he lets out a yelp.

"Oh my god." With his mouth full of cake, it sounds like *ormagore.* He unhinges his jaw and fans his hand rapidly in front of his lips, giving us a full show of half-chewed dough. "It's *hot.*"

"You're a mess," Cleo says, reaching around him to rip off a piece for herself. I try to swivel out of her way, but I'm not quick enough.

"I thought this flavor was *boring*," I say, watching her blow on the sugar-dusted chunk of cake.

"You said it was the best one." She chews thoughtfully as Silas comes to stand beside us with his own caramel-slathered plate. "I need to see for myself."

"And?" Silas says. He looks between her and Mick, who's sticking his tongue out like the hot July air could un-burn it.

"*Mmmmm.*" Cleo tilts her head back and forth. She motions toward my cake. "You try."

Silas looks up at me, his eyes bright in the glow of the funnel cake stand. "Can I?"

And my head nods on its own, my arms extending the plate toward him. I have a flash of Ethan in the dining hall at the Summit School, standing up to get me my own fork so I could have a bite of his lasagna. *It's cold and flu season*, he'd said. He could kiss me but not share utensils, like the germs were somehow different. I wonder what he'd say if he were here now, watching three separate people put their hands on my food.

"Don't burn yourself," Mick warns as Silas lifts the bite to his mouth. But instead of burning himself, Silas commits the cardinal sin of powdered-sugar consumption. He inhales.

The aftermath unfolds in slow motion: the sugar going up his nose, the pitch of his body as he lurches forward, the gasping cough that sends an enormous rush of air in my direction. The powdered sugar from my funnel cake lifts in the gale of Silas's breath and splatters all over my dress.

"Oh my god," Silas says, his voice raspy and strained. Cleo howls with laughter as he steps toward me, one hand outstretched. "I'm so sorry."

I look down at myself. There's sugar all over my chest, down my cleavage, fanning my shoulders like freckles.

"Are you okay?" Silas asks, hand falling to his side as he leans closer to me. I look up at him. Draw a breath. His eyes dart back and forth over mine. "Audrey?"

When I jerk forward and blow, the remaining sugar flies off my funnel cake and promptly coats Silas's T-shirt. It lands on his cheekbones, his chin, in the dip of his collarbone. When he blinks at me in shock, it snows off his eyelashes. There's a single beat of stunned silence, and then he starts laughing. Chin tipped back, the length of his sugar-flecked throat exposed. I do, too—surprising myself with it—loud and unlike me.

"*Audrey*," Cleo says, sounding breathless and thrilled. "You little minx."

"Now we see why she wanted powdered sugar," Mick says, reaching over with a napkin to brush off my shoulders. I take it from him and start working on my dress, laughter still hiccuping out of me. "It's a weapon."

"For real." Silas swipes at his shirt collar, sugar raining onto the boardwalk between us. He finds my eyes in the dark and grins through sugar-dusted lips. "You're full of surprises."

I shrug. Think, *So are you.*

26

"Since when do you have a boating license?"

Magnolia looks up at me, adjusting her sun hat as she settles in behind the wheel. She's wearing a gauzy sarong over a purple one-piece—the exact same style as the one my mother's wearing, just in a different color.

"Since 2013," she says. "Do you need to see proof, Officer?"

I feel my nose scrunch—the last thing I need is cheek from Magnolia Jones, busybody extraordinaire. But I can hear Mick laughing behind me, and when he nudges me with an elbow I turn in his direction.

"Grab these for me?" he asks, and I take the grocery bags he's holding out. They're full of chips and candy and trail mix—enough food to feed a small army for a whole weekend, decidedly overkill for six people with a four-hour boat rental.

"Think you bought enough?" I ask, and he jerks a thumb over his shoulder at Cleo, who's still on the dock with Silas and my mother.

"Ask Cleo, she did the shopping."

Which tracks, considering the three—yes, *three*—separate packs of Twizzlers I can see through one of the thin plastic bags.

"Don't knock my shop!" Cleo shouts. She's in a neon-blue bikini and a white bucket hat, wearing giant heart-shaped sunglasses. Next to her, Silas holds Puddles—her little sausage body stuffed into a bright yellow life jacket. "I didn't hear anyone else volunteering for snack duty."

The truth is this plan came together so last-minute I can't believe anyone had time to prepare anything—Magnolia knocked on all our doors at ten this morning and told us Camilla had rented a boat beginning at noon. The show last night went off without a hitch—sold-out theater, enthusiastic signing line—and my mother wanted to celebrate with an afternoon on Lake Michigan. Sadie bowed out, citing seasickness, but the rest of us are here.

It does feel like the *Letters* tour has hit some kind of stride; even I can begrudgingly admit it. One of the women at Preeti's book club in Winnetka turned out to be the Lifestyle & Leisure editor at the *Chicago Tribune*, and the day after we met she published a piece about Camilla and me and what she called "the synergy of our summer together." It detailed all my plans with Sadie, the fall shadowing position, the reasons I want to be a doctor (in my own words, for once). *In taking her someday daughter on the road*, she wrote, *Camilla St. Vrain has set them both up for successful somedays.*

It's an overexaggeration, sure. The most successful setup for my *someday* would've been the Penn program, and that's not where I am. But it's the first press piece all summer that's talked about me like anything other than my mother's pet—like an entire human being with aspirations beyond appearing in the gilded social posts on her feeds.

And, for the first time, the questions I got at last night's show weren't all about self-care. They weren't about how basking in Camilla's glow has made me just the luckiest girl to ever live. No one brought up the Sex Summit. The article painted me as my own person, and in its wake I was able to step on the stage as myself, instead of as the character Camilla has made of me.

"Check it," Cleo says, climbing onto the boat and sneaking a hand into one of the bags I'm holding. She pulls out a hot-dog-folded magazine, some glossy rag from the checkout aisle. There's a picture of Camilla and me on the cover, seated side by side at last night's show. *Camilla St. Vrain's Valedictorian Daughter Holds Court in Chicago*, the headline says. "You're famous."

I take it from her, flipping open to the article as everyone else settles around me.

Camilla St. Vrain's given us a lot, the article begins. *Yoni eggs, life-affirming Inner Saint retreats, permission to love ourselves just as we are. But as she traverses the country on this summer's* Letters to My Someday Daughter *anniversary tour, St. Vrain is giving us something she hasn't before: an up-close look at the someday daughter we've heard about for so many years, a future doctor named Audrey. And if last night's sold-out show in Chicago proved anything, it's that Camilla's eighteen-year-old daughter is impressive in her own right—not just someday, but already. After graduating at the top of her class from Colorado's prestigious Summit School, Audrey is—*

"Take a seat, honey." I look up, find Camilla watching me from her perch behind Mags. "I don't want you to fall when we start moving."

"Come up here," Silas calls, waving me toward the front of the boat. "Everyone's in the back, we should balance the weight."

Balance the weight, I think. Is that some kind of euphemism?

But no—it's just Silas being freaking *normal*, sliding over to make space for me next to Puddles on the leather bench seat. I think of him with powdered sugar on his lips and force myself to stop.

"Thanks," I say, and Magnolia powers up the motor, and Silas holds out a hand.

When I look up at him, he wiggles his fingers. He has to shout over the noise. "Let me see?"

I pass off the magazine, feeling suddenly nervous as his eyes track across it. The thought of Silas reading the words *yoni eggs* and *Audrey* in the same paragraph makes me want to pitch myself off the front of the boat, but eventually he's finished reading and hands it back to me.

"Can I ask you something?"

He slides closer when I nod, pulling Puddles into his lap. The Midwest wind whips around us, ripping curls loose from beneath his *GG's Gardenshare* hat.

"Why'd you agree to this tour," he asks, leaning in so we don't have to yell, "if you thought it would be so horrible?"

I tilt backward, regaining space between us. "Why did you?"

"Why wouldn't I?" Silas grins, the wind wrenching his T-shirt tight across his shoulders, the planes of his chest. I don't think I've ever seen someone so comfortable in their own body, watched another person move through the world as easily as he does. "When your mom offered the internships to American, the three of us applied right away." He waves a hand toward Cleo and Mick, who are already eating Twizzlers at the back of the boat. "A summer-long trip, eight weeks with my friends, work experience to put on my résumé—win, win, win."

"Résumé for what?"

He shrugs. "Whatever comes next. Making documentaries, maybe."

"Maybe?" I repeat. "You don't know?"

Silas studies me. Behind his shoulder, Lake Shore Drive recedes, its high-rises growing smaller and smaller. "Does anyone get to know for sure?" he says. "It'll be what it'll be."

I scoff. "It'll be what you make it."

Silas shakes his head, smiling, and looks down at his feet—big and bare on the floor of the boat. "Okay, Audrey. Your turn to answer the question."

It's out before I've thought it through: "I came because she wanted to spend time with me." Something I never thought I'd say out loud and yet here I am, saying it. Silas looks back up at me; I know, in the same way I know I'll draw breath, that he's a safe place to put this. "Because she doesn't usually want me with her."

His lips part, but I look down at my hands. Keep talking so he can't pity me, can't tell me how sad that is. "But I've always been this pawn, and that's really what she needed from me this summer. Someone to help bolster her image."

When he's quiet, I finally hazard a glance up at him. The high sun's right in his eyes and he's squinting at me—like our roles are reversed, like he's the resting mathematician now. "Can both be true?" he asks. "She wants to spend time with you *and* do the public image thing?"

"Is that love?" I say, and his eyes don't leave mine. "When there's a transaction involved?"

He tilts his head, and Puddles shifts on his lap. We both look down at her. "Maybe. I think love can probably be a lot of things."

150

We hit the wake from another boat, smacking so hard against the water that Cleo screams. We both turn to look back at her, watch her dissolve into a laugh as she leans hard into Mick.

"It's my biggest weakness," I say finally.

"What is?"

"The way I am with her." I meet Silas's eyes and then look away, out across the water. "Always hoping something's going to be there." I press my thumb to my pinky finger, not quite counting but ready if I need to. "I act stupid for her."

"Doesn't really sound like a weakness," Silas says. When I look back at him he's close to me, leaning in so I can hear him over the motor but also, it feels, so I know he's there. Listening. "Sounds like you love her."

I pull my lip between my teeth and we keep looking at each other and the wind lashes around us, somehow both warm and biting.

"Silas!" Mick shouts, and we both look away. "Where'd you put the—"

Mags cuts the engine, and suddenly Mick's voice is ten decibels too loud. He dips his chin, quiets down, and finishes, "—sunscreen?"

"Under the seat," Silas says, pointing.

"Yeah, I can't find it."

Silas sighs, holding Puddles's leash out to me. She's sitting between us, peering out over the water, and looks up at him when he stands. "Watch her for a sec?"

I take the leash wordlessly, and then he's gone. I'm distantly aware of Magnolia talking to my mother, an anchor being drawn out from somewhere, a great splash as it hits the water. Another boat trawls by and Puddles leaps to her feet, suddenly on high alert. I'm still thinking about the fool I've made of myself—about everything that bubbles up out of me when Silas is around, unfiltered and embarrassing, never what he asked for, so much more than anyone should have to listen to—and Puddles is halfway down the bench before I realize she's moving and think to tighten my grip on her leash.

But I'm too slow, and the leash is slick with lake spray, and it slips through my hands as Puddles climbs onto the boat's back ledge. Faster than I've ever seen her move, spryer than her eleven years would lead you to believe. She's hopping up, and she's letting out a croaking bark, and she's taking a great leap over the water in furry, wrinkly pursuit of the passing boat.

I scream. I move so fast I slip, my knee smacking the hard plastic of the deck. I think of what Silas said at that park in Austin—*Puddles can't swim.*

And I'm in the water before my brain's caught up enough to remember that I can't, either.

27

It's like this: the water is cold but it *burns*. For half a triumphant second I'm lifting Puddles from the wake, but then, of course, I'm not. I don't know how to tread water; I don't actually know what people mean when they say that. The water isn't even saline. It doesn't buoy me at all. I sink like a stone, something inhuman, all my limbs moving in useless, unfamiliar ways. I gulp for air and it's liquid. It does the opposite of what it's meant to, scorches me all the way down.

And it keeps getting denser—like the lake is solidifying around me, going thick between my clawing fingers. I'm reaching for something, I think I am, I'm so sure I'm fighting to save myself but there's just the walled-in darkness around me and the white-hot gurgle of Lake Michigan down my throat and then the slow blackening, seeping from the outside in, the aperture of myself winding down.

I think of Fallon's flash of a laugh, the room we lived in together all through high school, the home we made there. My dad's face in the glow of stage lights filtered through the curtain. The scratch of his stubble under my five-year-old palm. My mother, reaching for me—I'm small, I'm barely walking, I'm barefoot in her living room and she's grinning, unrehearsed, both hands around my ribs to lift me up, holding me so tightly, and I'm laughing and I'm turning through the air and I'm—

Throwing up. Acid wash of it, liquid nightmare, eyes pressed shut.

"Oh, Jesus," someone says—hazy, hardly there. Something big and solid between my shoulder blades, holding me still while the third-largest Great Lake pours out of my open mouth. "Oh, god, thank fuck."

I cough, tears streaming from my closed eyes. They're salty, hit my lips as I retch again.

"Good," the voice says, clearer. A little calmer. The hand on my back moves along my spine. "Get it all out."

I open my eyes and instantly close them again, everything too bright—the sunlight, the white belly of the boat, four pairs of ankles attached to four pairs of feet clustered in front of me. And the arms locked around my sides, the hard wall of human person I'm pressed against, the one I just puked lake water all over. It's too much to look at. It's Silas.

He pushes wet ropes of hair out of my eyes. "Audrey, can you breathe?"

I nod, eyes closed, gasping for air. It's the best thing I've ever felt—perfect, perfect air. Gusting down my windpipe, expanding my ribs into Silas's chest. My throat hurts so badly.

"Mick," Silas says, and I crack my eyes open enough to see him turn away from me, water streaking down his neck. The sun catches it, glinting in the space between us. "Can you grab a bottle of water?"

The boat sways, Mick's footsteps moving away.

"Audrey," my mother says. Her voice shakes, and behind my closed eyelids the sun's flare is shaded by her crouching in front of me. I open my eyes and she's right there, so close, plain fear on her face. Behind her, Cleo's covering her mouth with one hand. "Are you all right?"

Am I? I nod anyways, and Mick cracks open a bottle of water. When he passes it to Silas, my mother stands.

"Everyone just—" Silas breaks off, holding out an arm. He's breathless, panting. His T-shirt is drenched through. "Just give her some room, okay? She's okay."

The legs retreat, all of them except for Camilla's. I feel her move around me, sit on the bench behind my head and rest a hand on my shoulder. Silas presses the water bottle into my palm, curving my fingers around it with his own.

"Drink this," he says, and when I start to shake my head he cuts me off. "I know you don't want to, but you'll feel better. I promise."

He tilts me off him, helps me lean up against the seats so I can drink. There's only one reason he'd be this out of breath, that his clothes would be this soaked.

"Did you—" I rasp, and it hurts so much that I stop. I don't need to ask; I know he jumped in after me. I'm so ashamed that when I close my eyes again there are already tears building behind them. But then I remember, and they snap open. "Puddles."

He stands, pulling his drenched T-shirt over his head. It hits the deck with a wet smack just as Puddles comes running toward us, traipsing across my legs.

"Jesus, Audrey, she had a life jacket on." Silas looks down at me and then away, a muscle flexing in the corner of his jaw. He sounds angry, the words crackling like heat on metal. "What were you thinking?"

Puddles is fully in my lap now. She's soaked, too—she sits right on my stomach and I just let her stay there, panting. I don't know what I was thinking. I wasn't thinking at all.

"I'm sorry," I whisper, and the anger breaks from Silas's face. Like a cresting wave, like an exhale of relief. He lowers himself to the floor in front of me and when he draws a huge breath I watch it move through him—lake water beading clear between the thin bones of his ribs. Tracing wet lines down his torso.

"Audrey," he says quietly. His eyes low, looking at Puddles instead of at me. "Please don't—"

He breaks off, jaw tensing again. When he looks up at me there's water in his dark eyelashes. "Please don't ever do that again."

"Of course not," I whisper, and when the sun hits his eyes they go gold-green at the centers. His eyebrows twitch together the tiniest distance, half a wince, and I'm sure he's going to say something else. But suddenly Cleo is there, and when she drops to her knees beside me she pushes Silas out of the way. Her arms close around my neck, squeezing so tightly I let out a wet cough.

"I know I called you borderline horrible," she says. "But that was before you risked your life for a gross old pug."

28

"Ouch," Sadie says, eyes on my leg as we step out of a rideshare onto the sidewalk. "You've got a whole rainbow happening there."

I look down, clocking the gruesome bruise on my knee. I should've worn pants; I wore an ankle-length dress to last night's *Letters* show even though it's in the mid-nineties here in Denver.

In the days since Chicago, the side of my knee I smacked on the boat's deck has phased through the entirety of the color wheel, transitioning from a maudlin purple to a pukey kind of green, and now to this hellish yellow bordered with pink splotches. It looks like I have some kind of flesh-eating disease. Like I'm being consumed from the inside.

Which isn't so far off, really. The whole spectacle on Lake Michigan was so mortifying—so unthinkably idiotic—that it's been licking through my insides like hellfire ever since. I almost didn't tell Ethan about it at all. But on video chat that night, before running through a Penn lecture on emergency medicine, Ethan had interrupted my description of an idyllic and entirely fictionalized boat trip to say that my voice sounded weird. "Hoarse," he'd said. "Are you getting sick?"

In the head only, I could've told him. But instead it all came pouring out of me—how Puddles made a break for it, and the intolerable thought of her tiny, old body sinking to the bottom of the lake, and how I'm fine, really, completely fine, just kind of shaken up, but that's to be expected.

Ethan listened to the story with his mouth half-open, blinking rapidly. And then he said, "Why would you do something like that?"

The *I'm so glad you're all right* was implied, I'm sure. But it was Silas's voice echoing in my quiet hotel room as he said it— *What were you thinking?*—and the way he looked at me on the boat, terrified and accusatory, breath heaving out of him. What he'd said to me in Austin: *I can't do hospitals after what happened.* And that I'd scared him, maybe.

"Because I thought the dog would die," I told Ethan. It sounded defensive, and it was. I knew I was bristling; clearly it had been an idiot move, but was it really so hard to imagine a single reason I'd do something like that? The question made it sound like saving a dog from certain death was a choice completely off the table for someone like me. Like I was some kind of heartless monster. Ethan didn't know Puddles had been wearing a life jacket, and I didn't tell him.

"But you could have, too," Ethan said, his brow furrowing. "Audrey, that's so illogical. You can't—"

"Okay but I'm fine." It came out as one word, loud and graceless. The truth was it *had* been illogical. It had been completely instinctual, screaming from some primal part of me I didn't recognize. I didn't know how to explain that to Ethan; I didn't think I even could. But I hated how he was looking at me, like I'd somehow let him down by doing something he couldn't un-

158

derstand. I couldn't understand it, either, and his reaction only made it worse.

"You feeling okay, otherwise?" Sadie asks now. We're standing in the lobby of an obstetrician's office in downtown Denver, surrounded by pregnant ladies. "Silas said you were pretty shaken up."

Oh, just throw me back in Lake Michigan. Just pitch me off the top of the Willis Tower. The thought of Sadie and Silas discussing how *shaken up* I was, like a four-year-old on a Tilt-A-Whirl, is the most humiliating thing I can imagine.

"I'm fine," I say stiffly, and when we drop into waiting room seats side by side, my open backpack slides straight onto the floor, fully upside down. Of course.

I'm reaching to collect my truly enormous collection of scattered pens when Sadie leans down next to me. She picks up the used copy of *Letters to My Someday Daughter* that I bought in the airport, somehow already a month ago, the last time I was in Denver. Between all the unpacking and repacking this summer, I've left it at the bottom of my bag.

I watch as if from behind glass as she stares at it. That picture of Camilla on the cover, the dedication—*To her*—all the annotations in the margins. Similar, maybe, to the secretive notes she was taking in her own copy at Dr. Bautista's office in Chicago.

"Audrey," she says softly. "Did you take all these notes?"

I snatch the book out of her hand, hating the way she recoils like I hit her. "Of course not."

"Who did?"

"A criminally insane person, clearly."

She hesitates, and my cheeks are burning too bright to look at her. How senseless of me to carry it around like this, like someone wouldn't see. I feel like a teenager in a summer blockbuster, like my parents just found my porn stash or a giant bag of weed under my bed.

"I know that *you* do, but I don't take this book seriously enough to take notes on it."

Sadie's cheeks go scarlet. Her eyes flicker down to her lap and stay there. Shame tugs my heart into my rib cage like a riptide, battering it. This is my mentor, the one person who's buoyed my dream along all summer. I should apologize, but instead I shove the book into the very bottom of my backpack. When I look at Sadie she's still staring at her hands, pink-cheeked, like she's embarrassed to know that I saw her writing in *Letters*.

I should throw my copy away. There's a giant trash can across the waiting room, but even as I stare at it my legs don't move; my body won't let me. I want that book like I want a weighted blanket—something rooting me down.

"Sadie?"

Thank *god*. Sadie and I both look up, find a serious-looking woman with dark hair in a sleek bun. *Dr. Sun*, her name tag says, next to a yellow illustration of a baby footprint.

"Alice," Sadie says. When she stands there's something shaken up about her, like now *she's* the one on the Tilt-A-Whirl. It takes her a few tries to get a smile on her face, and when she waves a hand in my direction her voice stutters. "This is—um, this is Audrey."

I stand up, taking Dr. Sun's hand when she offers it. Shove down what just happened, push my mother out of my mind. "Thanks so much for having us, Dr. Sun."

"Welcome," she says, smiling. She leads us toward a back office, weaving past exam rooms. "Sadie told me about your big shadowing position this fall—very exciting. Nothing quite so fast-paced happening here, I'm afraid, but I hope we can still be of some help."

Hopkins Hospital releases their ICU selection in four days. It's been the only thing getting me through the aftermath of my unhinged behavior on the boat, knowing that in fewer than 100 hours I'll be in contact with the hospital, planning my fall semester.

"Oh, I'm thrilled to be here," I say when Sadie stays silent. I flit my eyes in her direction and she's looking down at her shoes, her mouth pinched. "I have so much respect for obstetrics."

Dr. Sun laughs, sitting behind her desk and motioning Sadie and me into seats across from her. "Respect for it," she says. "But not an interest in the pursuit, yourself?"

I feel myself flush. "Well, I'm not sure yet, it's still—"

Dr. Sun holds up her hands, smiling. "Obstetrics isn't for everyone; it hasn't even always been for me. When I started medical school I thought I'd be a cardiologist."

She starts to tell me about it, how bringing new life into the world suits her better than fiddling with hearts, and when I glance over at Sadie she's staring at the wall next to Dr. Sun's head.

There's a picture there, framed in matte white like everything else in this neutral office. In it, a woman lies on her side in a hospital bed, draped in a teal gown and smiling in a fully exhausted sort of way. She has one hand reached into the bassinet next to her—a newborn baby sleeps there, its eyes shut.

It makes me think, completely against my will, of Camilla knocking on my hotel room door the night of the Boat Incident. She asked if it was all right for her to take the spare bed beside mine, and I'd kind of just said okay, and we'd fallen asleep in the same room for the first time in more than a decade. When I woke up in the morning she was already gone, and she didn't ask to do it again. It was so weird that I'm not entirely sure it actually happened.

Sadie doesn't look away from that picture the whole time we're sitting with Dr. Sun. Lips pressed together, hardly blinking. I think of what she told me about Elliott—*he was eighteen months old when we adopted him*. And I know that there are as many reasons people choose to adopt as there are people. But I wonder if that picture hurts her somehow. She stays quiet for the rest of our visit. I'm not brave enough to ask.

29

Sadie's still acting weird that afternoon, quiet and window-gazing in the back seat of the rental car we take to Silas's grandma's place. I'm too ashamed of my outburst at Dr. Sun's office to look at her for the entire drive.

We take the road forty-five minutes from Denver at a different angle from the Summit School, a stretch of mountain-ringed highway I've never driven before. When Silas told me, back in Taos, that I should come meet GG, it sounded like the most ludicrous idea in the world. But then he saved my life, and when the interns knock on my door to round me up, he only has to look at me once to get me to cave.

Every time I come within twenty feet of Silas I hear it again— the hazy, half-alive way his voice brought me back from the brink. *Oh, god, thank fuck.* His hand between my shoulder blades. The betrayed way he looked at me.

We're going to the mountains, Mick had said, and I'd closed my Penn textbook and that was the end of it. Magnolia was chauffeuring my mother between interviews, but the rest of us would spend the night at GG's house in Switchback Ridge—a lake town halfway between Denver and Mount Blue Sky.

I texted Ethan that we were going to the mountains for a night, to which he'd said, Camping? You? And obviously not camping, me, but what if I did go camping? All the things Ethan thinks me so incapable of are starting to pile up, making me feel trapped by the idea of myself. Cabin, I'd sent. Just the one word, and still no reply. We lose cell service halfway through the drive, which feels just as well. For the first time this summer, I find myself grateful for the distance between us.

Silas drives, though apparently Sadie also knows the way. They've been here before, together—"Once, for Christmas," Sadie says when Cleo asks. But otherwise, she stays quiet. Guilt grows in me like a seedling, unfurling one green leaf at a time. Guilt, and shame, and fear. Sadie feels like one more person I've managed to alienate—even after she's done so much for me, even after she made room for me at Camilla's shows. One peek into the truth of my messed-up relationship with my mother and I've bungled all of it. But there are three other people in this car with us, and what would I even say? And still, there's a whispered question beneath the buzz of my regret: What's Sadie been writing in *Letters* that made her so embarrassed?

When we get there, Switchback Ridge is the exact version of Colorado you imagine when you haven't been here before. Thick with pine trees, surrounded by protected forest land, centered on a lake that's ringed with a walking path and busy with paddle-boarders. The weatherworn sign at its edge reads *Gossamer Lake* in faded white letters. When we roll past, Mick says *Ooooooooh* like a kid at the zoo.

"This," Cleo says, checking her lipstick in a palm-sized mirror, "is cute as hell."

The Summit School is in Boulder, red-bricked against the backdrop of the Flatirons. Well-groomed, imposing, institutional. Boulder's a college town full of tourists and beautiful people on mountain bikes. Everyone wearing the same brand of two-hundred-dollar windbreaker, applying the same tinted formula of Saint sunscreen. Switchback Ridge feels different: like the manufactured Denver–Boulder corridor hasn't crept in quite as far. It's a little wilder—gnarls of pine roots upending the edges of the asphalt, a tiny building at a lightless intersection with a hand-painted sign out front that says *Yak meat—if yer brave!*

"You should see it at the holidays," Silas says, and I don't want to picture it but I do. This small town covered in snow, winter light hitting the tree ice like glitter. And Silas in front of a fire, somewhere—wearing a sweater and laughing his low, easy laugh. My holidays are usually something catered at Dad's or, last year, in New York City with Ethan's family. A penthouse apartment on the Upper West Side full of first-edition books, formalwear to Christmas dinner, midnight Mass. That's what lies ahead of me, holidays like that.

"*Annnnnd,*" Silas says, hand flat against the wheel as he turns us off the road, "here we are."

The gravel drive is so choked with trees it seems to swallow us up: a tunnel of green with sunlight glancing through.

"Narnia," Cleo whispers from the back, and Mick laughs. But when the car emerges from the trees it doesn't feel like Narnia at all, or anywhere else I've ever been. This place is wholly its own: a stone-and-wood mishmash of a cabin with a robin's-egg-blue door, curved at its top like a hobbit house. The whole thing thick with trellises, blooming vines arcing toward the sun. And the garden—

spreading what must be two acres wide through the flat meadow surrounding the house. Groomed into careful rows, clutches of green radiating in straight lines like sunrays.

"When you said *garden*," I tell Silas, "I thought you meant, like, five planter boxes in a backyard."

He leans his head back, barking a laugh. "Clearly you haven't met GG."

"No time like the present," Cleo says, and when I look back through the windshield there's a woman waving to us from the cabin's open door. She's tall and wiry: tanned, muscled arms and faded denim overalls over a lavender T-shirt. When Mick opens the car's back door, Puddles waddles toward her and GG crouches to the ground, reaching both arms out.

GG hugs Silas before saying anything to the rest of us, Puddles sandwiched between them.

"Hi, baby," GG says, closing her eyes over the curve of Silas's shoulder. It's so intimate I find myself looking out over the garden, at anything but the two of them. No one's ever called me *baby* in my entire life. But then GG turns her green eyes on me and says, "You must be Audrey."

Must I be? Cleo could be Audrey. I glance at her, but I guess it's obvious: the knockout Japanese girl in platform boots and neon-pink eyeliner isn't Camilla St. Vrain's daughter. And GG already knows Sadie, so that leaves me. I reach to shake GG's hand but she pulls me in for a hug instead, squeezing me tight and quick like a chest compression. When we separate she studies my face like she's looking for something there, eyes tracking over my cheeks and my mouth and my hair. She says nothing else, just lets me go and reaches for Sadie. I watch her murmur something in Sadie's ear; Sadie closes her eyes and nods. Silas is watching them, too. But when our eyes meet he just smiles a little, rounds up Puddles, heads into the house.

A girl bounds toward him from the kitchen, all red hair and freckles. She's maybe our age, in a white sun dress that slips off one shoulder as she throws her arms around Silas so forcefully he lets out an *oof*. Puddles leaps at the girl's ankles.

"Maren," Silas says breathlessly, laughing. "I didn't know you were home."

"Of course I'm home." She lets him go and reaches for Puddles. The kitchen is full of white tile and wooden cabinets, flowers tied up to dry upside down over the sink. "It's summer, dummy."

"My cousin," Silas says, gesturing at her. "We were born two days apart."

"But I'm older," Maren says, grinning at me. She thrusts out a hand and I take it, detecting some Puddles slobber. I wipe my palm on my jeans as soon as she lets go. "Cuter, too."

She cackles as Silas rolls his eyes, reaching up to tug at his hair. He bats her hands away and everyone else files in from outside, Maren introducing herself around and then leaping over to crush Silas in one last hug.

"I'm meeting Ro and Miller at the lake," she says. She casts a glance around the room, looking at each of us in turn. "You'll all join later? You brought swimsuits?"

"Audrey, uh, doesn't swim," Mick says, half laughing. It's not quite funny to me yet, but I force a smile anyways. And I did bring a swimsuit, just like everyone else.

"You can simply *sun*, then," Maren says, shooting a smile at me as she walks backward toward the door. "I'm already late, anyway,

Miller's gonna throw a fit. I'll see you over there. GG!" She lobs a dramatic wave in her grandmother's direction. "Bye!"

"Take care, Mare bear," GG calls, singsong, already filling a teakettle from the tap. And when Maren's gone, "A freer spirit each time I see her." She says it fondly. "She's really coming into her own at that art school."

"How are the boys?" Silas asks. "You still see them for Sunday dinners?"

"Of course," GG says. She puts the kettle on the stove and turns to us, motioning everyone into chairs around the kitchen table. "Andrew starts high school this year, if you can believe that."

"Barely," Silas says, and GG laughs.

"He'll be just like the rest of you soon," GG says, then raises her eyebrows pointedly. "Gone."

"GG," Silas says warily, eyeing her. She shrugs, pulling open a drawer and rooting through it.

"I'm just saying, you could come see me more."

"Called out," Mick says, elbowing Silas, who sighs.

"I'm here now." Silas waves a hand at Sadie. "And I brought your favorite person. Doesn't that earn me some points?"

GG smiles at Sadie and Sadie smiles back at her, something passing between them. There's a line of framed pictures on the table against the wall, a grinning woman with dark hair appearing throughout them like the thread tying everything together. She has Silas's eyes, his nose. I know without having to ask that GG is Silas's mom's mom; that Sadie stepped in when all of them lost her daughter.

"A few points," GG finally concedes. She drops tea bags into the kettle and then brings it over to the kitchen table, lining up a row of mugs.

168

"Not to be rude," Cleo says, "but it's like eighty-five degrees outside. Do you have anything colder?"

GG's eyes flick up to her, but she just starts pouring in silence. It's Sadie who finally speaks, for nearly the first time since we left Dr. Sun's office this morning.

"Trust me," she says, looking at Cleo. "You want this."

"My homemade peppermint tea," GG says, just as the smell hits me. Fresh and green. "Healer of all ailments."

"We're not ailing," Mick says, and everyone turns to him. But GG's looking at Sadie, and I think, *Maybe not all of us.*

"It'll heal you anyway," Silas says, reaching for a mug and passing it to me. I breathe it in, feel the steam all the way down to my lungs. I watch him take a sip and close his eyes, lashes fluttering just once before he opens them again. "GG's been pushing this stuff on us my whole life. Cut to me being the only seven-year-old asking for herbal tea at his birthday party."

Cleo snorts, but then she lifts the mug to her lips and I watch her eyes go comically wide.

"Oh my god," she says, putting it back down. "This is amazing, Ms. G."

GG shrugs, but the little smile on her lips is proud. She sits, wrapping tan hands around a mug of her own. "Well," she says, looking at Silas. "Tell me all of it."

His eyes flick, almost imperceptibly, to me. And for some reason I think of that first night, of counting my fingers in the back alley in Los Angeles, of Silas unzipping my dress. *All of it.* I keep quiet, let Mick and Cleo and Silas fill the silence. Listen to Silas tell GG about his freshman year at American, and Cleo regale her with the tale of their night out in San Francisco that I spent alone in my hotel room. Listen to Puddles lap at the water bowl in the kitchen.

And I think about my summer: studying for a class I'm not even taking, staring into the pixels of Ethan through my computer screen, sending one thank-you email after another to doctors who might not even remember me enough to write recommendation letters down the road. The word comes to my mind unbidden, all on its own: *waste*. A waste of the precious few months before college. I bite my lip, and when I start counting my fingers under the table I feel Silas look at me, like maybe he knows. I just have to get through these next few days, get to the ICU acceptance, get to planning.

"Sadie," GG says, reaching to put a hand on her forearm. "What do you say you and I visit in the garden while the kids go have their fun at the lake?"

Sadie nods quietly, and we all stand.

"We'll see you in a bit," GG says, already guiding Sadie toward the back door. "I'm making meatballs for dinner."

"Time to lake it up?" Cleo asks, raising her eyebrows and looking between us.

Mick points a warning finger at me. "You're not getting in this time."

As if I need a reminder.

30

Maren's gone by the time we get to the lake. When Silas texts her, she says they left to get ice cream. The beach is small, not quite Chicago's North Avenue—just a sandy stretch along one little blip of the waterline, busy with spread-out towels. We brought some from GG's house, a mismatched collection she seems to have acquired at Disney World. When Mick unfurls his towel, it has a giant cartoon ant on it.

"Just my style," he tells Silas, who shrugs.

"Everything in that house is for the grandkids." He shakes out his own towel, two tigers in a jungle. "Seven older than me, eight younger."

Both my parents are only children, both the parents of an only child. I don't have a single cousin or sibling. The only family I have that's not on this tour is essentially Dad, who's been so busy since Austin I've hardly heard from him—and Fallon and Ethan, if they're allowed to count.

I pull out my phone and take a picture of the water, debate sending it to both of them before opening a text to just Fallon instead. Not our Colorado, but close, I send. Miss you.

"Can we all picture Camilla on one of these for a sec?" Cleo says. She sits on Rapunzel's face, crossing her legs. "Imagine her dismay, if she were here."

"The opposite of her aesthetic," I agree, tucking my phone back into my bag. "All of her towels are neutral Turkish cotton."

Cleo shudders. "The opposite of *my* aesthetic." She's in the same blue bikini from Chicago and a bucket hat covered entirely in rhinestones that makes it almost impossible to look at her—the sun's reflection in it makes her blinding.

"I'm going in," Mick says, and before I can even get my sunscreen out of my bag he's hoisted Cleo over his shoulders and started running toward the water.

Silas shouts, "It's cold!" But there's no way they can hear over Cleo shrieking. When they plunge into the water her bucket hat flies off, floating on the lake's surface like a beacon. I glance at Silas to find him shaking his head but smiling, Puddles bookended between his knees.

"I think I messed up," I say, and he turns to me. His eyebrows draw together, head tilting to one side. He's got his *GG's Gardenshare* hat on and a pair of dark swim trunks and no shirt. I draw a steadying breath. "I kind of snapped at Sadie during our obstetrics visit and she's been acting really weird ever since."

"You snapped at her?" he says, and I fight my body's urge to fold into itself. "About what?"

I bite my lip. Worry it between my teeth until it stings. I could lie, but I don't. "My mom's book. How she's been writing notes in it."

Silas hesitates, glancing at the water before turning back to me. I get the sense that he's weighing something, that maybe he'll push me away now, too. "What did she say?" he asks finally.

"Nothing," I tell him. "That's the problem. I think—I think I hurt her feelings? Or embarrassed her, maybe, about the notes? Do you know what she's been writing in there?"

His eyes find mine, sun glancing across them. And for a moment he looks like GG when we arrived at her house. Like he's searching for something in me. "Audrey," he says quietly, but suddenly Mick and Cleo are back, and he's standing to contain Puddles, and the moment is over. I curl my fingers into my palm.

"You absolute *turd*," Cleo says, pulling her soaked-through bucket hat back over her hair. "My sunscreen hadn't even set yet."

"You loved it." Mick grins wickedly, reaching for his ant towel and dragging it over his wet face. "Audrey, you next?"

"Very funny," I say flatly, and Cleo nudges me with her foot.

"You going to at least take off your clothes? Or too scared to even be in a swimmie these days?"

I sigh and stand up, shimmying off my pants. They're long and gauzy, specifically selected to hide my—

"Killer bruise," Mick says, letting out a low whistle. "You okay?"

"I'm fine," I say, pulling the hem of my T-shirt over my head. "It looks worse than it feels."

Cleo lets out a theatrical gasp. "What about *those*?"

I follow the line of her gaze to my rib cage, where—oh. Right. I try to lift my balled-up T-shirt to hide them, but Cleo's quicker than me and bats my hand out of the way. For a minute all four of us stare at them in silence: the five mottled bruises pressed to my ribs. Blue-green and tender. I've been sleeping on my other side, wearing wireless bras. This morning, I stood in front of the bathroom mirror and lifted a hand to line them up with my own fingerprints.

"Did I do that?"

When I look at Silas his lips are pressed together. He reaches a hand toward me and I imagine it landing on my skin, his palm in the empty space between the bruises, his fingers fitting them just right. But then he lets it fall and looks up at me, his eyes dark.

"Firm grip," I say. He looks back at my ribs, and I spread the shirt around my torso so he can't see. "Silas."

"Does it hurt?" he asks. It does, but not as much as it hurts to imagine the bruising itself—the act of it, Silas dragging the dead weight of me out of Lake Michigan.

"No," I tell him. He's still staring at my side, like he can see his fingerprints on my skin even through the T-shirt.

"Jesus, Si," Cleo says. "You really grabbed her, huh?"

He swallows, and when his eyes move to Cleo I hate how guilty he looks. "I mean, I really didn't want her to die."

Cleo snorts. "Fair."

"Audrey," Silas says, quieter, and when he takes a step closer to me his hand lifts again. Like a reflex, like he's not quite aware of it. "I'm sorry."

"Silas," I say. "Without you I'd be at the bottom of that lake."

"Don't say that," he tells me, and I know he means the lake part. That it hurts him, maybe, to imagine me underwater. But that's not the part that scraped my throat on the way out, the part that felt painful to articulate. *Without you.* I make myself think it again. Like exposure therapy, like an idea I'll maybe get used to if I think it often enough. The way I will need to be, after this summer. For the rest of my life. *Without you, without you, without you.*

When we get back to GG's house, everyone smelling of lake water except me, Sadie's at the kitchen table with a glass of wine. She smiles as we trudge in, everything about her easy and relaxed. Like the rest of this day didn't happen; like GG flipped some kind of switch to bring her back to herself. Like maybe I won't need to unearth that moment at Dr. Sun's by apologizing to her after all. GG stands in front of the stove stirring a pot of pasta sauce.

"Showers!" she calls, hardly turning to look at us. "All of you. Dinner's in twenty."

It twinges in a way I'm not ready for, the expectation that I'll be at a table at a certain time for a meal someone's made me. At the Summit School dinner is from six to eight, three entree options and open seating and a conveyor belt that swallows your tray open-mouthed when you're done. At my dad's, dinner is takeout on a counter and maybe an overlap in our schedules but more likely me eating alone, forking lo mein while the Pacific sun sets through the living room windows. I can't remember eating dinner at Camilla's even once since going to school. The rare occasions I'm home we go to restaurants with Laz, with loud packs of her friends who fill up private back rooms and don't ask me any questions.

"Audrey," Cleo says, and when I look up I realize I've stalled out by the kitchen table. Mick and Silas are gone; she's halfway down the hallway to the back of the house. "You coming?"

I nod, catching GG's eye before I go. She smiles at me, like she knows.

By eight thirty Mick's roped everyone into a loud game of Apples to Apples, which he inexplicably calls *App-lays to App-lays*. When he wins Cleo's "Graceful" card with "Swimming," I excuse myself to go to the bathroom. Ethan still hasn't texted me, though we usually video chat around this time. Waiting for me, maybe, to reach out first.

When I leave the bathroom, Silas is waiting in the hallway.

"It's his love language, you know." He's leaning against the slatted-wood wall, arms crossed, barefoot in shorts and a hoodie. At first I think he means Ethan, which of course he doesn't, and what would that imply, even? That Ethan's love language is silence?

"What is?" I ask.

"The teasing," he says. The hallway is growing dark with the sunset and smells like shampoo, the same one from GG's guest bathroom that both of us used. Our hair's still wet. "Mick. You scared him, in Chicago. He has to make a joke out of it or he'll just start crying."

I pull one sweatshirt sleeve over my knuckles. It's incomprehensible to me, that Mick could care so much after half a summer together. That Silas could. That I'm standing here, silent in this hallway, choking on how much I care.

"Can I show you something?" Silas says.

My voice comes out quiet. "What is it?"

"A surprise," he says. "I know you don't like surprises, but I think you'll like this one."

For a moment we just look at each other. When I finally nod he steps around me, the fabric of our sleeves touching and nothing else. I check my phone one last time, but Ethan still hasn't reached out. I follow Silas toward the back of the house.

There's a door there, pale wood with a curtained window in its middle. Silas holds it open behind him and I step through, the air cool with dusk. The garden is a storybook in the falling dark—

moths moving through the rows of vegetables, the whole meadow ringed in trees that move gently in the wind. He steps into the grass and I hesitate.

"My shoes."

He looks down at my bare feet, then his own. "You can't go barefoot?"

Bare feet are for the beach, and even then—with sandals waiting on my towel. The garden is all dewy grass and rich-smelling earth. I showered not even two hours ago.

Silas laughs, a breathy noise that sounds like it's at my expense. "What's the worst that could happen?"

We look at each other, and it pops right out of me. "An earthworm touches my toe."

There's a short, surprised silence, and then Silas starts laughing in earnest. Head tipped back, mouth open so I can see that crooked canine. His whole face changes when he laughs, a version of him that looks even more like himself.

"I will personally ensure that no earthworms touch your toes," he says, looking at my feet and then up at me.

"You can't promise that."

He smiles, soft, close-lipped. "I can promise, Audrey."

"Okay," I say then. And I step into the grass.

31

It turns out to be a tree house, tucked in the woods at the end of the garden. One tree-layer deep, so you're mostly in shade but can just see the house through the pine boughs. There's a little ladder up to it, rope that feels rough and frayed on the soles of my feet.

"This is maybe more unpleasant than an earthworm," I tell Silas. But he just grins and lowers a hand down from the tree house to pull me the rest of the way inside.

"This is my favorite place in the world," he tells me. It's small, a platform with three walls and one open side looking out over the garden. The walls are covered in pencil drawings, tangles of messy kid handwriting and hangman games and stick-figure scenes. I think of Cleo's dragon on that chalkboard in Austin.

"The whole world?" I say, and he looks over one shoulder at me. Sitting at the edge of the platform with his feet dangling over, framed by the meadow of GG's garden.

"The whole world," he says, and I come to sit beside him. Our arms are a few inches apart. He points to the ceiling, the far corner where a drawing of a flower stands out from the pale wood in fat black lines. "My mom drew that one. She grew up here, with GG and her siblings and my grandpa when he was still alive. Her name was Daisy."

He smiles at me, and I study his face in the soft dark. "That's why it's your favorite place?"

Silas shrugs. "It's part of it—imagining her here, that small. So long before she got sick that it wasn't part of her at all."

I nod. "It must have been hard to see her like that."

His eyes move over mine, and he hesitates before finally saying, "It was, yeah. I try to, um—just try not to remember her that way. It was such a small part of her life but it feels like the biggest part sometimes, because it was at the end." Silas lets out a rush of breath and glances back at the daisy. "But that's not fair. And when I'm here, it's easier to remember the rest about her, too."

"Like what?" I say, and when he looks back at me I wonder if I shouldn't have asked. But eventually a smile tugs at one corner of his mouth, shy and lopsided.

"Like she desperately wanted GG's green thumb, but she didn't have it. And every summer in Michigan she'd plant tomatoes and we'd wind up with literally *one* dime-sized tomato that she'd make this big show of 'harvesting' in August." He shakes his head, and a moth flits between us. "She'd use this fancy steak knife to cut it into fourths so we could all try it. It was this stupid ceremony every year."

"That's not stupid," I say. I'm picturing it: Silas, younger, standing next to that woman from the dining room pictures. His dad there, too, a middle-aged man with his same face. A kitchen island in the Midwest, summer sun slanting through the windows, Silas's little sister hanging off his elbow. "That sounds really nice."

He smiles at me. "Yeah, it was." He looks down at his feet, swinging slowly through the dark. "What's your favorite place?"

I wipe the soles of my feet with my hands, then my hands against each other. Blades of grass and rope thread drift into my lap. "I'm not telling you."

"Is it embarrassing?"

I glance at him, trying to not to smile. Which just makes him smile wider, and when he leans closer to me I can't quite bring myself to move away. "Audrey, is it a library?"

I laugh, surprising myself with it. "No, but close. It's a reading room."

He's still smiling, eyes holding mine. I think he's going to make fun of me, but he just says, "Tell me about it."

There's a hair tie on the floor next to me, white elastic with a pink flower bead. I pick it up, think of Silas's eight younger cousins. "It's on the third floor of the student center at the Summit School. Just this really imposing, academic space with beams in the ceiling and floor-to-ceiling bookshelves and lots of long tables with moody lighting." I glance at him, trying to track if he's bored yet. But he's just watching me, same as before. "It's the best late, like at midnight, when you get to be alone there. And it's so quiet, and you're surrounded by books full of other people's smart ideas."

It feels new, talking about this with him. Not Audrey studying on tour or Audrey in Camilla St. Vrain's shadow, but the Audrey I actually am, in my own life. It feels like crossing a line I maybe can't uncross. And the way Silas is looking at me—like he sees that space, just as I've described it—I find myself scrambling to change the subject.

"What about you?" I say. "With school. Tell me more about these documentaries."

"Someday documentaries," Silas says, and I tense at the phrasing. "I don't know. When I think about the rest of my life, it's the one thing I can't see getting bored with. The one thing I could imagine having fun with even if I had to do it every single day."

I study the side of his face, soft in the quickly falling dark. "What?" he says, and I shake my head.

"I've never factored fun into it, I guess. When I think about my career."

He lets the words sit there between us, and I'm so sure he's pitying me until he says, "But it's also about that feeling, right? The one you get when you know you're putting your energy in the right place." He nudges his knee against mine, then moves it away. "How you'll feel when you help a kid with a broken leg, or cure a lady with cancer, or whichever way you choose to save the world. I'm so scared of that." Our eyes meet. "Seeing people hurt. And I think it's pretty incredible that you're volunteering for it."

I curl the hair tie in my palm. Think of him in Chicago, drenched through, how angry he sounded in the hull of that boat. How afraid.

Silas makes me feel bigger than I am, sometimes—the way he talks about me, the ache in my bruised ribs that reminds me just how alive we both are. I bite my lip and turn the conversation toward him.

"What is it for you? The feeling that makes you want to make movies."

"It's like—" Silas breaks off, moving a hand through the dark air in front of us. "You know when you're watching something on film and it's just human people having a human experience but it hits you in the throat?" He looks at me. "And you feel overwhelmed by the experience of being a person?"

Right now, I think. He makes me feel overwhelmed by the experience of being a person.

"That's what I want to make. That feeling, where you're watching something alone on your couch but you realize we're all connected in this completely fundamental way that we don't even have to ask for—it's just there." He looks at me. "And we aren't alone, ever."

I squeeze the hair tie, feel the bead bite into my palm. I've spent so much time feeling alone.

"Do you believe that?" I say quietly.

"Which part?"

"That we're never alone."

"Of course," he says, and then he hesitates. "You don't?"

I open my hand, and both of us look down at the elastic. "I guess not. But it would be nice to be that type of person, to see the world that way."

"'That type of person,'" he repeats, and I look up at him.

"What?"

He blinks, dragging his teeth across his bottom lip like he's trying to land on the right way to say this. "I don't know, Audrey, it's like—you're categorizing both of us. Giving us these labels as certain kinds of people." It's dark enough now that the distant light from the house is pooling in his eyes. "Things can just be what they are, right? People, too. You could surprise yourself. You could change, and feel differently, if you didn't see yourself only one kind of way."

It feels, suddenly, like we're talking about something else. Like I've lost the thread, and I'm out of my depth, and I wish that it weren't so dark so I could see better. I wish that I weren't barefoot.

"Well, I hate surprises." It sounds more defensive than I mean it to, but when Silas shifts away from me I keep going. "This is how my brain works. I'm a science person, and I'm on this path, and it just—" I break off, button back into myself. What the hell are we even doing out here? Hopkins Hospital releases its decision in three days and I'm sitting in some tree house in the middle of nowhere. "I have plans, and I need to be a certain way to achieve them. This summer is just an interlude—"

"An interlude?" Silas cuts me off. The emotion on his face is so unfamiliar that I struggle to clock it for what it is—anger. "This summer isn't just an interlude, Audrey, it's your life. As much a part of it as every other part." He pauses and it's loud, crickets screaming in the woods. "Don't put all of this on pause. Don't—" He breaks off, eyes on mine. I have no idea what's coming next but I'm not expecting it to sting as much as it does. "Don't count us all out just because we don't fit into some plan you thought you had."

"I do have a plan," I say sharply.

"Okay," Silas says. It's more of a sigh than a word. "Look, can we try something?"

"You always ask that when you're about to make me try something anyways."

His eyes rake across mine. He says, "Can you tell me what you're actually thinking right now?"

What? I blink at him, try to bring his face into sharper focus. It's so dark out here it's like we're looking at each other through water.

"I'm thinking I made the plans I made for a reason," I say. "And I just met you. And you don't know me at all."

Silas is quiet then. I can't meet his eyes, but I do see him hold his hands up in the dark, like I'm some animal gone feral in front of him. Like he's showing me his surrender.

"I'm tired," I say, and when I leave the tree house, he doesn't follow.

But I'm not tired—not descending the rope ladder, not crossing the wet grass in my stupid bare feet, not slipping into the house too quietly for anyone to notice.

I'm not tired. I'm lonely.

32

I've already been awake for an hour when Magnolia calls me, a hazy distance to her voice like she has me on Bluetooth.

"We're twenty minutes out," she says, which makes so little sense I don't respond for a few long seconds. "Camilla would love for you to join us at this bookstore—if I text you the address can you meet us, or do we need to pick you up?"

I'm under a thin quilt in GG's office, a tiny back room with a Murphy bed that folds down from the wall. Mick and Silas are in a guest room on the other side of the house, and when I used the bathroom half an hour ago, Cleo was still asleep on the living room couch with her mouth open. My eyes track over the wall opposite the bed: a corkboard cluttered with pictures of grandchildren.

"You're coming to Switchback Ridge?" I say. "Why?"

"I want to see it." That's Camilla, her voice even fainter. She's probably sitting in the back seat like a debutante. "Silas made it sound idyllic."

Something churns in my stomach, guilty and sour, at the sound of his name.

"The bookstore's in a houseboat on the lake," she continues.

"The Bard on the Barge. Mags called yesterday and they're going to put together a little group for ten o'clock."

I look down at my lap, where my computer's open to the notes Ethan emailed me just after midnight. His email is short, but it doesn't necessarily mean he's mad. Ethan's always succinct.

7.12 lecture notes, he's written. *Let me know if/when you want to discuss. E*

It's the *if* I keep tripping on, the implication of doubt. That he isn't sure, anymore, where we stand with each other. And the fact that I'm not sure, either. Ethan, the bedrock of my life for the last two years, feels like a murky *if/when*. Inevitable, but in what way?

"What do I need to do for the group?" I ask, resigning myself to it. Maybe this is a gift, a reason to slip out of GG's house before anyone else is awake. Avoid whatever it was that happened in the tree house last night.

"Nothing, this time," my mother says. "Just come as you are."

Sadie's awake when I finish getting dressed, and when I tell her where I'm going she asks to come, too. I stare at her across the kitchen, waiting for a flicker of the tension from yesterday, and it never comes. I'm certainly not going to bring it up if it's blown over, so we just call a rideshare and walk the long, tree-tunneled driveway from GG's cabin to meet it at the road.

"Sleep okay?" she asks, and she's probably just being polite but something about it feels pointed. I wonder if Silas told her what happened, if somehow she knows that I absolutely did not sleep okay because I was thinking about the unhinged way he makes me feel, like I'm coming apart at the joints. I lay in the dark staring at the ceiling, sleeping in fits and starts, imagining Ethan across the country—the person who's always made me make sense. The opposite of how I feel around Silas, like the world is so much bigger than I thought and I'm not sure which part's mine to own.

I tell Sadie, "Sure."

"Did you hear the owls this morning?" She's wearing jeans and a windbreaker, hands in the pockets. It's cool, still, the morning air clean and new. "Two of them, calling to each other in the woods."

"No," I say. "I sleep with earplugs."

She smiles down at her feet, like she and her sneakers are sharing a private joke. "Efficient," she says.

"It is." I glance at her, an apology rising in me. *I'm sorry I freaked out at you. I'm sorry I'm so messed up about her.* But I can't make myself draw out the words. When the trees open up to the road, there's a red car waiting for us, and Sadie motions me in ahead of her. We drive to the lake in silence.

Camilla's already there when we arrive, three minutes past ten. I'm expecting a few people clutching copies of *Letters to My Someday Daughter*, but this "little group" turns out to be twenty women sitting on the wood floor with their legs crossed. The Bard on the Barge is a converted houseboat, connected to the lakeshore by a floating dock with rope railings that make me think, against my will, of the tree house ladder.

It's small and swaying, every wall lined in books behind horizontal dowels to keep them from falling off with the movement of the water. There are porthole windows and a few anchors hanging from the ceiling, like we're on an ocean liner instead of a landlocked lake small enough to see both sides from anywhere you're standing.

My mother cuts across the room to us, and I watch a few of the women track her. When their eyes catch on me, they smile.

"Good morning," Camilla says, dropping a hand on my shoulder and then letting it fall to her side. She looks between Sadie and me. "How was the visit yesterday?"

I glance at Sadie, suddenly terrified that she's going to bring it up. My used copy of the book, the notes she's been taking in her own copy, how nasty I was about it.

But she just says, "Great. Audrey charmed the pants off Dr. Sun, as always."

Camilla smiles. "What's the best thing you learned?"

I study her, consider her phrasing. The *best* thing. For me, the best would be the most useful—something tangible I can put into practice. For my mother . . .

"Dr. Sun delivered the Broncos' quarterback's baby."

Her eyebrows lift, eyes widening a bit. "How fascinating. Was it an easy birth?"

"I . . . have no idea," I say. "We didn't get into it."

"Was yours?" Sadie asks, and we both turn to her. Her face is neutral, pleasant. But I'm thinking of her eyes in Dr. Sun's office, how they didn't move from that photo on the wall—a new mother in a hospital bed, her baby sleeping beside her.

Camilla hesitates. "With Audrey?" I think, *Who else?*

Sadie's eyes flick to mine, and she hesitates herself before saying, "Yes, with Audrey."

"Not particularly," my mother laughs, pressing a hand to her stomach. I know I was weeks early, that she lost enough blood to stay in the hospital for a few days. That my dad was the one to hold me in all those first hours, to give me somewhere warm and close to meet the world.

"Oh." Camilla looks across the room, where Magnolia is giving her a signal. "Looks like it's time to get started." She flashes a little smile before turning from us, picking her way between all those women sitting on the floor.

She lowers herself onto some kind of bejeweled pillow at the front of the group, crossing her legs.

"I always find it hard to get into a state of mindful presence *mentally*," she begins, "without first getting there *physically*. If you'll all indulge me, let's close our eyes together and breathe into our bodies." Everyone closes their eyes when she does, but I keep mine open. Sadie's next to me, the two of us leaned against a community board full of flyers for dog walking and music lessons and summer tutoring. I glance at her, and her eyes are open, too.

"Identify a feeling," Camilla tells the group. "Any single one, whatever's bubbling up for you. None of them right or wrong. That's the thing about feelings—they don't come with value judgments, they just *are*. A feeling cannot be wrong, it can only be. Honor the feeling you're identifying right this moment."

And—okay. It's froofy, right? This is therapy soup. This is the hot, intangible, emotional roil that pushed me into the sciences. That has me reaching two-handed for the factual at literally all times. But standing here, the room full of books and quiet and only Camilla's soft voice, I kind of believe it for a second.

Or maybe it's that I *want* to believe it. Because all the feelings I've been having lately—the panic that pushed me into Lake Michigan after Puddles, the hurt of Ethan acting like he doesn't understand me anymore, whatever it is that consumes me any time Silas is around—I hate them. I've been absolutely roasting alive in how much I hate the feelings tornado my brain has turned into this summer. I've been desperate for the Audrey I knew even a month ago, so sure of all of it—how I feel, who I am, where I'm going.

But here's my mother, saying any feeling is okay. Telling me to honor that mess. And *god*, isn't that tempting? Wouldn't it be so good to move through the world that way, without policing yourself? Standing there on that swaying book boat I feel it for the very first time: a modicum of understanding. Why all these women love her so much.

"Now," Camilla says, "let's breathe one layer deeper. Fill your lungs, and as you inhale try to identify the voice of that feeling. What is she saying to you?" She pauses. Giving everyone time to find the voice, apparently. "If it's kind, thank her. Thank that voice for bringing you here today, to this space we're creating together. If it's unkind, offer her sympathy." She inhales. "She didn't choose unkindness; something taught it to her."

When Sadie looks over at me, I realize my eyes are stinging. I duck my chin, blinking the tears back into my brain. What the *hell* is happening right now? As my mother keeps talking, I turn to face the community board so I don't have to look at her, or at Sadie, or at anything else.

"Ask the voice how she might change if she were speaking to someone she loves," Camilla says.

My gaze is burning a hole in the community board, laser-beaming a tutoring flyer. It's some hand-drawn, mass-copied thing, shouting *Coding Tutoring!!* with two fat exclamation points.

"If, for example, that unkind voice was giving the same message to a young girl—to your own daughter—would she rephrase it? Would she deliver it with more grace, more love?"

Middle/high school students, the flyer says. *Caltech student home for the summer. rdev@mailspace.com for details.* I mouth the words to myself, try not to hear what Camilla's saying.

"And if she would, tell the voice: I am deserving of all that same grace and love."

Sadie shakes her head, movement in my peripheral vision. When I look at her, she leans into me and whispers, "She's kind of amazing, huh?"

I swallow, flick my eyes over to my mother. Hers are open now, surveying her little group. She's holding one woman's wrist, and as I watch she squeezes it and then reaches for another woman, taking the hand she has upturned on one knee. The woman's eyes open, and Camilla smiles at her.

So much of my mother's life is performative that I've forgotten, maybe, she's an actual human being. She's a living fifty-four-year-old person. She's here in this room, where there are no cameras and no lists of talking points, holding some stranger's hand to make her feel like her inner self is deserving of grace or love or whatever it is.

It hits me in the roof of my mouth, thick and choking. What this reminds me of. It's GG's dinner table last night—sauce-stained plates pushed to the side, Apples to Apples cards strewn over the uneven wood, Mick howling with laughter, evening air breathing through the open windows. This feels like that. Warm. A moment carefully gathered to make everyone in it feel like they belong there.

I think of Sadie in Santa Fe: *It was you pushing her away.* Of Dad in Austin: *We're your parents. We love you.* And of myself, so angry at Camilla for so long, so desperate for her to see me as I actually am.

And so unsure, suddenly, if I've ever done the same for her.

33

We're somewhere over Kansas when Sadie nudges my elbow. I have headphones in and my laptop open, scrolling through the Johns Hopkins course catalog. Aside from finger counting, nothing calms me down quite as quickly.

"Hey," she says. We had to bump up our flight last-minute to accommodate some A-list book club visit in Nashville, so our seats are scattered all throughout the plane. Sadie's in the window and I'm stuck in the middle next to an eleven-year-old who's spent the whole flight loudly smacking bubble gum. The interns are in a row at the very back. I haven't spoken to any of them since GG's.

I raise my eyebrows at her, pulling out one earbud.

"You doing okay?" she says.

I feel myself stiffen, my spine arcing off the back of the seat. "Why?"

Sadie smiles a little. "Don't be so suspicious, Audrey, you've just been quiet since the bookstore yesterday."

I blink. I've been quiet since the bookstore, or Silas finally said something to her? I've been quiet, or she wants to talk about how I literally *teared up* during that bananas meditation situation like some kind of kombucha-drinking earth mother?

"I'm fine," I say, and when she narrows her eyes I repeat it. "I'm *fine.*"

"You sure?"

I close my laptop, shifting a little to look at her head-on. "Can I ask you something?"

She waves a hand, like, *proceed.*

When I swallow it feels cartoonishly dramatic. "What do you take notes on, in *Letters?*"

I swear I watch Sadie's pupils dilate in real time. She looks like I just asked her how recently she committed first-degree homicide. Why does this matter so much to her?

"What do *you?*" she says.

I tilt away from her. "I told you, I don't. That was a used copy of the book. Someone else's notes."

"Why were you carrying it around, then?"

I blink rapidly. "I just, um." I think about lying, about making something up. Telling her that I was holding on to it for Camilla, or that someone gave it to me at a show and I'd forgotten to throw it out. But I remember what my mother said, yesterday in that houseboat bookstore: *Honor the feeling you're identifying right this moment.* And I feel like I want to tell Sadie the truth.

"I read it a lot," I say finally. "*Letters.* To try and understand her."

The plane hums around us. Sadie holds my eyes. "That's why I'm reading it, too."

Before I can ask what Sadie could possibly want to know about my mom, she says, "What are you hoping to find?"

The question settles in me like sand, not so heavy in itself but suffocating in its power to fill me. The way it blankets everything. *A sign that I matter to her,* I think. But I don't say that to Sadie. Instead, I ask, "What's your mom like?"

She stares at me. "My mom?" When I nod, she clears her throat. Looks down at her hands. "She's, I mean. She's an elementary school teacher in Grand Rapids. She has bangs and she thinks the only place worth vacationing is Mackinac Island. She's sixty-five."

She looks back at me, clocking my reaction like this is some kind of test.

"Okay," I say slowly. "Are you close?"

The seat belt light plinks on, and Sadie glances up at it before answering. "Yeah," she says. "I would say so, yes."

I press my thumb to my pinky, counting down from four. "How do you know?"

"What do you mean?"

I draw another breath. "What does it feel like? How do you know you're close to each other?"

Sadie's eyes slant with something so close to sympathy I have to look straight down at my lap.

"I'm sure you've caught on by now," I say. "That Camilla and I aren't, exactly. Close."

She's quiet for so long that I finally look up at her. But she doesn't look sympathetic—she looks uncomfortable. Like it's as awkward for me to admit the truth as it's felt for me to live it. Like she doesn't want to hear this, just like the rest of the world. Like we'll all be better off if we just keep living the fiction.

"Never mind," I say quickly. The sear of rejection is hot and black, liquid tar over my shoulders.

"Audrey—" Sadie tries, but I stick my earbuds in and wave her off. What do I think I'm doing, anyways? I'm the *someday daughter*. No one wants to consider that I might be anything else.

We're silent for the rest of the flight, for the wait in baggage claim, for the drive from the airport to our hotel in downtown Nashville. I keep my sunglasses on and my headphones in so no one will bother talking to me. I know I'm stewing, absolutely languishing in the mud pit of my own feelings.

I'm staring out the tinted window when we pull up to the hotel. When my phone pings with an email notification. When I get news that's two days early.

Dear Audrey, the email begins. *Thank you for your recent application to the Fall Semester Freshman ICU Shadowing Program. We sincerely appreciate your interest and regret to inform you that we're moving ahead with another student at this time.*

I'm going dark before I've even finished the first sentence.

34

The last time this happened, I had a dorm room. I had a place to tuck myself away, a twin XL bed with white cotton sheets, a heavy comforter to pull up and over my head.

This time I'm strapped into a shared van. I'm surrounded. I have no way to make myself invisible.

Shame claws through me, screaming at the pace of my heart-beats, and when the van stops in front of the hotel lobby I slam open the sliding door so fast it jams my elbow. I run for the lobby bathroom and someone—Camilla, maybe—shouts my name.

The lobby is cavernous and cool, aggressively southern. Ornate carved arches from the floor to the towering ceiling; plush velvet furniture; elaborate chandeliers. It's like stepping back in time. I think, distantly, that if I'd existed in the Gilded Age, I wouldn't have even wanted to be a doctor. I wouldn't be failing, because I wouldn't be trying to do this at all.

The bathroom is empty. When I beeline for one of the enormous stalls I break out in full-body goose bumps; I am simultaneously freezing and on fire. I close the heavy wooden door behind me and click the lock and slide to the floor with my back against it. I pull my legs to my chest and jam my cheeks into my kneecaps until my bones hurt. The breath is rushing into and out of me so erratically that my ribs ache, those five finger-shaped bruises. Panic floods me like the lake all over again, hot down my throat, drowning me alive.

My fingers tingle, numbing. I wrap them around my forearms and dig my nails into the skin until it breaks. A logical pain, and one I deserve. Sweat prickles at my forehead. I'm so hunched over my spine is digging into the wooden door. It hurts, and I press back even harder.

The person I knew I'd be this fall recedes, like a specter or a stranger. The best in her class, the one with the job everyone else wanted. The one with the perfect setup for her college career, ahead of the pack from the moment she set foot on campus. I've been her for so long in my own mind that now I feel hollowed out, hardly human at all. That person will be someone else. And I will be me, less than.

I think of Ethan, convincing me to stay on this tour to bolster my application. How I've oriented my entire awful summer around this one thing and it didn't even work. How maybe if I'd gone to Penn like I was supposed to we'd be celebrating right now—we'd be in the dorm room I've only ever seen through video chat and he'd be wrapping his arms around me. The familiarity of him. The relief of being the person he knows me to be.

I need a bed. I need a room with curtains to draw and a door to lock and the promise of isolation.

I wait long enough that no one who knows me will still be in the lobby. And then I wipe the blood off my forearm with toilet paper and go in search of my room key.

I hold the key to the reader and it hesitates, blinks red. I've got the key card in my right hand and I'm counting my fingers on my left, low and breathless, so fast I'm not even processing the numbers. I try the key again—red. I need to get behind this door before anyone sees me, before I'm swallowed by myself in the middle of this hallway. There are tears pressed against the backs of my eyes. I know they're coming.

"Please," I whisper, trying the key again. My voice sounds like it belongs to someone else. "Pleasepleaseplease."

Red light. I tap the card again, jiggle the lock, counting out loud. Again. Red light. Door handle digging into my palm I'm pulling it so hard. Red light, angry beep, and I'm about to sit down on the floor when the door opens inward. I almost fall into the room, right into Silas.

"Audrey." He breathes my name, his whole face broken open with shock.

"Oh my god," I hear myself say. My eyes dart around—his suitcase, open on the foot of one bed. Puddles, peering at me from the ottoman of a mustard velvet chair by the window. And the room number, on the wall right next to the door: 407. I'm 408. I'm 408 and I'm so, so intolerably stupid.

"What happened?" Silas says, eyes wide. I need to move and I keep not doing it.

"I'm fine," I say. My thumb is still tapping my fingers, counting wordlessly.

"Okay, Audrey, you're shaking." He reaches for me, careful, like I might spook. When his hand lands on my arm it's so warm and so gentle I feel the tears choke me from the inside—this is too kind. I need to be alone. "Come sit down."

"No," I say, but when he moves I do, too, and suddenly the door is closing behind us and I'm sitting on the edge of one bed and he's sitting on the edge of the other one and it's so much, it's too much, I'm so far from enough.

Our knees are touching. I can feel Silas's eyes on me, the absolute head-on angle of his body directed at mine.

"Don't look at me," I whisper. I don't deserve to be looked at. I don't even want to occupy the space of my own body. "Please don't."

He's quiet, and when I hazard a glance up at him he has a hand pressed over his eyes. Arm in the air, elbow cocked at an angle. His hair wavy and wild and a blue T-shirt I'm so familiar with by now and the way he smells—like woods and soap and GG's house.

"Not looking," Silas says, and something swells so huge in my chest that it practically pushes me off the bed toward him. Even after what happened in Colorado, even like this. Everything inside me wants to be close to him.

"Tell me what happened," he says. "I won't look."

I don't want to tell him. I don't want it to be true.

"I didn't get it," I say, and the words shred from me like violence. Like something that'll leave me different. "I know you think I've been this rigid, soulless robot—"

"I don't think that."

"—and it wasn't even worth it because I failed."

Silas says, "The ICU position?" and when the sob gasps out of me I lift a hand to my face so we're mirrors of each other.

Silas moves, then—coming to kneel on the carpet in front of me, his hips between my knees. My eyes are squeezed shut so tightly it hurts.

"Can I?" he whispers, and when I manage a nod his arms

come around me, nudging my elbow up and out of the way so it's rested on his shoulder. I exhale and his arms move into the space it leaves, pressing even closer to me so the bruises on my rib cage ache. He's holding me so tightly there isn't room for my shame, or my fear, or anything else between us. I push my face into his neck, knowing he can feel the tears stuck to my eyelashes but incapable of moving away. And he doesn't, either, and time doesn't pass, and when his fingertips dig into the tops of my shoulders something shifts inside me. A change I'm too afraid to name.

"Everything's falling apart," I say, and when he pulls back to look at me the collar of his shirt's all wet. I reach for it, like I could dry it with my fingers. "God, sorry," I sniff, and Silas traps my hand in his. He rotates my wrist, eyes tracking over the set of cuts on my forearm—four crescent-shaped slivers, red echoes of my fingernails.

"Audrey," he says quietly. I try to pull my arm away but he smooths his thumb over the cuts, his fingers folded around my palm. His gaze moves back to mine. "Everything?"

"Everything." Failing at the only plan I have, the only thing that was mine to control this summer. The off-kilter way I felt yesterday at the Bard on the Barge, like maybe what I've always understood about Camilla is wrong. And Silas, right in front of me—*god*, and Ethan, who's going to hate this when I tell him. Ethan's disappointment seizes inside me, wrings me out. "I'm ruining everything."

"Name one thing," Silas says, and I wipe roughly at my eyes. This is the most embarrassing moment of my life—worse than Lake Michigan, worse than the Sex Summit.

"I didn't get the shadowing position," I say. Hasn't he been listening? "I haven't achieved a single thing this summer."

Silas is quiet for a minute, studying me. "That's not true," he says. "Two days ago you walked barefoot through GG's entire garden without an earthworm touching you."

The laugh that bubbles out of me feels indecent, obscene. Silas smiles, but he looks sad.

I draw a rickety breath. "I'm serious."

"I am, too," he says. I realize my hand is still in his, resting on my knee. "You've met all kinds of doctors and impressed the shit out of every single one of them." I can't meet his eyes. "Sadie always tells me how you blow everyone away. And you've spontaneously road-tripped across the country, and seen the biggest field of mailboxes in America, and done a bunch of shows that have made a lot of people really happy." I look at him, and something goes loose and squishy and vulnerable inside me. "Audrey, that's the opposite of nothing."

But those things aren't the same as this, the brutal truth rattling behind my teeth. It wants to come out, so I let it. "I let myself down."

"But you tried your best," Silas says. "Their choice wasn't yours to control."

Tears fill my eyes and I press them shut. "I just wasn't good enough."

"No," he says, and when he squeezes my hand I open my eyes again. "They're strangers and they don't know you and this is just one thing. There will be so many other things."

"Yeah," I say quietly. "It's just that if I can't be the best at things like this, I'm not sure who I am."

He hesitates, eyes moving back and forth over mine. They're flecked green in the light from the windows, deep and brown and endless. "So you have to hit the mark every single time, or you might as well not exist? There's no middle option?"

Yes, I think. That's exactly it. I don't have a loud, loving family like Silas. I don't know how to connect with people like he does, or to move through the world so easily. I have school. I have my place there, at the top. The tears are so thick in my throat now that I can't speak through them.

"That's too much pressure for anybody," Silas says. "This is *one* job you didn't get. It doesn't mean anything about who you are."

"But it does," I say. There's a magazine in the pocket of his suitcase, the same one Cleo showed me on the boat in Chicago. I pull it out, hold the headline up to him: *Camilla St. Vrain's Valedictorian Daughter Holds Court in Chicago*. "The whole world knows me this way. Valedictorian." I point to the word, and it feels more like a punishment than a compliment. "That's who I am."

Silas's eyes track over the magazine, and he sighs through his nose. "But the whole world doesn't really know you, Audrey. This is one piece of who you are, and it's not even close to the most interesting thing about you."

I don't believe that, not even a little bit. And when I pull my lip between my teeth and clamp down I try so hard to hold in the words. I really do. I know how they'll sound—indulgent and desperate. But I say them, in the end.

"What is?"

A muscle works in Silas's jaw, like he's weighing what to say next. And his voice is quiet when he finally, carefully speaks. "That you came here this summer to be close to your mom even though it scares you." I close my eyes—maybe not ready, after all, to hear this. "Even though it's felt really shitty sometimes. Because you're hopeful for it."

Silence spreads between us, fills the room. It takes everything I have to keep breathing.

The AC kicks on from beneath the windows; Silas clears his throat and keeps going. "That you know how you want to do good in the world, and the way you trust yourself to make it happen."

My heart is beating so hard I'm sure he can feel it, all the way through my bloodstream to my palm pressed against his.

"And," he says softly, "that you jumped in that lake after Puddles. Your heart's bigger than your fear."

The tears are leaking onto my cheeks now. When I open my eyes Silas is completely blurred out in front of me, like an illusion, like something so good I could only have dreamed it up.

"You don't need to earn it," Silas says. "Or prove it with some job. I lost my mom before I was ready and it—" He breaks off, looking away from me. He presses his lips together, swallows, draws a breath. "When you lose someone like that, you just know." Our eyes meet. "We don't have to do anything to earn it, Audrey. We matter to the people who love us just by existing."

His words land in a soft, scared place deep inside me. And I realize that the feeling I've been tripping over all summer, like a splinter stuck through me sideways, is fear. I'm terrified that I built a whole life at the Summit School and that I have no place anywhere else. Not with my mother, not at Penn with Ethan, not with the interns. That maybe I don't belong anywhere. And that if I can't even get this job, I won't matter in college at all.

"Listen," Silas says. His voice is low and serious. "Fuck those guys, okay? You're going to be the best doctor."

I want to thank him. I want to tell him that I'm so, so sorry about his mom. I want to hide my face in his neck again—the only place I've felt safe this whole, entire summer.

But in the end, the only word I manage to get out is his name. *Silas*, whispered between us like an apology. And he just nods, like he heard the rest of it, and pulls me into him.

I close my eyes in the warm dark against his neck, and I count into the quiet, and I breathe. He breathes with me.

35

miss YOU!!!!

The text from Fallon wakes me up, the double buzz of the mattress next to my face. My eyes feel desiccated and sharp, like they grew thorns while I was sleeping.

where is this?? i miss CO so much it's nutso

It takes me a few solid seconds to orient everything: dark hotel room, pink velvet drapes pulled across tall windows. Yellow glow of the desk lamp in the corner and the curve of Silas's shoulder there, just blocking the light from the laptop he's looking at. Puddles, warm and breathing near my feet. And what Fallon's even talking about—the photo of Gossamer Lake I sent her two days ago in Switchback Ridge. Back before I'd made a failure of myself.

sorry i've been so MIA wifi's a little all over the place but i have indeed birthed another beautiful well baby in the time since our last correspondence

My phone buzzes a few more times, photos coming through. And then: fill me in aud how you doing over there?

I close my eyes again. Where would I even start? I can't believe I fell asleep here. I can't believe this is my life at all.

There's a knock on the hotel room door, and I keep my eyes closed so whoever it is will leave me alone. Puddles shifts, lifting her head, and we both listen to Silas's footsteps track across the carpet.

"Ms. St. Vrain," he says quietly, after the door clicks open.

"Silas, honey." My mother sounds tired. "How many times? *Camilla*, please. Is she awake?"

The headache clustered at the front of my skull gives a dull throb. They talked about me at some point—she knew I was in here, sleeping. I feel like someone's ward. Like I'm being babysat.

"I don't think so," Silas says, and Camilla says, "Let me check," and I brace myself.

"I'll give you a minute," Silas tells her. When the door opens again I swallow the realization that I don't want him to go. He's not mine; he doesn't owe me anything. But the room feels darker and more desperate without him in it.

"Audrey." My name is accompanied by Camilla's cool hand landing on my forehead, her body sinking the mattress next to my waist. I let the cold from her fingers seep through to my headache—it feels so good and for once I just let it be. "Are you still sleeping?"

I don't know what makes me do it. Maybe the moment at the Bard on the Barge, the flicker of the secret person my mother might actually be. Maybe the memory of her sleeping in the bed next to mine that night in Chicago, wordless but watchful. Whatever the reason, I open my eyes and look at her.

"Hi," she says. When our eyes meet I see it all: the Audrey she's made me, the *someday daughter*. Captured contextless on her social feeds, all of my wins cataloged there for the world. The last time this happened and it turned into the Sex Summit instead of what it actually was. There's no place for this version of me; I've let both of us down. "Do you want to talk about it?"

"No," I whisper. Her cool hand moves into my hair, brushing it off my forehead. It makes me feel very young.

"All right," she says. Her hand keeps moving, rhythmic. "I'll just say this, then. You can honor this feeling. Grieve the loss of something you wanted very much." In this dim, unfamiliar room she could be a dream; a version of herself I've never known to exist. "But these feelings are like waves. We're better for acknowledging them, for leaning in as they sway us. Allow this to move you but don't let it drag you under, Audrey." Her thumb traces a line between my eyebrows, up into my hair. Cool and centering. "It'll pass, honey. And you'll still be standing."

I don't believe her, but I nod anyways. Maybe so she'll leave, maybe so she'll see me as the person I want her to see me as: stronger. Still standing.

"And consider moving," she says, her cool fingertips leaving my skin. "A walk outside, or something fun somewhere other than this hotel room. The world isn't this job, though I know it feels that way now. You might need to see it with your eyes to remember."

I nod again. I can't imagine moving.

"What do you want to do?" she asks me. And I don't quite

answer, because what I want to do is disappear. I tell her what I have to do instead. The inevitable *if/when*.

"I need to call Ethan."

It's not something we do unprompted. Call. We always text first: *Is now a good time?* As if we are both something the other needs to prepare for. Calling Ethan feels like I'm ambushing him.

"Hello?" he says, and I close my eyes. The room is empty except for Puddles and me; she's still at the foot of the bed, breathing steadily in the quiet. It's dark. It feels like I'm occupying a different universe from Ethan, and hearing his voice in this space splits some kid of chasm right between my ribs. Like I am two Audreys: the one Ethan knows and the one in this room, a stranger and a failure.

"Audrey?"

I've been quiet for too long. I love the way Ethan says my name—I always have. He has the kind of calm, even voice that makes any word sound like it's worth the world.

"Ethan," I say softly. "How are you?"

A pause. It's perfectly quiet where he is; maybe his dorm room. I picture him there alone and hate the way it makes me feel.

"I'm studying," he says, and once that would've been answer enough. But it's not an answer, really. "What's going on?"

Everything's changing, I think. That's what's going on, but if I say it it'll be true. And I still want to be Ethan's Audrey, reliable and sure of herself and right. Constant and constantly enough.

"I didn't get it," I say.

And Ethan does the worst thing he could do, which is that he makes me say it again. "What?"

I drag the words up like dead weight. "I didn't get it, Ethan."

Silence. It stretches and stretches and I can't believe he's doing this to me.

"Ethan, I didn't—"

"I heard you." I know him well enough to know that the way he says it means he's thinking. That my words are actively processing through him, problems he's already working to solve. "Did they say why?"

I realize then that I haven't even read the whole email. But I can't bear to look at it, so I just say, "No."

"Have you tried calling? There might be someone in the admissions office who could help. Reconsider."

It's incomprehensible to him. He sounds like he did all the way back in Los Angeles, when I called him from Camilla's backyard and he couldn't believe Penn had given my place to someone on the wait list. For a brutal flash of a moment, I see myself the way he does: a shoo-in for this spot. And I know that this outcome doesn't match his idea of me, and that my failure to meet this expectation is intolerable. He can't even process it; his first reaction is to change it.

I don't have it in me to talk him into what I know to be true, which is that they aren't going to reconsider. One student gets this shadowing position out of an entire incoming class and it's not me. They chose someone else. I don't want it to be true, either, but it is.

"No," I say. My voice cracks on the word and Puddles lifts her head, cocking it to one side like I've surprised her. In the silence before Ethan speaks she stands and pads toward me across the mattress.

"The office opens at nine o'clock tomorrow morning," he says.

Puddles sits beside me, leaning all her weight against my thigh. She's so warm. "I'd call first thing, before they get—"

"Ethan." He stops. "I didn't get the job, okay?"

He's quiet for an endless, endless minute. I don't know what I wanted him to say when I picked up the phone but I should have known that it would be this. What did I expect? Ethan was never going to tell me it's okay; in the world that we share, it's not okay. I missed the mark and the only thing to do now is fix it.

"You'll find something else," he says finally. My nose burns with tears, and when I put my hand on Puddles's back she leans into me even harder. "When I see you in Miami next week, we'll find something else."

"Okay," I say. My voice is thin and absolutely pitiful. The thought of him seeing me like this feels impossible. The door opens and light floods in from the hallway, cut with Silas's shadow. "I have to go."

"Audrey," Ethan starts, but I can't do this—I can't shoehorn something else into the hole where the ICU was, not yet. I can't strategize this with Ethan, not while Silas stands ten feet away. Not while the waves are still this wild, threatening to pull me under.

"I have dinner," I tell him, the lie coming so easily it scares me. "With my mom. I have to go, Ethan."

When I end the call a sob hiccups out of me, painful, angry for being held in through that whole conversation. I feel worse than I did before we talked—just like I knew, somehow, that I would. When Silas sits on the bed across from me he sets something on the nightstand and turns on the lamp. He doesn't touch me, not like before.

"Whatever he said," Silas says quietly, "he's wrong."

I press my fingertips into my eyes, draw a steadying breath. When I push my tears across my cheeks and look at Silas he's holding something out to me: a paper cup, watery green liquid steaming into the space between us. Thin string hanging from its edge with a *Peppermint* tea tag.

"GG would be horrified that I'm giving you this knockoff version," he says. "But it's all they have here."

"Thank you," I whisper, and when I take it from him my hands shake. Silas reaches to rub Puddles's head, and the edge of his palm brushes my leg.

"What are you thinking?" he finally asks, eyes coming up to mine. His hair's like it was that very first night in Los Angeles: pulled back, a few pieces loose around his face. I remember thinking he looked so wild, then. So unknowable to me, like we didn't and could never have anything to do with each other. *It's just a summer*, my dad told me when I called him from San Francisco. But here we are.

I take a sip of the tea and it's so hot it dislodges something inside me. "What do I do now?"

He pulls his hand back into his lap, draws a breath. "Can we try something?"

I think of the tree house, his angry eyes in the dark. I nod.

Silas says, "Come out with us tonight."

36

"A honky-tonk," I repeat. I'm sitting on the toilet in Cleo's hotel bathroom, some kind of frozen eye mask elastic'd around my head. I can barely see her through its eye holes.

"Yes, Audrey." She's leaning over the sink, gluing a sparkly blue set of eyelashes in place. When I agreed to go out with the interns I didn't really know what I was signing up for; when Silas dropped me off at Cleo's door she took a long look at me and said, "Yep, I've got this."

And now, the ice mask. I don't ask what it's for because I know it's to run interference on the red, puffy catastrophe of my face. There's a black wrap dress set out on the bed for me, Cleo's. There's the news that we are, apparently, going to a honky-tonk.

"I didn't know that was a real thing," I say. "I thought it was, like, a joke term."

Cleo glances at me. She hasn't once asked what's wrong or tried to hug me or given me a lingering sympathetic look. She acts like she always does—like I'm irritating her and she's on the edge of her patience. It feels like a gift.

"You thought 'honky-tonk' was a joke term?"

"It's too corny to be true."

She sighs, turning back to the mirror. "You know, Audrey, shitting on universally beloved things doesn't make you cooler than other people. It just hurts their feelings."

I blink. "Are honky-tonks universally beloved?"

"Yeah," Cleo says, lowering back onto her heels from where she's been leaning into the mirror. "Like gas station candy and Disney World and all the other basic shit refined people pretend they're too good for."

"I'm not a refined person," I tell her, and she snorts. Glances at me.

"Maybe not in this exact moment, Captain Underpants." She gestures at the ice mask, and I pull it off my face.

"Captain Underpants doesn't even wear an eye mask."

"Ah," she says, returning to the mirror. "So you're familiar with his work."

My phone buzzes, sitting on the bathroom counter next to Cleo's makeup bag. We both look at it.

DAD-O: I'm proud of you, mouse

I grab the phone off the counter and Cleo looks away, swallowing. The text makes me hate myself. The fact that I'm someone who needs to be comforted at all, that Dad and Camilla must have talked. What that conversation must have sounded like. And that there's nothing to be proud of now.

I stare down at my bare feet on the tile floor. The white polish on my second-to-last toe is chipped and I hadn't even noticed, which makes me feel completely out of control. Cleo draws a breath and I think it's finally going to happen; she's going to say something to console me and it's going to send me right over the edge.

But she just says, "So can I call you 'mouse'?"

And I laugh—this wet, halfway-to-tears sound—and Cleo smiles, reaching over to flick me in the shoulder.

"Go put that dress on," she tells me. "We're outta here in five."

Broadway is a neon vein in the dark, so loud I think we're there when we're still three blocks away. The street is wide and carless and packed with people, shoulder to shoulder like the starting line of a charity 10K or some sort of postapocalyptic pileup. Everyone leaving town—the final, frantic beeline for the evac helicopters.

"What're we looking for again?"

Mick's right next to me, but I can hardly hear him. He's wearing jeans and cowboy boots he bought this afternoon and a white T-shirt so thin and tight that I can see every hard line of his abdomen straight through it.

"Lady June's," Cleo shouts. Her cowboy boots are pearlescent, shining red and purple and blue as we pass the lit faces of three-story bars spilling country music into the street. Every building's windows are open, thick with bodies dancing inside. I can't hear myself think, and when I glance at Silas I understand that was the point of this.

"Do we know the cross streets?" he asks, and when Cleo shrugs he does, too. His eyes find mine as Cleo forges ahead, and I watch them catch on the dress she gave me—short and tight, though much less so by comparison on this street than it felt back at the hotel. I feel very warm. Silas smiles and tips his head after Cleo.

"Don't dawdle, now." Mick wraps an arm around my shoulders, steering me out of a bachelorette party's line of fire. Their bride is in a white cowboy hat and looks like she's been crying for a solid hour. "If we lose you, Camilla will kill us."

"You won't lose me," I say, in the same moment Silas says, "We won't lose you."

"Can never be too careful," Mick says, and I let him take my hand when he reaches for it. It makes me feel less out of place here—physically connected to someone who belongs. The bar lights play across his face and I think of his last name, moonlight, and how Mick really is that way—always shining, even in the dark.

"Glenna here?" Cleo shouts it at the bouncer half-propped on a stool under a sign shaped like cowboy boots. It's pink and neon, buzzing into the dark, *Lady June's* splashed across it.

"Who's asking?" he says, and when he looks at Mick it's so careful and so prolonged that I realize he's checking him out. Mick grins wickedly, and Cleo waves her hand in front of the bouncer's face.

"Hello? Tell her it's Cleo Mori."

"Tell her yourself," he says, and when he juts his chin over Cleo's shoulder a short Black woman in a tight denim dress materializes with a stamp in her hand. She hugs Cleo, rocking her back and forth, the entirety of her face split into a smile.

"Hey, you," Glenna says when they pull apart. She stamps the back of Cleo's hand, then motions for Mick to stick his out. "Y'all be good in there and don't make me regret this."

"We'll be honorable as a pack of church ladies," Cleo says, and when Glenna takes my hand she barks out a laugh that's so huge and unselfconscious it makes me want to stay next to her all night.

"Maybe not that good," she says, and Cleo's hand darts out for my wrist.

"My big sister's best friend," she shouts, dipping her mouth close to my ear. Her fingers are still locked around my arm, pulling me into the crowd, and I can feel a hand on my back that I sincerely hope belongs to someone I know. It's mobbed in here, hardly room to breathe. "They cut holes in all my bras when I was in middle school and now we love each other. So it goes." She presses me against the bar next to her. "Beer?"

"Um, I don't—" but there's already a plastic cup of it in my hand, foamy and wet.

"To Nashville!" Cleo screams, loud and yet barely registering. The four of us cheers high in the air, like we're about to play a soccer game and this is the huddle. "To being fucking hot and young and free!"

When everyone else takes a drink I do, too. It's fizzy and cold, and it makes me feel like someone else. The stamp on the back of my hand is a cowboy boot with the letters *OK* inked inside it; I blink at it and decide that maybe I can be, just for now.

"I want to dance," Mick says, his hips shimmying with the words. Cleo takes another big gulp of her beer and nods, pointing through the crowd toward a stage where three women are performing under pink lights.

I watch her mouth move to the words *let's go*, and when they part the crowd away from the bar Silas looks at me.

"Dance?" he says, and when I reply he can't hear me. So he ducks very close, his cheek right next to mine and my lips at his ear. His hair brushes my temple.

"I said I don't."

Silas pulls back to find my eyes.

"You don't dance?" he says, and I shake my head. He smiles, and when he leans his mouth close to my ear I feel him breathe every word. "Not that type of person?"

Things can just be what they are, I hear him say. His voice soft in the tree house, his bare feet in the night air next to mine. *You could change, and feel differently.*

I want to feel differently. I want to claw out of the cage of myself.

"Maybe we could just try," Silas says, and when someone squeezes into the bar beside me his arm comes around my back, pulling me gently toward him and out of the way. I think of his arms around me at the hotel this afternoon, holding me so tightly that I couldn't unravel.

"Maybe," I say. Silas smiles: easy, crooked, honest. He takes my hand to lead me toward the stage and I try to remember what this is: functional, way-finding, a way to keep me from getting lost. Mick held my hand in the street and Cleo's constantly grabbing me. I don't think about how different this feels, or the tether that snaps when Silas lets go.

He turns to face me in the center of the teeming crowd and I think I get it, why people like this. That there are so many of us we get to feel anonymous. That I can see Cleo and Mick nearby but only in fits and flashes, not enough to make them out or form a judgment or discern whether they belong. They just do.

The song changes and in the breath of silence Silas takes a sip of his beer, licks the foam from his lip. He has hair stuck to his cheekbone and as the woman onstage starts singing again I reach for it, someone outside myself just like everyone else in this room.

I brush it away, and Silas looks at me in the red-and-orange dark. My hand falls and he catches it, his thumb moving over the fingernail marks on the soft underside of my arm. They're red and angry but they're small and I know he can't see them in here. I know he finds them by memory.

"I don't want to talk about it," I tell him.

"I know," he says. And then he moves closer to me—by necessity maybe, the crowd pressing in as the song gets louder. His hand is still on my arm and he lifts it around him, dropping my wrist across his shoulder so I'm holding him in the pulsing dark. Our faces are very, very close. Silas looks at the floor and I look over the arch of his neck and when he starts moving to the music my body goes with his.

Mick is five feet away, kissing a tall man in a cowboy hat with big hands wrapped around Mick's waist. They part and Mick's head tilts back, a laugh moving through him. Cleo dances next to them with both arms in the air, screaming along with the song.

I close my eyes, feel Silas put a tentative hand on the middle of my back. Think, *What am I doing?*

And then, for once, I let myself get away with not having a good answer.

Ethan calls when we're walking back to the hotel, at nearly one o'clock in the morning. Nearly two where he is. I'm so stunned to see his name glowing up at me in the middle of Broadway I nearly don't answer in time.

"Hello?" I say, and Silas glances back from where he's walking with Mick. Cleo has her arm hooked through mine, and when she sees the way Silas is looking at me she says loudly, "Who's that?"

Her head's right next to the phone pressed into my ear. Ethan says, "Audrey?"

"Yeah." I pull my arm out of Cleo's and take a few steps away from her. We just left the bar and Cleo's pink-cheeked and bubbly; when I let go of her she wedges herself between Mick and Silas instead. Mick spent most of the night making out with His Tall Cowboy™ and Cleo's had more to drink than I could quite keep track of. Silas puts a steadying arm around her waist, and when he looks at me again I look away first.

"Who was that?" Ethan says. Broadway is still loud and I have to press a hand over my other ear to hear him.

"Cleo," I say. "She's the photography intern."

There's a pause, and I swear I can hear Ethan thinking. I know him so well it feels skeletal, like we share the same bones. "You sound different," he says finally.

A man trips backward through the open door of the bar ahead of me, and I sidestep to avoid him. "Different how?"

"Breezy," he says, and I feel my face screw into itself. "Maybe inebriated."

"I had a beer and a half."

Another pause. I draw a loud breath just to hear something on the line between us.

"Where?"

"With the interns."

More silence. "I thought you were at dinner with your mom?"

I watch Silas's heels ahead of me, the even pace of his footsteps. Ethan's caught me in the lie but I can't make myself give it to him. "And now," I say, "it's one in the morning."

"I don't understand," Ethan says. "We don't drink. I didn't

think you—I thought. I thought you'd be trying to find another position for the fall."

There it is. Something sours at the back of my throat and I swallow it down. For a few fleeting moments I'd actually forgotten.

"Tonight?" I say, and I know I sound mad. Know, too, that I've never been mad at Ethan. "You thought I'd be doing that tonight?"

"When else?" Ethan says. His voice rises to match mine. "I called because I found something I thought you might be interested in. It's only lab work but it starts in September and they're still—"

"Ethan," I say, and this time when Silas turns to look at me Mick and Cleo do, too. "Please stop trying to fix me."

"Fix you?" His voice is immediate in my ear, incredulous. "I'm trying to help you, Audrey. This is what we do. If you don't want my help, just say it."

It's the beer, maybe. It's the way Cleo is looking at me, openmouthed. It's that Ethan has reached inside this moment and reminded me of my shame—of who I really am when this night is over. And it's the fact that I'm so, so excruciatingly sick of myself.

I say, "I don't want your help."

Ethan's quiet for too long. It's unlike him, to be at a loss for words. I know I've fucked up as soon as the words are out, and I know it more when he draws a breath so sharp it's audible.

"Okay," he says. "I'll just see you in Miami, then."

37

But I do need help, is the thing.

In the crowd at Lady June's it felt like morning wouldn't come. That's the lure of it, I understand now—a suspended moment, colored lights, how a night like that makes a world of itself. It convinces you it'll last forever. But it's so short, and then it's morning.

When I wake up, life feels nothing like it did last night, dancing anonymously in the dark. It feels realer. And much, much worse.

There's the email, for one thing. No subject line, just a blue hyperlink to the research position Ethan brought up on the phone. The line of text beneath it: *I think we should take a break until Miami so we have space to think about what we both want from this.* The way I read it as: *I don't want this.* And the white-hot humiliation of how quickly I click the link anyways, apply for the job, wait for it to take some kind of edge off.

There's Sadie knocking on my door at ten o'clock. The epidemiology lab we're supposed to visit at Vanderbilt. The way I can't get out of bed to speak and how I text her instead. The fictional fever I fabricate. How every time I breathe, I feel more like a coward.

The day seeps darkly by: the shades drawn, the sheets at my chin, my eyes dry and bloodshot. The clack of my laptop keys and the ache blooming in my lower back from how my body's twisted, propped awkwardly on one elbow as I submit the lonely PDF of my résumé over and over and over. I apply to six more on-campus jobs and I get up to pee and I mouth tap water from my cupped hand in the bathroom.

Food? Silas texts me at two, and the hot shock of shame sucks my lips between my teeth. It's day now: stark and sure and indisputable. This isn't Broadway at midnight. This is the world I need to occupy forever, the one where I let him see me the way that he did. I keep my eyes closed for thirteen whole, slow minutes. When I open them I can't even read the one word of his text message through the blur of my tears. Later, when he knocks on the door, I pretend to be sleeping.

I run the hotel room TV all night long. Every time I wake up someone's talking: strangers playing out fictions who have no idea who I am or the depth of my humiliation. I order room service when they open at six o'clock in the morning and pick at cooled, rubbery eggs from under the comforter, the fork feeling foreign in my hand.

When Cleo slips the ice eye mask under the crack of my door I'm on a deep dive of the Hopkins ICU website, searching for any crumb that'll tell me who they picked. I can't find anything, any evidence of what this person has that I lack. Cleo doesn't say anything; I watch the shadows of her feet disappear and finally pull myself out of bed. There's a handwritten note on top of the mask, instructions for how to use it scribbled on a Post-it. She's drawn a little lopsided heart. I stare at it until the AC kicks on and my legs get cold.

It's nearly evening again when Camilla knocks on the door. Ten minutes to five, still hours from that safe zone when the sun sets and it makes sense for me to be in here like this.

"Audrey," she says. We're due at the War Memorial Auditorium in thirty minutes, I know. All two thousand sold-out seats. *Camilla St. Vrain's Valedictorian Daughter.*

I say nothing, and she says my name one more time. And then the door clicks open.

I have my laptop next to me, power cord draped over the lump of my body under the covers. I haven't changed my clothes or run a hand through my hair since Sunday night, nearly forty-eight hours ago. The ice eye mask is pushed up onto my forehead, room temperature and useless. I'm disgusting. She doesn't flinch.

"Have you eaten?"

I gesture to the room service cart, motionless at the end of my bed, silver dome covering the picked-over remains of the breakfast I barely ate twelve hours ago.

"Can you eat now?"

I shake my head. When I pull up the words they scrape my throat; I've hardly spoken since Sunday, either. "I'm sick."

My mother doesn't check me, though I know it's obvious to both of us that I'm lying. She crosses the room in her show clothes—silk wrap dress, so pale pink it could be cream—and sits next to me in my filth. Her hand on my forehead is cold as it was two days ago, cold as Dr. Osman's hand in San Francisco, as comforting and dry as the hand of every doctor I've ever met. I remember that my mother is a doctor, too.

"You're not a child anymore," she tells me. That's the hollow, heavy truth: no one is responsible for my deterioration but me.

"I can't tell you what to do. But please don't pretend nothing happened."

We stare at each other. My bleary, bloodshot eyes on hers—rose eye shadow, dark mascara. I wonder if she's thinking about what I'm thinking about: that week sophomore year that I didn't get out of bed. The Sex Summit. The last time we were here.

"That's what we do," I tell her. Her eyebrows twitch toward each other just the tiniest distance, a question she doesn't ask. I feel, suddenly, like I'm back underwater in Chicago—like my lungs are pressed fully flat under the weight of everything we aren't saying to each other. "We pretend."

Her lips part but I don't want to listen. "Go do your show." I wave one hand toward the door and it feels unwieldy, not mine. "I'm fine."

"No," she says, and the dull headache I've had all day throbs against my skull. Right between my eyes, so painful I have to close them.

"Mom," I manage. "You're going to be late."

"So I'll be late." Her hands are clasped in her lap and the way she's looking at me—full attention, basically unblinking—makes me want to hide. I want to be alone, to go back to my internet scroll, to absorb into this mattress and exist here in its cushioned shell. "Tell me what you mean."

I don't want to tell her what I mean. I can barely even think straight I'm so dehydrated. I can feel every pore on my body sucking inward; I've cried so much in the last two days I'm desiccated and empty. I have nothing left to give her, nothing left in me to have this conversation.

But when I don't speak, when my throat constricts like a

clenched fist, Camilla moves toward me. Her hand brushes through my hair, curls it around my ear. It feels like something I want to lean into, against all my better judgment, and I think of her on that houseboat in Colorado—the way she looked at those women. The way she's looking at me now.

"Mom," I whisper. It's strangled and thin; it hurts on the way out. Her eyes don't leave mine. "What's wrong with me?"

"Audrey," she breathes, and I start sobbing. My own name feels like an offense, something I can't bear to be associated with. When she hugs me I let it happen; I'm layered in sweat and tears and she presses me directly into her silk dress anyway.

"What's wrong with me?" My voice is loud somehow. Breathless and wet. "You're a therapist. Tell me what's wrong with me."

"Honey." Her arms are tight around me, stronger than I know her to be. "What are you talking about?"

"*This*," I practically scream, obscene, rearing back so I can motion around us at the squalor I've made. This stale room I'm hiding out in like some kind of pox-ridden recluse. "Why am I like this? Why can't I handle things that other people can handle?"

When I fling my arm into the space between us her eyes track over the fingernail cuts on my forearm. She takes my wrist in her cool hand and lowers it back to the bed, looking up at me.

"Tell me what it is." I sound like I'm begging; I probably am. "Why do I do this? Tell me what it is. Please." Her eyes slant in a sad way that cuts right through my chest, breaks every rib on the way to my heart. She pities me. I ask again anyway. "*Please*, Mom."

"There's nothing wrong with you, Audrey."

The sound that I make is a wail, inhuman. "Don't pretend. For once, don't pretend—not like last time."

"In Colorado, you mean."

Of course I mean in Colorado. I sniff, wet and graceless. My head hurts so badly it feels thirty seconds away from falling off entirely. "When you pretended nothing happened. When I did this before."

"I didn't—" She hesitates, gathering herself. "I wasn't trying to pretend nothing happened, I—"

"Then why did you do that? Why did you turn that whole entire thing into the Sex Summit story and this big media hit and just fucking ignore—you acted like it never even, I mean, we *never* talked about it, Mom. Never." When our eyes meet again, hers are as blurred as mine. Shit.

"I'm sorry," she says. Simply, with no qualifiers. It loosens something inside me. "I knew you didn't want to share how you were feeling then. I took you to the counseling center because I wanted you to have private space to work through those feelings, away from me and the—" She breaks off, sighs in a way that sounds so, so tired. I watch her struggle to find the words, like this is as hard for her as it is for me. "Everything that follows me. The magnifying glass people take to my life, and yours in turn."

"But instead you lied," I say. I can't believe I'm saying this out loud, finally, after so long. But what do I have left to lose? "You pretended you were there for some Saint sex ed stunt, like what I did was so wrong we couldn't even speak of it, ever. Like it was so shameful. So—" My voice squeaks off, going so high so suddenly it's impossible to keep going.

"I'm sorry," she says again. "Audrey, I'm so sorry, that was never my intention. I thought having a different story about that week-end would give you space to talk about what you'd gone through on your own terms, or not talk about it, if that's what you wanted. I wasn't trying to hide it; I was trying to leave the choice to you. I didn't mean to cover it up, honey, I was only trying to let you decide." Our eyes meet, and it all shifts in me like dominoes. Tiles clicking into place. How little we've understood each other. "There was nothing shameful about that, just as there's nothing shameful about this. I'm sorry."

"There was," I whisper, breath shaking out of me. "And there is. I don't know what's wrong with me."

"Honey." She pulls me into her again, and this time I can feel her heart hammering. I've never, ever seen my mother cry. "There's nothing wrong with you."

"Then why am I like this?" I say, straight into her dress.

"I know you want a simple answer." She pulls away so she can look at me. Wipes a tear from one carefully mascaraed eye. "Something hard and fast, but the truth is we can't always cleanly categorize ourselves. Nothing is that simple. This is your experience, Audrey. It's not wrong; it just is."

"It feels wrong," I say, straight down at my fingers twisted in my lap. "I thought I'd fixed it. I thought—I worked so hard to become an EMT, and I never messed up like that again, and I just—I thought I was better than this but here I am, again, doing the same thing."

"Honey," she says, ducking her chin so I'll look at her. "There is no value judgment. No *better*, because you are not bad." I feel the tears rise in me. "And no matter how much you've learned, how smart and impressive and self-possessed you are, you can't white-knuckle yourself out of anxiety. You can't pretend a panic attack away."

I close my eyes. *Anxiety. Panic attack.* When I open them, Camilla is blurred by my tears. "I wish I was different," I whisper.

"No," my mother breathes. "Audrey, I don't wish you were different."

My throat is too tight to speak through.

"You've always pushed yourself so hard," she says. "And your perfectionism, it—it motivates you to excel but it also comes out this way sometimes. It tells you things that are untrue. That certain losses are a reflection on *you.*"

I think of Silas: *That's too much pressure for anybody. This doesn't mean anything about who you are.*

"I'm so embarrassed," I whisper.

"There's nothing to be embarrassed about."

"There is." I swipe my eyes with the backs of my knuckles. "Right after I got the email, I went to the wrong room by accident." I swallow, trying to dredge up the words, but my mother just nods.

"Silas," she says.

I wince; I can't help it. "I made a fool of myself."

She cocks her head to the side, eyes never leaving mine. "By showing him how you really feel?"

The memory floods me with thick, licking heat. "I didn't want anyone to see me like this."

"Audrey," she says slowly. "Needing help is part of what makes you a person."

It rises in me so fast, a deep-coded response: *I don't need help.* But I do. God, I do.

"We aren't made to manage our emotions all on our own." My mother takes my hands and squeezes them. "We need each

228

other—it's in our brains, in our DNA. Needing help from the people around us, and giving that help back to them in turn, isn't a sign of weakness. It's what makes us human."

I look down at our fingers locked together, maybe the first time in my sentient memory that we've touched each other like this. Maybe she's right: maybe what happened between Silas and me was normal, the natural order of things. Maybe I only imagined how enormous it felt. Overestimated both how horrifically I imposed on him and the weight of the gift he gave me in handling it how he did. His hand pressed over his eyes, his elbow jutted out beside him. His arms locked tight around my rib cage. The wet mess of his shirt collar.

But I'm thinking, too, of Sadie on that airplane. The way her whole body tensed the minute I tried to open up to her about Camilla. How uncomfortable she became the second I showed her the scared, unsure part of me.

And I know that even if my weakness is what makes me human, not everyone wants to see it.

Not Sadie, not Ethan. Not even me.

"Audrey?" The voice is muffled, but I'm so on edge it makes me jump. My mother and I turn in unison to look at the door. "It's me. Um, Silas."

Camilla makes to stand, but I stop her. When she looks at me, I shake my head sharply and she lowers herself back onto the bed.

"I just wanted to make sure you're okay," he says. "Will you open the door?"

My mother and I stare at each other, holding our breath. Neither of us move.

"Okay," Silas says finally. "We're, um. We're about to head out for the show and it—it feels weird to leave you here. I get it, if you want your space. I just—" He breaks off, and I feel a sharp twinge of guilt. I picture him standing in the hallway, speaking to my closed door, and hate myself. "I just hope you know I'm here. And I hope you're okay. There's something I need to tell you, so, um. I'll try you again in the morning."

I close my eyes. *There's something I need to tell you.*

"Puddles is in my room," he says. A flat white rectangle slips beneath the doorframe—his room key. "If you need her, okay?"

He taps a knuckle on the door, soft echo in the quickly falling dark. "Okay. See you soon, I hope."

His footsteps retreat. I tip my forehead against my mother's shoulder and cry.

38

In time, the heaviness lifts. My limbs start to feel like my own again; I draw deeper breaths and sleep more soundly and start to eat. Just like after the Sex Summit, I come back to myself with time. Eventually, the marks on my arm feel like they were made by someone else.

Camilla did the show without me. When I asked what she would tell everyone, she said: the truth.

Audrey couldn't be here, she told the audience in the clip Mick posted to her social media after the show. No one pressed; I guess it was reason enough. But I knew, watching it on the blue rectangle of my phone, who had recorded the video—and that he knew exactly why I wasn't there.

In Colorado my shame circle was small: Fallon. Here I've let the storm of myself wing wide: Silas, Ethan, Sadie. Cleo and Mick, maybe, if they're disappointed in me, too. My dad, whose calls and texts I haven't been answering. And Fallon, again, who I finally texted Doing okay over here! Which was an absolute lie and felt like some cowardly kind of betrayal, especially considering she'd seen me do all of this before. But she didn't have service, it seemed, and I hadn't heard back from her.

I've let so many people see into my darkness this time. I don't know how to move past it except to pretend that it never happened, which—now that I'm out of it—is nearly how it feels. I don't recognize that person, unshowered and alone in her hotel room. I want her to be fictional. I want to separate myself from her. I want, for the first time in recent memory, my mother.

The day after the Nashville show we do yoga together in her hotel room. We video call my dad. I watch the smile spread across his face at seeing us side by side and I feel young and safe and different.

I send an email to the epidemiology lab at Vanderbilt and apologize for missing our appointment. I cc Sadie, and she replies directly to me: *Can I come by?* I'm thinking she's going to chide me for messing up a visit she worked hard to set up for me. Tell me that I need to get my act together for the rest of them. I'd deserve it if she did.

But when I let her into my hotel room, my chin ducked, apology already halfway out of my mouth, Sadie doesn't say anything at all. She just reaches for me—like it's what she came here to do, like it's something we've ever done before. I let her hug me, maybe because I'm too stunned to stop it. Maybe because it feels good, after what happened on the airplane, to have her see my sadness and hold it against her instead of pushing it away.

"It's okay," she tells me before she leaves. Like I said anything, which I didn't. "Take your time."

So I do. When Silas knocks on my door again, I don't open it. When Ethan keeps not calling me, I brace for what's coming when I see him in Miami. The *if/when*.

The moment—not quite here yet—when I'll finally have to face myself.

My mother is leading a guided stretch when the power goes out. Theater lights clicking off in one great wave, audience gasping into the dark.

I'm suspicious the whole thing's for my benefit, anyways: we've been in Miami for twenty-four hours and she's tried to get me to do yoga with her three times already. Weekly Flow doesn't feel as bad as it used to, but a girl can only handle so much yoga. Besides—a backyard workout makes it nearly impossible to avoid people seeing me, which has been my primary modus operandi for the last few days. The house Mags rented in Miami Beach has six bedrooms and an infinity-pool'd backyard surrounded by trees; the yoga mats have been waiting out there for me like docking stations. Visible from every single back window.

"Emotional pain doesn't live in our brain with our memories," Mom told me. "It lives in our bodies. You need to move and tap into it." She stood across from me in the massive, granite-sheathed kitchen, watching me pour a second cup of coffee before anyone else was awake to intercept me. She knew that Ethan and I were on a break because I'd told her—which isn't something I do, historically. But we've tiptoed into some new kind of territory where we say stuff to each other. It feels scary in an edging-on-good way.

"I'm not in pain," I told her. It was true: I'd rounded the gloomy curve out of Nashville and I didn't want to keep focusing on it. I had action to take now: more jobs to apply for, fall courses to enroll in now that I was less than a month out from the start of school. I'd been emailing back and forth with my assigned premed adviser, laying the tracks to optimize my course load across all four years of undergrad. It was like a puzzle, fitting together my prereqs and electives and the professors I wanted to study under. It gave me purpose. I felt like myself again, and I didn't want to run into Nashville Audrey while hanging inverted in downward dog.

"Let's arch our left arms up and over," Camilla says, now. "Breathing deeply into our bellies and—"

The stage lights click off all at once, silence falling in that eerie, ancient way—when not even the central air's still running, and you realize that the whole world has been white noise until now. I blink into the sudden dark, letting my arm fall out of its arch as emergency lights click on down the theater aisles. There's lots of gasping from the invisible audience. Above the domed roof, thunder rumbles.

"Please move calmly toward the exits!" A voice rises above the murmured panic, someone from the theater appearing in front of Camilla and me with a flashlight trained on his face. He looks like he's about to tell us a ghost story, and I think for the millionth time of Silas in his tree house in Colorado. The sun setting over the garden and all those crickets clicking in the woods and the promise, still, of the life waiting for me in the fall.

"The hurricane is coming early."

Magnolia appears from nowhere, her face hazy in the dark. She puts a hand on my shoulder and then Camilla's, helping to guide us from the stage. "It's supposed to make landfall tonight—we need to get back to the house."

Mags has been tracking Lola for days, a tropical storm gathering angrily in the Atlantic. It was a blip and then a smear and then a cyclone, hurtling straight toward Florida because of course it is. Why wouldn't this happen? When I pull my phone out of my skirt pocket Ethan has texted me for the first time in a week: Not sure if you'll have service to see this, but my flight's canceled. Just as I open it to respond—though to say what, I don't know—I lose my last bar of cell service.

"*Power outage.*" Cleo's voice hisses so close to my ear that I jump. She cackles and wraps a hand around my elbow, tugging me along behind Mags as we move through the backstage maze. "This is gonna be fun."

"What if we die?" Mick's voice is high, not quite *panicky* but close.

"No one's dying," Mags says firmly. "The management company has already boarded up the house. We'll be completely safe."

I glance behind me—a black, endless tunnel back to the stage. "Where's Silas?"

"I'm here." His voice is soft and close, but I can't tell where it's coming from. The other side of Mick, maybe. Cleo squeaks as we brush past the stage curtains, pulling me closer, and all of us follow the pinprick of Magnolia's phone flashlight toward a glowing exit sign.

The rain is thrashing outside, palm trees arching ghoulishly in the street.

When I find Silas's eyes in the waterlogged moonlight, he looks away first.

39

The house looks condemned when we get to it: plywood boarded over every window, driveway already thick with plants ripped from their roots and palm fronds blown from the sky. The property manager is waiting for us inside: a tall, thin man in a baseball cap holding a flashlight. He apologizes to my mother four times in a row, like he called down this hurricane himself.

"Y'all stay in the office," he says. "Fewest windows in the house. Lots of flashlights in the TV console."

I glance at Silas; his arms are folded over his chest. *There's something I need to tell you*, he'd murmured through the door in Nashville. I think of all the things I'd tell him, if I were brave.

"You got a dog in here?" The property manager looks between us, and Silas lifts a hand.

"Yeah, she's mine."

"Don't let her get outside, all right? One bad clap of thunder, she spooks and you never hear from her again. Seen it a hundred times."

Silas swallows, looking over the guy's shoulder like he wants to get eyes on Puddles ASAP.

"And that goes for all of you." The property manager hands his big yellow flashlight to Mags and makes for the front door. "Stay inside till it's over. Storm always ends, you just got to ride it out and be smart."

"Thank you," Mags says. When the front door closes behind him, the house feels cavernous and forbidding.

Silas says, "I'm going to grab Puddles."

Cleo says, "I have an idea."

"I found it this morning."

Cleo smooths a hand over the Ouija board, set in the center of the circle we've made of our bodies. The house's office is cool and sprawling, and we sit in its middle on the plush carpet. As far from the two windows as we can get. They're boarded and dark. "In the linen closet off the kitchen."

"How do we play?" my mother asks. She's directly across from me, next to Silas. He has Puddles in his lap and it's taking every ounce of my resolve not to look at him.

Cleo's mouth drops open. "You've never Ouija'd?"

Mom shrugs. She's still in her show clothes: white slacks, blue blouse with raindrops drying at the shoulders. "Can't say that I have."

"It's a spirit board." Cleo's words run into each other, like she's so excited she can't get them out quickly enough. In the stark yellow of the flashlight on her face, her eyelashes look spiders'-leg long. "We put our fingertips on the planchette and ask a question, and the dead tell us what they know from beyond."

I think my mother's going to scoff—it's what I'm trying not to do. But she smiles in the shadowy light and shimmies her shoulders like a kid at a birthday party, the excitement wiggling right out of her.

"We should light candles," she says, and a clap of thunder booms above us so loudly it nearly drowns her out. She's already standing. "I saw some in the master bathroom."

"I'll help," Mags says, and then they're gone.

"Wow." Cleo places the planchette in the center of the board. "She's amped."

"I haven't played this since I was in high school," Sadie says. We're supposed to see a dermatologist tomorrow, but I imagine that's not happening now. "My sister asked for the name of my future husband and instead of spelling something out it just said 'no.'"

Cleo snorts. "Incredible."

"I guess I should've known," Sadie laughs. "But of course I just thought it was telling me I'd die alone."

Mick glances at his phone, bright in the dark. "Can you believe we're about to play Ouija with Camilla St. Vrain during a hurricane? A video of this whole situation would do *numbers*. This is the shame of all shames."

Cleo lets out a sympathetic noise, and when I look at Mick I realize that for someone so wired to social media, he's been uncharacteristically private this summer. "You haven't posted about her," I say, and everyone turns to look at me. "Not once since the tour started."

"Of course not." Mick swipes open his phone camera just as we hear Mags and my mom open the door. "We signed NDAs. Doesn't mean I can't record it for myself, though."

I don't know why it didn't occur to me before; of course they signed NDAs. What's happening here isn't normal—it's a business arrangement, and one they aren't even allowed to talk about.

"That's more like it," my mother says, settling back into her place in the circle. She sets a candle on either side of the board, and I don't point out to her that now we're all at risk of burning our wrists when we touch the planchette.

"Do you believe in this stuff?" Sadie asks, looking over at her. Their eyes meet, and in the flicker of candlelight the way they smile at one another feels like a mirror. It occurs to me that I'm not the only one who's grown closer to Camilla this summer.

"In another plane beyond our mortal world?" Mom says, leaning sideways to nudge her shoulder into Sadie's. "Sure."

"I guess I more meant the premeditation of it," Sadie says. "That someone in the great beyond might know our futures before we do."

"Like fate's a book everyone gets to read when they die," Cleo says. Mick angles his phone to catch her face in the candlelight. "And only us mortals have to learn the story as it comes."

"I'm not sure." My mother looks at me, smiling. "I don't suppose there's any harm in imagining that, though, is there?"

"It's kind of comforting," Silas says. He's running a hand over Puddles's wrinkly head, her eyes closed under his palm. "That someone knows how the story goes, even though it's going to be what it's going to be."

"Why do you always say that?" Finally, like a magnet catching by inevitable force, Silas looks at me. Everyone else does, too. "'It'll be what it'll be.' It takes away our freedom of choice. Leaves us no agency at all."

"Oh," he says flatly, "you're talking to me now?"

The silence that drops over us is like the power going out at the theater: unnatural. A strange break in the order of things. Sadie stares at Silas but he doesn't look away from me. It feels like he's punched me in the throat, though I know I deserve it.

My mother opens her mouth, but before she can get any words out there's a crash from outside. The plywood has come loose from one of the windows—it wrenches and slams with the wind, letting in rain that lashes the glass.

"I'll fix it," Silas mutters. He drops Puddles into Cleo's lap and before anyone has time to react he's turning away, moving into the pooled darkness toward the office door.

"Wait, what?" My voice sounds like it belongs to someone else—someone shaken and unsure. Nashville Audrey. "Silas, wait." I've stood up before I realize I'm doing it. "I'll come, too."

40

I catch up to Silas in the foyer, where it's so dark that the tip of my nose brushes his shoulder blade before I orient myself enough to rear backward.

"You can't go out there," I say, and he turns so abruptly that his phone flashlight slices into my eyes. I wince.

"I can't?" He turns back immediately, keeps walking. I scramble for my own phone and hit the flashlight to follow him. Ethan's text is still there on the screen: Not sure if you'll have service to see this, but my flight's canceled.

"If the wind was strong enough to rip off the plywood, it's strong enough to hurt you."

The entryway is all marble floors, thunder reverberating from smooth surfaces. With the windows boarded up, it's pitch-black.

"And if I don't get the plywood nailed back in that corner, the window could break."

"So it breaks," I say, but he's still moving away from me. Slipping his sneakers on, reaching for the hammer and a box of nails on the entryway table.

"Silas," I say, and he doesn't look at me. Just shoves the box into his back pants pocket, grabs the utility flashlight sitting next to it. When he reaches for the front door I take another step toward him. "Silas, *stop*—"

"You stop," he says, finally looking at me. He wrenches open the door and rain gusts in, startling and cold on my face. "Go back to the office."

He steps through the door, and when he yanks it shut behind him I promptly pull it open again.

"I'm serious!" I shout, the storm gobbling up my voice. It's apocalyptic out here—I can barely see the black back of his shirt in the drive of the rain.

Silas whirls around, hair already soaked through and sticking to his forehead. "So am I!" He waves at my legs. "You don't even have shoes on!"

I look down at my feet: pale in the grass, already dotted with dirt. I hadn't even noticed—every single part of me is drenched. I look back up at him. "I don't care."

"Great," he says loudly. "*Now* you don't care about being barefoot outside." He waves a hand through the rain. "Just go back."

Silas turns and makes for the window. The plywood's come loose in the bottom right corner, ripped right from the nail, and with each gust of wind it slams violently into the side of the house.

I follow him, yelling above the thunder. "Why are you so mad at me?" I've never been this wet in my life; when I breathe it feels like I'm drinking.

"I'm not mad at you." He crouches in front of the window without looking at me. His jeans are soaked and stuck to him; he struggles to get the nails out of his pocket.

"Clearly, you are." Rain pelts the top of my head. It's so windy that I press myself against the side of the house to avoid getting whisked away. Standing like this, flat-backed against the brick, we're facing each other.

"I'm confused," Silas says, pulling a nail out of the box. He still isn't looking at me; there's so much water running down his face he looks like he's crying. "You've been icing me out since Nashville."

I swallow, try to blink the stormwater out of my eyes. He's right, of course.

"You're still not going to say anything?" He lines up two nails, one on either side of the original one, which is still bolted into the window frame but holding nothing now. "Why'd you even follow me out here?"

"Silas—"

"I mean, we have that whole conversation, we do the Broadway thing, we dance at the bar and I was trying to be there for you—"

"You *were* there for me."

"Then what?" he asks. His eyes meet mine—dark, dark, dark. "Because I told you, multiple times, that I needed to talk to you. And you've just ignored me, like I'm nothing to you. I thought we were—"

He breaks off, holding my eyes for a moment before turning back to the window. He doesn't finish his sentence, just starts whaling on the nail. The storm's so loud I barely hear it driving into the side of the house.

"Thought we were friends?" I offer, wanting him to keep talking. He's the opposite of nothing to me. I'm a coward and a fool.

"Is that what this is?" He looks back at me, the second nail curled in his hand. "We're friends?"

Rain fills the space and the silence between us. I can feel my fingers pruning.

"I don't know," I whisper. Too quietly for him to hear, but he watches my lips move.

"Jesus, Audrey." He starts on the second nail, and the plywood kisses close to the house—a snug seal against the window frame.

"I'm confused about my feelings—"

"Yeah, me too." He stands, the job complete. Makes no move to go back inside. "And you just left me to work through that alone. We could have been talking about it." He waves the hammer between us, like he's completely forgotten it's attached to his hand. "We could have been figuring it out together this whole time."

"I'm sorry." It comes out scratchy and uncontrolled. "I didn't know what to say, I was so embarrassed, I—"

"Embarrassed about what?" His shirt's sticking to every line of his shoulders, the hard knots of his collarbones, wet lanes of rain racing across his skin like that day on Lake Michigan.

"About what I did," I say. "Are you serious? About how I broke down in front of you like some kind of—some—"

"*Person?*" Silas says. When he takes a step toward me, I don't think he's aware of it. "God, Audrey, can't you tell I want to be close to you?" The hammer's hanging at his side now, useless. "There was nothing embarrassing about that. If anything, it felt like the most honest you've been with me this whole summer. And then you just—" His eyes rake across mine, water dripping from his eyelashes. We're suddenly very close to each other. "You just disappeared on me."

He draws a breath and I look at his mouth and it's so loud out here—thunder booming, trees groaning in the wind. Everything is a disaster, natural and human and otherwise. I think, *Can we try something?* And my body moves all on its own, until there isn't room for the rain to fall between us and my chin is tilted in a mirror of his and my eyes are closing. To block this out, maybe, or to focus on it through the scream of the storm.

But I don't kiss Silas, because something stops me. And it takes a few full, thudding heartbeats for me to realize that it's his fingers, pressed to my lips. They're held up like a shield, gentle but entirely halting.

I look at him, but his eyes are closed.

"What—" I step back, and his hand drops to his side. His eyes open, dark and steady and something else, too—something that sinks like a stone to the pit of my stomach. "You don't want to?"

The breath he lets out sounds injured, like I punched him. When he speaks, it's angry. "Are you kidding me?"

But he's not looking for an answer, because he turns away from me and stalks across the grass back toward the house.

41

"Hey!" I shout, my toes squelching through the mud. "What are you doing?"

"I'm going inside so we don't get killed." He pulls the door open and I follow him through it, back into the lightless, echoing foyer.

"No," I say, and Silas trains his flashlight on the ceiling so it illuminates the room. "Out there. What was that?"

"You're asking *me*?" He thrusts a second flashlight into my hand, clicking it on and then letting go. "What was that, Audrey?"

Our voices are loud, bouncing from the marble. I glance at the office and Silas jerks his head toward the back of the house, where the bedrooms are. My footprints track mud and water the entire way to his room.

"Why are you mad?" I hiss when he leads me through the door and closes it behind us. "I thought you wanted this."

Silas laughs, but it's a bitter noise. "I've spent all summer shoving down how much I want this." My skin goes hot and he wipes a hand over his face, pushes soaked hair off his forehead. "Because I know you have—that you don't—" His eyes flick up to mine, unsure and then suddenly angrier, accusatory. "And now you're going to do that to me? You're going to come at me half-assed about it? No, Audrey, that's not what I want."

I blink at him, shocked silent.

"I don't want part of you in secret," he says. He's holding his flashlight loosely, trained at the floor, so the planes of his face are soft and dark. "I don't want to be some caught-in-the-moment mistake. A person you regret." Thunder rumbles, shakes the walls around us. "That's not what I want at all."

"What do you want?" I whisper.

A muscle works in his jaw. "I think you know."

I want to step closer to him, but I don't. "Tell me."

"I want this for real," he says. The fight's gone out of his voice; we could be back in his hotel room in Nashville, hands covering our eyes. "I want to be the person you go to on purpose, not by accident because you got the room number wrong." He exhales, sharp, but I'm not breathing. "I want you to meet the rest of my stupid cousins and I want to watch Puddles fall asleep on your ankle like that night in the car a thousand fucking more times, every single day if you'll let me. Audrey, I'm—" He swallows, scrapes a hand through his hair. "I mean, god, when you jumped in that water after Puddles I thought—*fuck*, if she doesn't die, she's going to kill me. This is going to kill me."

I squeeze the flashlight so hard my bones ache.

"So if you aren't serious, if you're just going to be with him, I can't—" Silas breaks off and shakes his head. "Please don't do that to me. I can't handle this if you don't mean it."

We stare at each other. I breathe and the air makes me shiver. I'm soaked and I'm freezing and I'm scared.

"Say something," he whispers.

"Ethan and I are on a break," I tell him finally. Silas blinks rapidly.

"What does that mean?"

"We aren't—" I stop, dig my teeth into my bottom lip. Silas looks like he's holding his breath. "We aren't speaking. We're taking a break. Which is why I—did that, I mean. And he was supposed to come here, but his flight's canceled, so I don't—"

I break off, and he takes a half step closer to me. "You don't what?"

"I don't know what happens now."

We stare at each other, wind buffeting the house. "I think that's up to you," Silas says.

I press my eyes shut. I know that broken things never fit back together quite the same way, that there is no returning to the Ethan I knew before. Standing in Silas's bedroom, storm swirling around us, the future feels dark as the bottom of the ocean. I can't see myself there—I can't see what I'm doing, I can't see who I'm with.

"How would it work?" I say, opening my eyes.

"How would what work?"

"How would we—" I swallow, can't believe I'm saying this out loud. The scenario I've gamed out in my own mind for weeks now, refusing to admit to myself what I was doing. "With you at American and me at Hopkins. I mean, we wouldn't—"

"It's a forty-minute train," Silas says. He steps closer to me, and I'm overwhelmed by the urge to tip forward and rest my forehead on his shoulder. I'm so, so tired. "Is he going to Hopkins, too?"

I shake my head. Wrap my arms around myself instead of reaching for Silas. "Yale."

"Okay," he says slowly. "Okay, I mean, that's farther—"

"But what about after?" I make myself look up at him, and it hurts. "There's med school, Silas. And residency. And I have all these plans—"

"And I don't? We can have plans together, Audrey." His gaze moves over mine, searching. "We can support each other's dreams even if they aren't the same. You know that's possible, right?"

"I don't know," I whisper. That was always the safety with Ethan: we had the same plans. We were going the same way and he'd be there at every point down the road. "Maybe?"

"It is." I've been talking to the dark ceiling and Silas moves in front of me so I have to meet his eyes. "Besides, 'after' is three years away. At least that long. Do we need to know, right this second?"

I bite my lip, silent. I always want to know, is the thing. I want a map for everything to come and a steady line to trace myself through it.

"I don't think we do," Silas says. His voice softens. "I just want to know you, Audrey. Now. I want you to know me, too. We can figure out the rest later."

It hits me then that Silas has seen me from the start. Not as someone he can mold into what he wants me to be but as someone he wants already, just as I've been from that moment in the back alley in Los Angeles. I squeeze my nails into my palm.

"Silas, it's going to hurt."

"What is?"

"All of it," I say, shivering so hard now that my voice shakes. "Being away from you at school and not knowing if we'll wind up in the same place and just—I mean, if it ends, I just don't—" I break off, stare up at him.

Because part of me knew that I could do it, with Ethan. That I could be apart, do a relationship like that, have him in fits and starts. I could stomach the weeks and months of separation punctuated by frenetic weekends linked by train. I've already lost so much of him this summer, and I've survived it.

But the way I am with Silas—the hook in my belly when he's close to me, the indefensible way I've needed him so much just this summer alone. It would be torture, wouldn't it? To have him only halfway. A greater torture still to have him and then lose him.

"Yeah," Silas says slowly. "We could get hurt, I guess, but doesn't this hurt?" He reaches for me and then stops himself, and in the moment before his fingers freeze next to mine I think, *please*. "Don't you hurt? Because I do." He swallows, his voice going soft and small. "I really fucking do."

I do. I do, I *do*. I squeeze my eyes shut. Thunder rumbles from the ocean.

"Can we try something?" Silas says, when I still haven't spoken. "Can you tell me what you actually want? Not what you're supposed to want, or what's going to set you up for some other thing." I open my eyes, and he takes a deep breath, and I realize he's scared to hear me answer. "Just what you actually want. Right now. Right this second."

I'm not brave. I can't say it so plainly, what's pressing at the roof of my mouth.

"I think you know," I whisper, echoing his words.

And he echoes mine, too. "Tell me."

I fill my lungs. I squeeze my elbows in my fingers, set my shoulders to stop the shaking.

And I look at Silas, who's wanted the truth of me from the start.

And I tell him.

42

The knocking wakes me slowly, distant but persistent. I open my eyes to the dark office, blue light just inching around the edges of the boarded-up windows. We slept on the floor, linens and pillows pulled from the bedrooms while we waited out the storm. It sounds quiet now, outside—but the knocking comes again.

There's something heavy and warm on my stomach; as my eyes adjust to the light I clock it as Silas's arm, thrown across me. He's sleeping right next to me, much closer than the polite distance where we fell asleep, his chest rising and falling rhythmically. I stare at his arm: tan from summer, a few ropy veins racing up from his wrist to his elbow. His fingers are splayed over my hipbone and when I sit up his fingertips press into me for just a moment, a reflex. Puddles is wedged into the space between our bodies, her face buried in Silas's neck. Mick and Cleo sleep a few feet away. Mom and Magnolia are gone.

When I check my phone, still without service, it's 8:03 in the morning.

I slip out from under Silas's arm as delicately as I can, and when he turns onto his back Puddles wiggles after him to keep her spot.

Her big brown eyes track me out of the room.

The house is still dark, hardly feels like morning. The knocking continues, and I grab a flashlight from next to the office door and use it to make my way across the foyer. I wonder, briefly, where my mother is. But then I swing the front door open and every single thought drops directly out of my brain.

"Ethan."

He's standing on the front steps in khaki shorts and a rumpled Yale T-shirt cut by black backpack straps. A duffel bag rests at his feet.

"Hi," he says. The one syllable sounds absurd, hanging in the humid air between us. It occurs to me, distantly, that the sun is out.

"You're here." Behind him, a landscaping truck sits in the driveway. There are at least four people picking up debris in the yard. My thumb is pressed to my pinky finger, silently counting.

"I took a bus," he says. He looks exhausted: purple smudges under his eyes, dark hair uncharacteristically unkempt. "And then another one. And then, um, a cab."

"I didn't think you—" I break off. My brain is hardly working at all. "When your flight was canceled, I didn't think—"

"You didn't think I'd come?"

I shake my head slowly.

"Well, I did." He shrugs, something so entirely defeated about it I feel tears gathering in my throat. "I think we need to talk, don't you?"

"Yeah," I whisper. A black SUV swings into the driveway and Ethan turns around to look at it, giving me a chance to stare at him openly: the familiar curve of his shoulders, the dark-framed glasses I've slid down his nose so many times before. *I think we should take a break. Space to think about what we both want from this.*

My mother and Mags pile out of the back of the car holding trays of coffee. When my mom sees Ethan her smile falters, but only for a moment. No one, after all, knows how to pull it together quite like she does.

"Ethan," she calls. "Honey, how did you get here?"

"Bus," I say for him, and my mom's eyebrows arch.

"I'm surprised they were running. We had to drive forty minutes just to find coffee."

"Could have been worse," Mags tells us as Camilla presses Ethan into a hug that looks, from his side, reluctant. "Fizzled out as a tropical storm before becoming a hurricane. Everything looks mostly okay out there, but who knows when the power will be back."

My mother hands me an iced coffee and then, inexplicably, passes one to Ethan. I wonder whose it was supposed to be.

"Thank you," Ethan says. "It's nice to see you, Ms. St. Vrain."

They've only met once before, at graduation.

"Oh, you too," Mom says. Her eyes flick, nearly imperceptibly, to me. "Are you two coming in? It's so dark with the boards up but cooler than this heat."

"Maybe we should take a walk," I say quickly. The thought of Ethan and Silas occupying the same space is untenable. Ethan looks like he's thirty seconds from falling asleep. "Or maybe just sit outside?" I gesture toward the water, ten paces across the yard. "If you're, um. Too tired."

Ethan swallows, glancing out at the ocean before looking back at me. "Yeah," he says. "Sure."

"Go on ahead." My mother touches the back of my arm. When she squeezes, gently, I feel a sharp pang of fear. "Mags and I will bring your bags inside, honey."

Ethan slides off his backpack, handing it to Magnolia. She

slings it over a shoulder, offers him a curt smile, and follows Camilla into the house.

And then there's no one else to look at, and Ethan and I stare at each other for a moment that feels so long it's torture. I draw a breath. He waves across the yard and says, "After you."

There's a seawall at the edge of the grass, and when I lower myself onto it Ethan hesitates.

"It's wet," he says.

The butt of my pajama shorts is already soaked through. I'm so overwhelmed by what's going to happen next that I didn't even notice. "Oh," I say, making to stand back up. "Um, okay. We can just, we can—"

"It's fine." Ethan lowers himself gingerly next to me, setting his coffee on the ledge. He hovers for a moment over the wet grass and then finally gives into it, wincing like the moisture hurts. *He's me,* I think. *I'm like that, too.*

"Thank you for coming," I say. My bare feet are in the water, but Ethan tucks his sneakers flat against the seawall.

He looks at me, eyes as blue and dark as the ocean. "I was worried about you."

The way he says it feels like an accusation. That I've given him something to worry about.

"The storm wasn't so bad," I say, and he shakes his head.

"Not that; everything else."

"Everything," I repeat.

His eyes cast over my face, like he's looking for something familiar and having trouble finding it. "What you said when you were drunk in Nashville."

My cheeks go hot. "I wasn't drunk in Nashville."

254

"You said you were."

"I said I had a beer."

"And a half."

"Are you serious right now?"

"I don't know, Audrey, are you?" His voice sounds frayed, like he's holding too tightly to himself and something's starting to rip. "Because this isn't you. The partying and not caring about the ICU rejection after—"

"Not caring?" It feels like getting an IV, how fast the fury diffuses through me. Sprinting into my bloodstream. "You have no idea what you're talking about."

"Okay, then help me understand," he says. "Because all I know is we had a plan, and then all summer you've been less and less committed to the Penn work. Then you get rejected from the ICU position, and you go out and drink instead of doing something about it. It doesn't make any sense."

"It wasn't *instead of*," I say, trying to keep my voice as even as possible. Something is clawing back up from the dark pit of my stomach, a familiar shame. *He's right*, it whispers. *You didn't do anything about it.* "I was really upset, and I needed to do something fun to get through that night. That's it."

"But that's not how we have fun," Ethan says. Our eyes meet and it's so plain on his face, how confused he is. "We aren't into stupid stuff like drinking or going to clubs."

I feel stiff, like there's metal shot through my bones. Maybe I *do* have fun like that. Maybe I've always had that in me. Hearing him use the word *stupid* in association with a choice I've made feels like a compound fracture. We've been on a break, and it's so clear sitting here beside him that we really are broken.

"Would it be so bad?" I manage. Wind moves off the water, fingering through his hair. "If I had fun like that sometimes?"

"I don't know," Ethan says. When I rear back, he holds up his hands. "I mean, no. I don't—no, I just feel like you're changing and I don't understand what you want. It's not making sense."

"Okay, well, I'm not a problem set, Ethan. You can't solve me." There's no one here to protect me but me. I feel like I'm watching myself from above, propped on the seawall in my pajamas as I'm told by someone I thought was on my team that there's no wiggle room between us. That I've fucked it all up by trying even one new thing. And it hurts, but it also feels untrue. I don't know a lot, I don't know what's next, but I know I didn't earn this. "It's as I am or not at all."

Ethan looks at me, draws a breath through his nose. "I guess it just feels like I don't *know* who you are anymore."

I blink at him, trying to find it. The feeling I used to get around Ethan, like he ordered the world for me. Like everything would make sense if I could just be next to him.

I've always thought he was helping me: editing my papers, encouraging me to apply for things, sending me links to research positions. But now, sitting by the ocean with a person who doesn't recognize me at all, I wonder if Ethan actually just needed me to be a certain version of myself. If he was scared of what might happen to us when I finally fell short of his vision of me.

"I think we're supposed to change, sometimes." My voice is quiet, swishing into the tide. "I'm sorry if you don't like the ways I'm changing. But you can't force me to be the kind of person you want me to be."

"I know," Ethan says. He sounds sad, and it hollows me out.

"I guess I've just always thought we were the same kind of person, until now."

I reach for my coffee and take a long, bitter sip. It's weak and watery. "You came here to break up with me."

Ethan hesitates. "Yeah," he says finally. If there's one thing I've always been able to count on Ethan for, it's the truth. "And I knew you would do it, if I didn't."

I nod, setting the coffee back on the ledge.

"Because of him?" Ethan says, and when I look at him I can tell that it hurts to ask the question. "The guy from that paparazzi photo."

I think of Silas, asleep with his arm thrown across me. Drenched by Lake Michigan. Moonlit in that tree house overlooking the garden. "A little," I say. I owe Ethan the truth, too. "But mostly because of us."

He nods, tracing the seam of his shorts with a thumbnail. When he looks out over the water, his eyes narrow into a wince. "It's probably my own fault, for encouraging you to stay this summer. That day you called me from California. Maybe it would've been different, if we'd been together at Penn." He turns back to me. "But I told you to stay."

He's right—it probably would've been different. I wouldn't have met Cleo or Mick or Silas and I wouldn't have drowned myself like a dumbass and I wouldn't have fallen so hard for that stupid dog sleeping in the office. I might have landed the ICU job. I wouldn't have had that conversation in Nashville with my mom. I wouldn't know so many things about myself that I know, sitting here, right now.

"I wanted you to want me to come," I say. His eyes track over mine, liquid blue in the sun off the water. "And there were so many times early this summer, and last year at school, that I—" I swallow, make myself say it now when I never have before. "That I wanted to tell you I loved you, or to hear you say it, but we never did."

Ethan hesitates, and I watch this process through him. I can tell, by how long it takes him to find words, that it's the first time he's thought about it. "I'm sorry," he says eventually. "I didn't think we—I thought we were focused on other things."

"Yeah," I say quietly. Focused, steady Ethan, who's never pretended to be anything other than himself. "We were. And I'm glad you told me to stay on the tour."

He looks at me, draws a deep breath before speaking. "Yeah?"

I nod. "Yeah."

Ethan looks out over the water. The wind moves through his hair and he lifts a hand to rub a fist between his eyebrows, working out a headache. "Damn it," he mumbles finally. "This feels like shit."

I reach for him and he lets me do it, wrap both arms around his bicep and lean my head onto his shoulder. I've always wanted more of Ethan than he was willing to give to me, and now we won't have any of each other at all. It feels awful and inevitable in equal measure.

"I'm sorry, Audrey," Ethan says, when we've been sitting for a long time staring out at the water. He draws a deep breath that nudges my head with the rise of his shoulder. "You're going to be a really good doctor."

My eyes prick with tears, and I squeeze his arm. "So are you."

43

After that, Ethan and I eat Frosted Mini-Wheats in the kitchen. It's the only room they've taken the boards off of, and golden light floods in to slice through it like some kind of Renaissance painting. This house is stunning—a different place in the daylight. Ethan is a sixty-year-old professor in an eighteen-year-old's body, but he loves nothing more than sugary cereal.

"No flights today," Mags tells us, scrolling her laptop at the island. She has her hair in a topknot and is wearing yoga clothes, not a speck of makeup. It's like the storm shook something loose in all of us, brought us down to a common denominator. She props a hand on her hip in a way that can only be described as *casual.*

"Even private?" my mom asks, popping a Mini-Wheat in her mouth. I gape at her. I don't think I've ever seen her eat processed food.

"*Mmm,*" Mags says, clicking around. "We might be able to do private."

"No private planes." I level Mags with my gaze. "No death traps."

Ethan rolls his eyes, nudging me in the side. "I can take the bus again," he offers, and Mags and my mother grimace in unison.

"Eight oh five tomorrow morning," Mags says, glancing at Ethan and then me. "United from Miami International. That okay?"

I watch Ethan sip cereal milk from his spoon. "I have an aunt," he says. "In Coral Gables. I can stay with her until then."

When my eyebrows arch, he smiles sheepishly. "I told her I was coming, in case you kicked me out."

"We'd never have kicked you out," Camilla says, and I look up at her. "Not with nowhere else to go." She sounds serious and sincere. Motherly.

Footsteps echo behind us, and when we turn around in the bar seats, Silas is standing in the foyer. He's in basketball shorts and the T-shirt he pulled on after we got soaked through last night, bright purple with a frenetic line illustration of a cowboy hat that he bought from a street vendor in Austin. His hair is wild and unkempt, loose around his cheekbones. Puddles circles his feet.

"Hi," he says, and Ethan's gaze swoops immediately back down to his cereal. Silas lets his eyes linger on mine for one held-breath moment—he looks simultaneously wrecked and resigned. He turns and makes for the door. I'm standing before it's fallen shut.

It takes me fifteen minutes to find him; Silas moved so quickly it's like he and Puddles simply evaporated into the muggy post-storm air. I check the backyard, the tangle of palm trees behind the pool, the side gardens where people in matching T-shirts gather fallen plants into garbage bags. I walk half the seawall. I've nearly given up when I finally circle back to the front of the house and catch sight of Puddles: twenty yards down the beach, chasing a seagull along the shoreline. Silas sits in the sand with his knees pulled up to his chest.

He doesn't see me until I'm right beside him, lowering myself onto the beach. It's quiet out here—no one in sight except Puddles and the seagull and the two of us.

"Hey," I say. Silas turns to me, his temple resting on one of his kneecaps. His arms are wrapped around his legs. We look at each other, the sun emerging from behind a cloud to cast his eyes green and gold.

I reach out to brush the hair off his cheek, same as I did on the dance floor at Lady June's, and it's not enough. I want to crawl into his lap. I never want to stop touching him. He closes his eyes.

"It's over," I say.

Silas keeps his eyes shut. He says, lowly, "I figured."

"No." I run my hand along his arm, fit my fingers around his wrist. He's holding his own elbows so tightly his knuckles are white. "It's over with Ethan."

His eyes break open. It feels like gasping for air in that boat on Lake Michigan. Like his arms holding me together on the hotel bed in Nashville. Like everything's all right.

"What?" he says, but I know he heard me. Every muscle in his face fights not to reveal itself, his lips listing sideways and his eyebrows drawing together and finally, total abandon, the smile breaking across his mouth on a breathless laugh. "But he's here."

"Yeah," I say. When I slide my palm into his, Silas grips on to my fingers, tight. "To say goodbye."

"I'm not—" He rights himself, focusing his features into a frown. Even as his body's turning toward mine, my hand wrapped in both of his. "I'm sorry. Are you okay?"

"Yeah." A warm breeze moves off the water, rustling hair into his face, and I push it back. Tuck it behind his ear. "I'm okay."

"Do you want to talk about it?" His eyes track over mine. "I mean, did he—are you—"

"Later," I say. "I do want to talk about it, later." I swallow, and Silas watches my throat move. "Right now I just really want to kiss you, if that's okay."

He grins. Wide and lopsided, flashing that crooked canine I noticed the very first time we met. Back in Los Angeles, when he saw the worst of me and wanted all of it anyways.

"That's okay," Silas says. He closes the distance between us before I have time to do it myself, dropping my hand so he can hold the back of my head. He kisses me gently and then, when I fist a hand into his T-shirt and tug him closer, not gently at all.

I'm still wearing the old *Summit School EMS* shirt I slept in and half-damp pajama shorts, but Silas doesn't seem to mind. He pulls me onto his lap and my knees dip into the sand. His lips are soft and insistent and when he arches to kiss the delicate skin behind my ear I feel it in my stomach: new and warm and wanting. His fingertips press into my rib cage. I run my nails over the back of his scalp and he groans.

"Audrey," he murmurs, right against my lips. "Jesus."

"Don't bring him into this," I say, breathless. Silas laughs and I smooth my hands over his hair, push it away from his face, hold him steady so we can look at each other.

"I like this," I say. It's the first thing I can think of and I just let it come out, no second-guessing. "I like you."

He smiles, brushes a thumb over my hipbone. "I like you, too."

Something wet nudges my foot and I yelp, tumbling sideways

off Silas's lap. It's Puddles, looking at me bewilderedly, and Silas picks her up to drop her onto my stomach. I let out an *oof* and he moves over us, lowering himself to hold all three of us in place. "Puddles likes you, too," he says, kissing my cheekbone, then the corner of my mouth.

I look at her, fuzzy little face so close to mine I can't get it in focus. "I will begrudgingly admit that I also like Puddles."

"Knew it." Silas rolls onto his elbow and Puddles wriggles away from us, snuffling over the sand. He watches her go, something moving across his face that I can't quite place.

"Silas," I say, and he looks back at me. Dips his chin, kisses me one more time. "What are you thinking about?"

"The mailboxes," he says. I turn my face so his head's blocking the sun. It haloes his hair, makes him look like a young god. "In Arkansas. Do you remember?"

"Of course."

"I left a letter to my mom." Silas curls a strand of my hair between his fingers, tracking the movement with his gaze. "Told her about you, a little."

"Really," I say, and he meets my eyes. Smiles in a shy sort of way that makes me want to eat him alive. "What did you say?"

"That I was hoping for this," he tells me. "I mean, not the storm, and not even the stuff with Ethan, necessarily. Not so specific, just. That I wanted to be part of your life." I reach up, touch his cheek, and he turns his chin to press his lips to my palm. "That I'd take any help she could give me."

"Do you think she made this happen?" I ask, pushing my fingertips into his hair. I can feel the tendons at the back of his neck, the hard knots of bone at the base of his skull.

"I don't know," he says. "Do you?"

"No." I shake my head. I can feel my hair growing sticky with sand but I don't move to fix it. "I think I'd have wound up here, no matter what. Wanting to be with you."

"'It'll be what it'll be,'" Silas says, grinning, and I roll my eyes. "Maybe this once."

"If only once," he says, "I'm glad it was this time."

44

"I don't want to oversell you on this, but Sadie's pancakes are a religion."

I eye Silas, pulling on the cardigan that hangs from my doorknob. "That sounds like an oversell."

He shakes his head, leans down to kiss me. "You'll see."

It's Sunday morning and we're in our pajamas; the power's back on and everyone's in a celebratory mood about it. Which means, apparently, Sadie's religious pancakes. When I follow Silas into the kitchen, she's pulling a carton of buttermilk from the now-functional refrigerator.

"Good morning," she says, smiling at us as the fridge door falls shut. "You're both up early."

It's 7:06. Puddles woke Silas to take her outside, and then he woke me—quietly opening and closing my bedroom door, nudging under the covers beside me. Getting to be close to him still feels like a trick every time; I've spent all summer wanting him and now here he is, mine.

"Puddles is obsessed with the beach," Silas says. She trots over to the water bowl, and all three of us watch her go. "She keeps acting like she needs to go out just to fool me into letting her get close to the sand."

"Willful girl," Sadie says, crouching to scratch Puddles behind one wonton-folded ear. When she stands up, she eyes Silas's hand on the curve of my hip and raises her eyebrows. He doesn't move it, but my cheeks go hot.

"Anything you want to tell me?" Sadie asks, rummaging through the upper cabinets and pulling out a paper bag of flour. Cleo and Mick spent the day with Silas and me at the beach yesterday, so they know—but it hasn't exactly come up in front of Sadie. She's been away from the house for the most part, working at a café with Wi-Fi nearly an hour away.

"Audrey's smitten with me," Silas says, and I twist out of his grip.

"What?" he cries, face split in a grin.

"You're embellishing."

"Am I?"

"Yes," I bite out, but when he yanks me back toward him by the drawstring of my pajamas I go willingly. He's not wrong, is the unspeakable truth. Ethan might have been my match, but Silas casts light into the shadow parts of me, illuminating rooms I didn't know I had. I feel different with him, and better.

"Are you using protection?" Sadie asks, waggling her eyebrows at Silas.

I say, "Oh my god," just as Silas says, "*Sadie*," just as my mom walks into the room.

"Who's using protection?" she says, and I lift a hand to cover my eyes.

"Are you aware your daughter's agreed to date this questionable figure?" Sadie asks my mom, waving a spatula in Silas's direction. They share a look, and it makes me feel known. Like I belong to both of them.

Mom does know about Silas, because I told her all of it after we dropped Ethan off in Coral Gables. *He's good for you*, she'd said, a response I wasn't expecting. Silas is everything Camilla St. Vrain isn't: spontaneous, candid, hiking-sandal-wearing. *Well, he's a boy*, I told her. *Not a leafy green.* She'd laughed in the passenger seat of our rental car. *Life's not salad, Audrey.*

"Are you communicating about your sexual preferences?" she asks now, looking back and forth between Silas and me as she makes for the coffee pot. "Asking for what you want?"

"Mom, *stop.*" I cross my arms over my chest, shrinking away from Silas.

"What, are you embarrassed?" She raises her eyebrows as she pours coffee into a mug. "There's nothing embarrassing about pleasure."

Sadie's laughing, her back to us as she stirs batter in a bowl. I absolutely cannot make eye contact with Silas, and when Puddles waddles over to lick my bare ankle, I just let it happen.

"Sadie, will you pass me the salt?" Mom's moving on to, apparently, more controversial topics: the horrific way she drinks her coffee. I watch her sprinkle table salt into her mug, but when I turn to Silas to catch his disgust he doesn't seem appalled at all. Instead, he looks nervous.

"Salt," he says, and Mom looks up at him. "I've only ever seen one other person do that."

He looks at Sadie, and she's already looking at him. Something inscrutable passes between them before the moment breaks.

"You too?" my mother asks Sadie, unbothered. "Rounds out the bitterness." She stirs a spoon in her mug and then steps closer to Sadie, peering over her shoulder into the mixing bowl. "Need any help?"

I feel my eyebrows lift. "You cook now?"

She glances at me. Shrugs. "No, but I can *sous*."

Sadie laughs. "Well, if you want to be French about it, you can pass me the *sucre*." Mom reaches for a bag of sugar on the counter, and as they both turn toward the stove I lean onto one of the bar stools. My hand lands on something hard and flat in its seat.

Silas has crossed the kitchen, looting through the cabinets for a coffee mug. When I peer beneath the island and lift the front cover of the copy of *Letters to My Someday Daughter*, there's only Puddles to see me do it. I recognize Sadie's handwriting instantly—her neat print, navy ink in the margins. I see my name, *Audrey*, scribbled mid-sentence, and snap the book shut.

"I need to use the bathroom," I say, slipping the hardcover under the hem of my T-shirt. When I start to turn away, Silas smiles in my direction. "I'll be right back."

45

That night's "book club" is a black-tie cocktail hour on the back deck of a country club overlooking the Atlantic. I'm not sure beach-front property can reputably refer to itself as "country" anything, but the women there who crowd my mother with their pristine hardcovers of *Letters to My Someday Daughter* certainly serve *Stepford* energy.

It's awkward but tolerable, mostly because Mom lets me slip out to the beach after the initial Q&A. I haven't had a moment truly alone to break into Sadie's *Letters* notes—I hid the book between folded shirts in my suitcase, so it'll be there when I'm ready for it. I feel criminal but justified—what's she doing taking notes on *me*? Collecting annotated copies of my mother's book has always been an inexplicable compulsion, and I'm equal parts fascinated and mortified to learn what Sadie's written inside. Someone I actually know. Someone who actually knows me.

I stand with my toes in the water and watch my mother illuminated in the frame of a warm-lit window, smiling with her captive audience. That book's been like a third person between us my entire life, telling stories only she knows by heart. I think about how much there is we don't know of each other, and how maybe we're chipping away at all that now.

Silas and Sadie stayed back at the house, but Mags is here with Mick and Cleo. The book clubs never get recorded; usually Mom and I go to them alone. But this one's high-profile enough for photography and social media support, apparently. Plus Mags, flitting around like some kind of Botoxed fairy godmother to make sure everyone has enough canapés.

Puddles greets us at the door when we get back to the house, all snuffly enthusiasm. Cleo picks her up and her sun-yellow nails disappear into Puddles's folds.

"Hello, angel," she says, kissing Puddles directly on the nose before holding her out to me. "Look who it is. Your mommy's home."

I narrow my eyes but she just smiles and deposits Puddles into my arms. Instantly, my black dress is covered in fur. This dog is a glitter bomb.

"Hey!" Silas calls from the living room. He stands as we come closer, a paperback in one hand. "How was it?"

"Fantastic," my mother says. She's pulling off her heels, one hand on Magnolia's shoulder for support. "They had this incredible croquembouche covered in caramel sauce, Silas, your sister would have *loved* it. I wanted to bring some home for you to try, but they were all out by the end of the evening."

I think of what Silas told me about his sister back in Chicago, her penchant for baking. That he must have told Camilla that story, too—and that she remembered it.

"Hey." Sadie's voice precedes her down the hallway. She's in a hoodie and leggings. "Did any of you grab a book from the kitchen this morning? Trying to pack up and I can't find it."

I swallow, fight the fire rising to my cheeks.

"Which book?" Camilla says, lowering back onto her bare feet.

"Um." Sadie blinks twice before smiling shyly and saying, "Yours."

My mother laughs. "I haven't seen it, but I'm flattered. And I'm certain we can get you another copy."

Sadie glances at Silas before the rest of us. He shrugs, and she says, "Anyone else?"

"Nope," Cleo says, and I manage to shake my head, and Mom declares, "I'm dying for a bath."

The moment breaks, and as my mother disappears down the hallway with Magnolia, Sadie does the same.

Cleo looks between the three of us with her eyebrows raised. "Ocean skinny-dip?"

I feel myself go rigid, spine lengthening and shoulders setting. I narrowly escape outing myself as a kleptomaniac, and now this? Mick lets out a whoop and a *fuck yes* that's so loud Puddles jumps. Her black nails skitter on the marble.

"Audrey?" Silas says, catching my eyes across the foyer.

And the thing is, I want to be this person. The one who goes to a honky-tonk in Nashville and tells her mother the truth and knows how to be fun in brave, public ways. But skinny-dipping feels like pushing the gas pedal through the floor of the car, and when I tap my thumb to my pinky finger Silas tracks the movement with his eyes.

"You know what," he says, "you guys go ahead. I think we're good."

Cleo snorts, hooking Mick by the arm. "Yeah, I bet you are."

My mouth drops open and Cleo shoots me an exaggerated wink, sticking her tongue out. By the time they cut through the front door I'm flushed all the way down to my toenails.

"Not so into public nudity, huh?"

I turn back to find Silas much closer, soft smile on his lips and his hand reaching for mine.

"Maybe we can work up to it," I say.

He shrugs one shoulder. "If you want."

"Thanks for being my out." When I prop onto my tiptoes his face changes, an expression I've come to know well over the last few days. The way Silas looks right before I kiss him—like I've surprised him so entirely, like every time his lips meet mine it's brand-new. Like even as it's happening, he can't quite believe it.

"Happy to be your out," he says quietly as I lower back onto my feet. His hand is warm on my waist and when my eyes flick down the hallway his do, too.

"Help me take this dress off?" I ask, and Silas smiles.

"Audrey St. Vrain," he says quietly. "Are you asking for help with your zipper?"

This time, there's no reeking Los Angeles alleyway. There's no unidentified liquid underfoot. It's not humid and I'm not angry and when Silas reaches for my zipper, I don't feel anything except his fingers on my skin.

"This almost made me pass out the first time," he tells me. We're in my room, door shut tight, and the bedside lamp casts a warm glow. "Just so you know."

"My zipper?"

"Mmm." He pulls it down, trailing one fingertip above it along my spine. "You were so mad and your skin was on fire and you were the most beautiful person I'd ever seen."

Silas smooths his palms through the unfurled sides of the dress until his fingers are splayed across my ribs. His thumb brushes a ridge of muscle in my back and then his lips land at the nape of my neck, the top of my shoulder. I shiver, goose bumps blooming down my bare arms.

"I wanted to kiss you so bad," he whispers.

"You didn't even know me."

"No," he says, and I lean back until I meet his chest. The motion of it pushes my dress up his arms and the rest of the way off, so it puddles at my feet. "And now that I do, I want to kiss you even worse."

Blood roars in my ears. Silas is warm in a way that swallows me whole. He doesn't turn me around for a moment—we just stand like that, his arms around my bare waist, his lungs rising gently into my back.

But then I lift one arm to wrap it around his neck, and we crash together in a rush: my body spinning to face his, his hand rising to my hair, his lips meeting mine. One warm palm pressed between my shoulder blades.

I reach for the hem of his shirt and he pulls it over his head, hair curly and wild as he leans back in to kiss me. I'm drowning in a way that feels like filling my lungs. I'm one, big feeling. *More.*

When his fingers skim the line of my bra I reach back and unhook it myself. Silas tips me toward the bed and I reach for the hem of his sweatpants, brushing my fingers against the soft, warm skin underneath. His breath catches and I watch him swallow.

"Hey, we can go slow." His eyes scan mine, pupils wide and dark. "We don't have to do anything you don't want to do."

"I don't want to go slow," I whisper. Ethan always made me feel like this was something we weren't ready for, but I know now that

Ethan not being ready didn't mean I wasn't. I was. I wanted this with him, once. And I want it now, in a way that feels like being set on fire. "Is that okay?"

"Yeah," Silas says, and when I lower the waistband of his pants he swallows again. "Yes."

I tilt my chin up and he kisses me, one hand around my ribs and the other in my hair. I feel him kick his pants off, the thin fabric of his boxers on my bare thighs.

"Audrey," he whispers. "You've done this before?"

I'm scared to say it, but this is Silas. So I say it anyways—quietly, like a confession. "No. Have you?"

His eyes move over mine, dark in the lamplight. His thumbs brush the sensitive skin between my ribs and my pelvis. "Yeah," he says eventually. Watching me carefully, like I might be hurt. But I'm not—he's here with me now, and it's enough. "But you—this is your—" He breaks off, drawing a big breath that I watch move through his rib cage, his chest. "Audrey, are you sure?"

"Silas." I take his face in my hands—the same one that I saw tight with anger on Lake Michigan, blank with shock in Nashville, now so worried and so careful. "I'm sure. Of you and of this."

"Okay," he says. He kisses my shoulder, the curve of my neck. I feel him against my leg and something clutches inside me, a whole new room in my body opening up.

"Then you have to talk to me," Silas says, his lips beneath my ear. "All right? You're the boss."

I'm scrabbling for the waistband of his boxers but he stops me, lifting my hands to his chest. He traps them there under his own.

"Audrey," he says, in a way that makes me feel like I've never heard my own name before. His eyes track over mine. "Okay?"

His lips are swollen and pink. I draw a steadying breath. "I'm the boss."

"You're the boss," he says again, softly, and carries the words to my mouth.

Later, Silas turns off the lamp and kisses my ribs over the faint ghosts of his fingerprints.

46

"What's next?" Mom says. We're in a hidden lounge at the Miami airport, all plush leather seating and built-in phone chargers. Cleo leans on Mick's shoulder as he scrolls my mother's socials, and Silas is at the enormous floor-to-ceiling window across the room, holding Puddles up to see the tarmac. Mags and Sadie stand side by side at the bar. I think of Sadie's book, nestled against my laptop in my backpack.

I scrunch my eyebrows at my mom. "Our flight to Boston?"

"I mean with you." She's wearing a baseball cap low over her forehead, and so far we've only received a few lingering glances. "What do you have planned with Sadie in Boston?"

"We're seeing an internist," I tell her. When I don't elaborate, she waves a hand in the space between us, like, *go on*. This is new—both her curiosity and my urge to satisfy it. Talking to each other is like a muscle we've let atrophy, and building it back up aches in a good way.

"I guess Sadie knows this person through Dr. Osman," I say. Mom lifts a to-go cup of coffee and takes a sip. "The pediatrician we met back in San Francisco. They went to medical school together."

"Does it appeal to you?" she asks. "Internal medicine."

I study her face for the trap, try to suss out what she wants me to say. If she thinks a specialty would be more impressive—neurosurgery, maybe. If there's an answer she's hoping I'll give.

"It does," I say slowly—like if I draw out the words, I might have time to catch her reaction and course-correct before going too far. But my mother only nods, attentive and neutral. "I wouldn't always get to dig as deep with patients, but, um." I glance up as Silas heads toward us, Puddles tucked under one arm. "A lot of times internists are the first doctors people go to when they need help." I look back at Mom. "And it would appeal to me, I think. Getting to be that person."

She smiles. "You'd be wonderful as that person."

"As which person?" Silas sits next to me, and Puddles clambers out of his lap onto mine. When he drops an arm around my shoulders, I lean into him like a reflex. Since that night in my bedroom I want to be close to Silas so desperately it leaves me breathless; already, I'm worried about August. About two short weeks from now—after Boston, after DC—when he'll be out of my reach.

"An internist," I say, looking up at him. He smiles, and when his eyes flicker to my lips it tugs deep in my belly. But my mother is three feet away from us, and he doesn't kiss me.

"The intern and the internist," Silas says. Mom laughs—a gusty, unrehearsed sound—and Silas turns to grin at her. "Sounds like a mediocre Broadway show."

She lifts a shoulder, drops it again. Waves a hand toward us. "I'm enjoying it so far."

Cleo, sitting next to me in the middle seat, finally falls asleep somewhere over North Carolina. Mick's in the aisle, nose inches from his phone screen as he plays a game that shoots the occasional *plink* sound effect into the humming space between us. I confirm Cleo's false-eyelashed eyes are firmly shut before reaching into the backpack between my feet.

I maneuver as inconspicuously as I can, working the dust jacket off Sadie's copy of *Letters* before pulling it out of my bag. Without the jacket the book is plain maroon canvas, indistinguishable when you can't see the spine. When I glance at Mick his gaze is still a magnet on his phone screen.

There's the dedication, familiar to me as my own name. *To her.* But circled here—a solid navy-blue line, like Sadie wanted to remember those two tiny words.

I start flipping. Slowly, to savor it like sweet poison. And faster, when I realize how few notes she's actually taken. They're sparse—an underline of *The fear of intimacy is the fear of ourselves* in chapter three, with Sadie's scrawled words beside it. My name, right where I'd seen it jotted down in Miami: *Audrey uncomfortable during Sex Summit Q/A in SF.* Later, penned in inexplicably next to the chapter five header: *C discussion of private vs. public lives in Santa Fe.*

The majority of the notes are in the book's third and final section, which is about reparenting your adult self. About making choices with conviction. There's a full page on deciding whether or not to have children—when I flip to it, my breath hitches beneath my ribs. The paper is filled edge to edge with pen.

It's okay to not desire the lifestyle you're told is desirable, Sadie's underlined. *It's okay to accept your desires as they are. If that doesn't include children,* listen. *Honor your own wishes. There is no one else to do it for you.*

Next to it, Sadie has written: *In Austin C mentions difficult "context" to her life while writing book.* And beneath that, my name again. *Asked C if her birth was easy & she said "With Audrey?"*

I flip the page, looking for more, but there isn't any. The rest of the book is blank—nothing but its commercially letter-pressed lines, every word where it's always been.

I look at Cleo, fast asleep. At Mick, who I haven't seen blink in the last hour. And back down at the book—snapped shut in my lap. I spread my fingers across it, watching the contrast of my pale hands splay over its bloodred cover.

The notes read like a case file. Like Sadie's compiling evidence. But what the hell for?

47

Boston's *Letters to My Someday Daughter* show takes place in a church just a few blocks off the Common. It's enormous and ornate, all flying buttresses and stained glass. The pews are packed. Our voices echo from the great stone ceiling.

Today's been our tightest connection—we left the airport in a shuttle that took us to the hotel just long enough to change our clothes. And then it was straight here; no time to pull my mother aside, no time to talk to Silas. He laced his fingers through mine on the ride from Boston Logan and I stared at the side of his face, words rising in me like acid. *This person you think you know*, I almost said. *She's up to something.* But Sadie was right there on his other side, scrolling the news on her phone. And besides: Silas loves her. I don't want to place myself like a wedge between them until I know what I'm looking at. Until I've processed it over and over. Worn its edges smooth.

But Silas already knows me, and when we parted in the dark beyond the stage curtain he trapped my wrist in the circle of his fingers.

"Audrey."

I turned back to him, heart like a snatched firefly behind my ribs—flickering and afraid. He took a step closer, his other hand rising to my waist. Warm palm on my hipbone.

His eyes moved over mine. "Are you okay?"

I wanted to tell him. He was the first person I'd ever met who I wanted to give every single one of my truths to. "Sadie—" I started, but then Magnolia emerged from the darkness.

"Ready?" she said, and I wasn't, but my mother had appeared beside her. "It's time."

"Wait." Silas's fingertips tightened into my dress. "Tell me what—"

"It's okay." I pressed a hand to his chest, dropped it, lifted my fingers to my lips instead. Stepped out of his arms to follow Camilla into the stage lights. "Talk after?"

His eyes tracked over mine, back and forth. "Okay," he said. Black Henley, black jeans, dark hair tied back. Camera at his side. The exact way I'd seen him so many times, on nights just like this one, all summer long. "Talk after."

Now I look over at my mother in the middle of the Q&A. It's our penultimate show, and it's not lost on me that we've survived it. That this summer is drawing shut—Camilla St. Vrain and her *someday daughter* are nearly off the menu. Soon we'll be back to the way it's always been: my mother in Los Angeles, me far away. I watch her smile under the lights and wonder how different it will be, now that this summer's had its way with us.

"I'm curious about the early years," a woman says, standing in the audience. She's holding the mic too close to her face; the feedback crackles like static. "What it was like raising a daughter after writing *Letters*, and talking to so many people about it."

Mom looks at me, smiling lightly, and clarifies, "The early years with Audrey?"

I think of Sadie's note, scribbled in blue pen: *Asked C if her birth was easy & she said "With Audrey?"* I look offstage, where Silas's camera sits all alone with its recording light blinking into the dark. He never leaves during a show, but he's gone now. My mother starts talking about me as a baby—*precocious and alert*—but I'm not listening. It's the last question, and when she finishes answering I excuse myself to the bathroom mid-applause.

Cleo and Mick are leaned against the wall past the curtains, their faces illuminated by the glow of their phones.

"Nice one," Mick says, smiling up at me. "If the doctor thing doesn't work out, you could take a crack at motivational speaking."

I look past him, scanning for Silas, as Cleo hums her agreement. "What did she say out there?" She nudges Mick in the shoulder. "'We do ourselves a disservice by self-labeling as any one kind of person. We need our own permission to grow and change.'" Her eyebrows hike up as she looks from Mick to me. "Right? Something like that. Hit me right in the chest, Aud."

"Silas taught me that one." I look between them. "Where is he?"

Mick jerks a thumb over his shoulder at a closed office door. "With Sadie. I'm sure you can go in."

I pad down the carpeted hall toward the door, carved wood with an elaborate metal knob. I can hear Silas and Sadie inside—when I tip my ear closer, I catch the tenor of Silas's voice. Low and urgent, like he's angry.

"—yeah, Sadie, but I told you she was acting weird before the show. Something's going on."

"Silas." Sadie's voice is soft, steadying. The voice of a parent consoling her child. "There's no reason to believe she knows."

"Even if not," he says, voice rising, "it doesn't even—things have changed, okay?" My body moves on its own, twists the doorknob. "You need to tell her or I'm—"

Silas breaks off, eyes widening when he sees me in the door-frame. Sadie, standing with her back to me, turns around.

"Audrey," Silas says. "Hi."

I look between them: Sadie's pale face, the steadying way she swallows. And Silas—how he looks ruined and resigned. Everything inside me goes rigid, bracing.

"What's going on?"

Sadie glances at Silas, and he says, "Tell her."

This room isn't an office after all; it's for children. Sunday school, maybe. All the chairs are too small, the walls covered in colorful construction paper. Sadie glances at a box of crayons on a nearby table.

I clear my throat. "Tell me what?"

"Silas," Sadie says, nearly begging. "Not here. I need to—"

"No," Silas tells her. "You've waited long enough."

Sadie looks up at me, drawing a deep breath. Her pause feels like torture, endless. "Audrey, there's something we should've talked to you about a long time ago."

We. I look at Silas, my safest place. Think of this afternoon, when I wanted so badly to tell him what I'd found. Of thirty seconds ago, how it felt to walk down this hallway and know he was at the other end of it—that no matter what was going on, it would be okay. It didn't occur to me even once that he wouldn't be on my side. But now, here he is: part of a *we* that's kept something from me.

"Okay," I whisper, so quietly it's hardly a word at all.

Sadie steps toward me, arms out like she might touch me. She doesn't. "I know you've had some hesitations this summer. About the tour, and the book, and your involvement in it."

I feel my eyebrows twitch together. I've spent my whole life thinking *Letters* actually has nothing to do with me, but after Nashville and Ethan and these two months with my mom, it feels at least a little closer to true. And our show tonight was good—we fake it so well now that I'm not sure we're faking it at all.

I press my thumb to my pointer finger. "And?"

"Well." Sadie hesitates, then finally looks into my eyes. "Audrey, I think Camilla might've written the book about me."

48

My eyes rake over Sadie: her jeans, her gold wedding band, her neat, familiar ponytail. The same safe, reliable person she's been all summer long. "Excuse me?"

"Do you want to sit?" she asks, gesturing to one of the baby chairs.

"No." I'm running my thumb over all my fingertips in turn. Not even counting, just using the motion of it to keep myself still.

"Audrey." Silas takes a step toward me, but I can't rip my eyes off Sadie. "Please sit."

"I don't want to sit. Tell me what's going on."

Sadie glances at Silas before looking back at me. "Okay," she says, drawing a deep breath. "Your mom had another daughter. Sixteen years before you."

I realize that I'm shaking my head, and make myself stop.

"When she was twenty," Sadie says. She takes a step closer to me, and I mirror it with a step back. It smells like cardboard and school supplies in here. "She gave her up for adoption. It was—" Sadie hesitates, lifts her hands to her own chest like she can't manage to speak the word *me*.

"No," I say, but Sadie keeps going.

"I got the court records when I was eighteen." When I'm silent, she says, "The book came out when I was nine—seven years before you were born. When I found out who she was, I sent a letter asking if we could meet. But she didn't want to meet."

"She didn't want to meet," I repeat, my voice flat.

"The response was from her team," Sadie says. "But that's what it said."

Her team. Magnolia.

"It's not true," I say. "She would have told me." But even as I speak, I feel something clicking into place: The black hole of my mother before *Letters to My Someday Daughter*, her life before the limelight that she never talks about. Sadie's notes in *Letters*—all those annotations about making your own choices about parenthood, about the "context" of my mother's life while she was writing, about her response—"With Audrey?"—when Sadie asked for her birth story. And the book's dedication, *To her.* Always allegedly about me, though I didn't exist to be "her" when she wrote it.

People describe rooms as spinning, when your whole life tips on its axis. But nothing spins around me—it's like I melt in the center of it all instead. Like I'm something less human than I was before I heard this, my atoms ceasing to exist the way they used to.

"*Would* she have told you?" Sadie says, and I squeeze my fisted hand so tightly the tendons over my knuckles ache. "Audrey—"

"Does my mom know who you are?"

"No." Sadie shakes her head. "I didn't identify myself in the letter. I didn't want her to know who I was unless she wanted to know me—and she didn't. I was hoping to talk to her before talking to you, but, well . . ."

She doesn't finish the sentence. My brain throbs inside my skull. I look at Silas, a hot sear of pain, and quickly away. "How did you—why are you here?"

Sadie looks at Silas. I know, even before he speaks, that what he says is going to wreck me.

"When Camilla offered the tour jobs to American, I—" He stops, swallows. Steadies himself. "I thought it would be good for Sadie to get closure. To meet her biological—"

"You did this?" My voice comes out hoarse. This summer bleeds behind my eyes: that back alley in LA, when I thought Silas and I were strangers but he knew exactly who I was. The doctors Sadie introduced me to, not because she saw promise in me but because—what, we're *related*? And the way Silas and Sadie must have compared notes at every stop along the way. Poring over that book together, talking about me and my mother and the specimens of us that they came here to study.

I take another step back from him, toward the door. My voice is low and broken. "You knew, and you kept it from me all this time."

I watch Silas's face fall. "Audrey, please." He reaches for me, and I shrink away. "Please don't look at me like that."

"Like what?"

"Like you don't recognize me."

Tears blur my vision, hot and sharp. I think of the person Silas encouraged me to become, one little bit at a time. The studying I didn't do, and the shadowing position I didn't get, and the boyfriend I made plans with who's gone now. "I let you ruin my life and you weren't even honest with me."

"Is that what I did?" Silas's voice catches. "Ruined your life?"

Ruin isn't quite right, but I nod anyways. Silas didn't ruin me; he betrayed me by turning out to be the same as everyone else. I'd thought, for maybe the first time in my life, that I'd found someone who actually sees me. But Silas was interested in Camilla, not in me. He wanted to be around me because of something she did. Just like always, just like every other person.

I let him in like a fool, and he hid the truth from me all summer long. I trusted Sadie. I thought I might actually have a shot at a relationship with my mom.

I've always known I'm not the *someday daughter*, that she doesn't exist the way the world believes her to. That even if she did, we were never one and the same. But this summer—with Silas and Sadie and my mom—I started to believe.

I shouldn't be surprised now, but I am. Standing here in this musty Sunday-school room with two people I thought I knew.

Silas didn't ruin my life; he gave me hope. I was better off without it.

I have myself to blame, really. The Audrey I was back in June would never have let herself be hurt like this, by these people. She'd never have let Camilla St. Vrain worm her way in. She'd never have fallen for the slobber-collared boy with no solid plans. But I let my guard down, and now I'm here: an idiot of my own creation.

I leave the Boston show in a rideshare by myself, shouldering past Mick and Cleo while Silas shouts after me down the hallway. I gather my things at the hotel and check myself into a different one, using the emergency credit card Dad gave me when I turned sixteen. When he calls me after midnight to say my mom's in a panic, I tell him to tell her that I'm safe and to leave me alone. Exactly how I should have been all this time.

He presses for the name of my hotel, my room number, the reason I'm upset. But I know he'll only tell her, and I don't want her anywhere near me. I've spent my life furious with Camilla for building her fame off our fictional relationship—I don't even know how to name what it feels like for her to have built her fame off pure fiction. If what Sadie's saying is true, Camilla didn't just embellish our mother-daughter relationship for her career. She lied about which daughter her career was built on in the first place. I'm more expendable to her than I could ever have imagined.

By the time morning comes, Silas has left me six voicemails. I delete all of them, one by one, without listening to them. I can't deal with him, not when everything else is falling apart. This betrayal isn't his—it's my mother's. But he's twisted in it like a bug in a web, collateral damage. He could have told me, but now he'll be devoured by my anger along with everything else.

When I text Sadie that I don't want to see her at the internist visit, that I'm going alone or not at all, she gives in without a fight. I think of her in Nashville: *Take your time.*

I call United and cancel my flight to DC. This will be my last doctor visit, and only because it's the one I've looked forward to most. I've given more than enough of myself to this tour, and there's no reason for me to see it through now. Tomorrow I'll fly to Baltimore a week early. Stay at a hotel until my dorm opens for move-in.

By the time I emerge from the T at Massachusetts General Hospital, Silas has called four more times. I put my phone on silent, straighten my blazer, walk through the hospital's sliding glass doors. I zip every awful feeling into the shell of myself. I do what I'm best at.

When I walk back through the doors two hours later, my mother is waiting for me on the sidewalk.

49

Camilla's standing immediately in front of the violent red *Emergency* sign, which is exactly what this feels like.

"No," I say, stopping in my tracks.

"Audrey." She moves toward me, and when she pulls off her enormous sunglasses there are dark circles under her eyes. She's wearing her same master-of-disguise baseball cap and her blonde hair in a ponytail. Jeans and a hoodie. The whole getup makes her look twenty years old, like someone young enough to have no idea what they're doing. But she's known. All this time, she's known.

"Is it true?" I say, and then she stops, too. There are ten feet of hot air between us, humid and stagnant. Sweat breaks on the back of my neck.

She doesn't beat around the bush, though it's what I expect her to do. She doesn't say, *Is what true?*, though there's more than one lie between us. She just says, "Yes. It's true."

"Wow," I say, the word punching out of me like a bullet. I don't know if I've ever heard myself hit this volume. "You're unbelievable."

I sidestep her, making for Fruit Street and the T station.

"Audrey—" She reaches for my elbow and I yank it out of her hand.

"Don't touch me."

Distantly, I'm aware of people watching us: a father and his child headed into the building, someone in a uniform glancing up from their phone. My mother shoves her sunglasses back on.

"Can we please talk about this?" she says, following me.

"No," I shout without turning around. "You've had eighteen years to talk to me about this."

"Honey, that's not fair—"

"It's not *fair*?" I whirl around, bag jerking off my shoulder into the crook of my elbow. "No, Mom. It's not fair. It's not fair that you kept this from me. It's not fair that you used me to boost your career without actually getting to know me." I suck in a breath. "It's not fair that I'm always trying to live up to some fictional version of me you've told the whole world about."

"Audrey," she says. I wish she'd stop saying my name, reinserting me into this conversation that I don't want to be part of. "I didn't—"

"Yes, you did." When I start walking again, she does, too. "You made me out to be someone in all your lectures and on all your social media, so I became that person, or she became me—I can't even separate it out." I'm waving a hand through the air in front of me as I walk. I'm not even thinking the words, they're just coming out—for once, I'm just letting them all come out. "And none of it was even true. And it feels like if I don't keep up with this story you've told about me, I'll just stop existing or something." I look at her, and it makes tears burn behind my eyes. "Sometimes I can't even tell if I chose my personality. Sometimes I don't even know who I am." We stop at a crosswalk and a car screams past, sending a gust of hot air across us both. "It's like you just made me up."

She looks stricken. Camilla St. Vrain, who has an answer for everything. But if anyone should get to be speechless here, it's me. I'm sick of waiting for the crossing light, and I'm sick of waiting for her. I turn on my heel and start up Charles Street.

"Audrey, wait." I hear her jog after me, pristine white sneakers cutting up the sidewalk. "Honey, I had no idea you felt that way. I wish—"

"You didn't ask," I say, looking straight ahead. We could be in a speed walking competition, we're moving so fast. "Maybe you were too busy thinking about your actual *someday daughter* to check in with your spare."

"Okay, enough." She takes my hand, and before I can pull it away, she locks our fingers together. I squirm my palm against hers and she squeezes even tighter. It's torture.

"Let go," I say, loudly enough that the person walking past us stops to stare. Then they keep staring, and when they pull a phone from their bag, I know they know who we are.

"Shit," my mother says, and starts tugging me toward the pedestrian overpass. We hustle up the stairs and over the sound tunnel of Charles Street, cars sprinting beneath us. When I glance back, the person is gone.

"It's fine," I say. When she keeps pulling my arm without slowing down, I say it again. "Mom, it's *fine*, they're gone. Let go of me."

But she doesn't. "If I let go, you'll run away, and we need to talk about this."

"Where?" I have to shout so she'll hear me over the traffic. "Suspended up here on top of the highway?"

"That park." She points down the stairs on the other side of the overpass, where a green strip separates Charles Street from the river. "Come on."

I strain against her hand again, and when I finally break free, she turns around to scrabble after me.

"I'm not running away!" I say, and for a moment we pause to stare at each other. We're both panting. "I just don't want to be led around like a kindergartner."

"Fine." She sucks in a breath and turns around, leading me the rest of the way over the street and into the park. When she motions me onto a bench, I sit at one far end and indicate that she should do the same. She does, turning her entire body toward me. She takes off her sunglasses.

"Audrey, I'm sorry." She lets it hang there between us, and I scoff out a laugh.

"For which part, Mom?"

"All of it." She folds her hands together and squeezes them. "I was wrong not to tell you about my first pregnancy, but it was another life. It was—"

"It's not another life," I say. "It's your life. The same one. And Sadie's here, right now."

"But I didn't know." Her voice scrapes, and she clears her throat. "I had no idea who Sadie was until last night, same as you."

"Because you pushed her away," I say. "When she reached out, all those years ago—"

"Magnolia," she says simply. It takes her a few minutes to keep going, like she's tamping everything down to make space for her words to come out. "Magnolia didn't tell me that Sadie reached out when she turned eighteen. I knew her birthday was coming up, of course, and that she'd have access to that information, if she wanted it." She draws a shaky breath. "But Magnolia handles all the mail, and she hid it from me, and so I assumed Sadie didn't want to know who her biological mother was. Or that if she did know, she didn't want to contact me. And that was absolutely her choice to make. So I let it go. I moved on, to focus on my daughter." Her eyes are steady on mine. "You."

I shake my head. "Why would Mags hide it?"

"A misguided attempt to protect my career," she says wearily. "She's as shocked as I am, believe me. She didn't know who Sadie was until last night, either." She looks up at me. "All those years ago, when Sadie reached out to her anonymously, all Mags knew for sure was that I'd spoken of *you* as the *someday daughter*. She thought that if the world found out I'd given birth to another child—"

"You'd look like a liar," I finish for her. "But it wasn't misguided; it was true. You did lie."

"Audrey—" she starts, but I cut her off.

"Who's the book about, Mom? Who's the *someday daughter*?"

We stare at each other. Warm air moves off the water, over the grass. My mother draws a breath.

"I wrote the book to process my own decision not to become a mother, that first time." She glances at the river, presses her lips together. "I was twenty when I gave birth to Sadie. My parents were gone, I had no family, I hardly knew her father. When I held her in the hospital, I knew I wasn't ready to be a mother. I knew giving her to her true parents was the right thing to do. I didn't question it then, while she was with me. It felt so clear." She runs her thumb over the back of her hand, pressing hard. "I only questioned it later, and then I questioned it for years. I wrote the book to help me untangle the choice I'd made, and to forgive myself for not doing what the world told me I was created to do: desire motherhood, choose it above all else." She turns back to me, holds my gaze. "And I wrote it as a kind of love letter, something to put into the world for the daughter I knew I'd never mother."

My breath is a desperate tangle in my chest. When I speak, my voice wavers. "So it was about her. I've never been part of this at all."

"Honey, you're part of everything." My mother leans toward me, sliding a little closer on the bench. "And when you were born, at a completely different stage of my life, people assumed that of course the book was written in anticipation of you, and—"

"And you let them believe it," I say. "You lied."

She doesn't defend herself. She doesn't seem to know what to say at all.

I swallow, trying to clear the tightness in my throat. "If you didn't keep her, why did you keep me?"

In the space before my mother responds the words bubble up in me, a pleading whisper: *Because I loved you, because I wanted you.* I want to hear them with searing, immediate shame.

"Because everything was different this time," she says finally. "Because it was a decision your father and I needed to make together."

But what I hear is: *Because he made me keep you.*

I make to stand, and she says, "Honey, wait. Please. *Please.*"

When I look back at her she's blurry, and I wipe my tears roughly away. She doesn't deserve them. I want so badly to be alone.

"Audrey, you're so smart." I sigh harshly, and she holds up a hand. "No, I mean it. You've always been so much smarter than me."

When I lower myself back onto the bench, she keeps going.

"You came out of the womb like that. Analytical. Precise and curious." She draws a rickety breath. "But it was easy to be your mom when you were small: scraped knee, Band-Aid. Midafternoon tantrum, nap. You needed me so tangibly." I look away from her, watch a party line of ants track across the walking path. "Sometimes I don't know how to be a mother to you, because I know you don't need me anymore. You're brilliant. I sent you to school so you could get what you needed." She swallows, looks down at her hands and then back up at me. "We expect our children to need the same things we do, but they don't. And I wanted you to have everything I didn't know how to give you."

I look at her. "What do you need that I don't need?"

She smiles, lets out a short exhale. "Permission. Other people's approval. I've always needed those things. I spent years hearing other people's voices in my head before I heard my own." She spreads her hands in the space between us. "That's part of the reason I wrote the book. I had horrible guilt over a choice that I *knew* was the right one for me. I didn't offer myself any kindness, or trust my own intuition. And you've never struggled with that. You've always honored what you want. It's one of my favorite things about you." She starts to tear up, and I have to look away. "You're incredible, Audrey. And so brave—not like me. I knew I had a daughter out there, somewhere, but I could only acknowledge it in this veiled way." She lets out a strangled exhale and I look back up at her. "I built a career on a book I wrote for her and I couldn't admit it—even though I wrote the whole book to tell myself that what I'd done was okay. I wasn't brave."

It feels simultaneously satisfying and devastating to hear her admit it.

"And when people came along and assumed the book was about you, I wasn't brave enough to correct them, either. Because you were right in front of me, and you were my whole life, and—" She breaks off, swallows. "I loved you so much. Love you so much. And it hurts me to hear that you feel I've shaped you into something you're not." She braces a hand on the bench between us, almost reaching for me but not. "Because that was the opposite of what I wanted. I chose the Summit School so you could have a normal life, out of the spotlight, and discover yourself away from any association with me." She clears her throat. "But it sounds like I was misguided on that front, too."

I look up at her, and for a moment we're quiet. I wonder if we've ever understood where the other's coming from on the first try. If we've ever tried at all.

"I liked school," I say finally. "I just wanted to have a mom, too."

She nods, and a tear rolls down her cheek. She brushes it away with the tips of her fingers. "I'm sorry. I know we haven't—" She hesitates, swallows. "I know I haven't been as present for you as I should be. We could have done this tour in a whirlwind two weeks, but I drew it out because I wanted to spend the summer with you." She draws a breath. "When I lost my parents, I'd been away at school for two years, wrapped up in my life, and suddenly they were just gone. I wanted to fix this before I lost you like that."

Something whispers, angry, from deep inside me. *But did you ever want me at all?*

"Audrey," she says, when I still haven't spoken. "I'm so sorry I kept this from you. I'm so sorry about all of it. I didn't handle it well."

"But how did you handle it *so* badly?" I've been holding my bag on my lap this whole time, and my thighs are going numb. "You're a therapist."

She breathes something that almost sounds like a laugh. "Being a therapist means I know better. It doesn't mean I always *do* better. That's why therapy isn't a one-and-done thing: you don't go to a session and learn the lessons and leave a cured person. It's ongoing work. It's lifelong." She looks at me. "You have to keep choosing the right thing—and it's usually the hard thing. I don't always make the right choice."

My eyes glaze with tears, and I blink them away. "Was it the right choice? Keeping me?"

"Oh, honey." She reaches for me finally, and I let it happen. My bag is a hard obstacle between us, and when she hooks her chin over my shoulder it presses into my stomach. "Of course. Of *course*. When I wrote the book I was imagining this daughter I knew I'd never raise. It was intangible—it was hypothetical." She pulls away, ducks her chin to make me look at her. "Having a child in real life isn't the same. It's so much more complicated and so much better."

I draw a shaky breath, pull back to look at her. "But there's two of us," I say. "In real life."

Her eyes scan mine, brilliant blue and blurry with tears. "Yeah," she says quietly. "And I think it's time we go talk to her."

50

The lobby of the hotel looks like an ER waiting room. Mags, Mick, Cleo, Sadie, Silas—all of them gathered in the carefully clustered armchairs like family hoping for news. Which is what I thought they were, in a way. My family of some kind.

"Audrey." Silas is on his feet the moment my mother and I walk through the doors. Puddles isn't with him, which is how I know he's beside himself. He's wearing the *GG's* baseball cap and a thin T-shirt and sneakers. His eyes are bloodshot. The lobby is freezing, and when he gets close enough to reach for me, I can see the goose bumps on his forearms.

"Don't." I hold up a hand, and he stops. Drops his arms to his sides. Something tugs, like an iron hook, through my belly. I want to fold myself against him, close my eyes in the curve of his neck, and forcing myself not to leaves my insides a massacre.

"Please," he says, so quietly, like it's only the two of us. Like every other person in this lobby isn't watching. "Audrey, I'm so sorry, if I can just expl—"

"Silas." I've been so focused on the tremble in his voice, on the smudged half-moons under his eyes, I didn't even see Sadie stand up. But she's right behind Silas, hand on his shoulder. "Let me, okay?"

He looks at her, his lips parting. And something passes between them—unspoken, the wordless way people communicate when they know each other so well. Sadie nods. Silas looks at me, fevered and searching, and takes a step backward.

"Upstairs, maybe," my mother says quietly from beside me. When her hand touches my elbow, I flinch.

"Camilla," Sadie says, "do you mind if I talk to Audrey alone?"

Blood courses, frantic, to my face. I look at my mom and realize I don't want to be without her for this. But when her eyes track over mine, she just nods. "Of course."

"What?" I say, but Sadie's already moving toward the elevators, arm reaching out but not touching me. My mother nudges me after her, silent and sure, like she and Sadie have already spoken. We ride the elevator in panicked silence. When Sadie lets me into her hotel room I stand, rigid, holding my own hands.

"Please sit," she says, motioning to the chairs in the corner of the room. There are two, high-backed and overstuffed, a lamp standing between them like a mediator. I sit.

"Look, Audrey." Sadie lowers herself into the other chair and runs a hand through her hair. I watch her wedding band catch the light. "I fucked up here. But there was no good way to do this."

"There was probably a better way," I say. I'm scanning her for similarities: she didn't get Camilla's blue eyes, like I did. She didn't get her blonde hair, but I didn't get that, either. The way they look at me is the same—that earnest, unflinching intensity. I assumed it was because they're adults, but maybe it's because they belong to each other.

"Yeah," Sadie says softly. "There probably was. But I couldn't figure it out in time."

The AC kicks on, and I let out a wavering exhale. "Why did you come here?"

It's a cruel thing to say, maybe. Maybe I shouldn't be pushing her away, questioning her motivations, when half our blood's the same. I have no idea what the right thing is now.

She rubs a thumb into the center of her palm. Studies her hands before looking back up at me. "To know you," she says simply. "And her. It's been this huge question, all my life. I mean, god, I chose to go to American just to feel like I was experiencing something she had." Sadie blinks across the room before looking back at me. "Maybe that's embarrassing, but it's the truth. The two of you have always been unreachable to me. And I wanted to see if I could figure out why she'd pushed me away, when I contacted her all those years ago. To see whether this book was about me, like I thought it might be."

I blink down at my hands. I know something about chasing Camilla in places she can't see you; trying to experience her in ways she'll never know about. My used copies of *Letters*, my stash of therapy reviews. She's made a mess of us both.

I look up at Sadie. "But you could've told me sooner."

"Yeah," Sadie says quietly. "Before we came here, Silas and I talked about it—if we would tell her, or you."

It's torture to picture it: Silas, who I thought I knew so well, plotting how to keep my own history a secret from me.

"I'm sorry if that sounds insensitive," Sadie says. She shakes her head. "Not *if*. I know it does. But I was operating under the understanding that Camilla knew her first biological daughter had reached out, and that she didn't want to meet me. It didn't feel obvious, that it was something I should share with either of you. It felt like a secret everyone wanted to keep."

"I didn't know it to keep it," I say, and she nods.

"I know that now. But I didn't, then." Sadie twists her wedding band around her finger. "Back then, we both just thought this was an opportunity for me to get some closure. To meet both of you and see what this part of my past, this part of my DNA, felt like."

"Well?" I say, and my voice has an edge that it didn't before. "How did it feel?"

She sighs, slow and controlled. "Really hard. Audrey, for years I've thought that you and Camilla had this perfect relationship—that you were so close. That maybe she didn't want to meet me because she'd had you by then. It hurt so badly to see how publicly she loved you when she didn't even want to know my name."

I shake my head, but I can't manage words. All lies, every part of all of this, from top to bottom.

"But then I met you, and I could see that you were in so much pain." I look up at her, and her eyes are full of tears. I think of those notes she took about me in her book—*Audrey uncomfortable during Sex Summit Q/A in SF*—and the way she's been watching over me all summer long. "That the reality of your connection to her was so different from what I'd seen filtered through the media. I hated myself for holding such a false narrative of both of you for so long."

"Yeah," I say quietly. "The stories are better."

"Not better," Sadie says. "Both of you are so much smarter, and so much more thoughtful, and so much more impressive in real life. And before I knew it, I was completely in over my head, holding on to this thing that no one else knew, and I'd come to care about both of you so much, and I knew you were hurting and that the truth would complicate everything in this really huge way, and it—" She breaks off, catches her breath. When she reaches for my hand, I let her take it. I stare at our fingers and think, for the very first time, that I have a sister.

"Silas wanted to tell you from essentially the first time he talked to you," Sadie says. "He knew right away, before I did, that we'd made a mistake. You didn't deserve to find out this way, Audrey, and it was me keeping the secret." I look up at her, and she squeezes my hand. "You have to know that it was me."

I swallow, and it hurts. "So what do you make of us? Camilla and me." My voice is tight and pitiful. "Not so perfect, after all."

"No relationship between a mother and their daughter is perfect," Sadie says. "Mine isn't, but I love her so much. Yours isn't, but—"

Sadie draws a breath, and it's not Camilla I recognize in her this time. In the way she sets her shoulders and steadies herself and brings her focus to center. It's me.

"But that doesn't mean," Sadie says, "that she's not worth forgiving."

51

We're talking about Elliott when Silas knocks on the door. About how Sadie and Cora didn't think twice about adoption; that it was something Sadie always knew she'd do. *I have the world's best parents*, she told me. *I needed to be that person for my own child.*

"Sadie," Silas says, low and exhausted. He knocks again, once, a heavy sound like his fist is still pressed to the door. "Can I please come in?"

Sadie's eyes flicker over mine. "It's your choice," she says softly. "But I think you should hear him out."

I stare at the door, like I could see Silas through it. I'm so bone-tired. I want him to come in here so I can lean the full weight of myself against him, let him catch me. And I don't want him here for the same reason: I don't know if I have the strength to keep this up. But I let him see parts of me no one else has, and he didn't even tell me the truth.

"Audrey," he says. It wrenches through me, the fractured sound of his voice. "Please."

"Okay," I whisper, and Sadie's eyebrows rise.

"Yeah?" she says, and I nod. Press my lips together. Count my fingers as she moves toward the door, as she opens it, as Silas finds my eyes over her shoulder. They maneuver around each other in the doorframe, Sadie casting one last look at me before she steps into the hallway and the door falls shut.

Silas stands three feet inside the room, one hand on the back of his hair. He says, "You didn't answer my calls."

I say, "You didn't tell me the truth."

He winces. Gestures to the chair opposite me that Sadie left behind. "Can I—?"

I just stare at him. Silas swallows before crossing the room and sitting down.

"Audrey, I'm so sorry." His eyes are dark and devastated. I'm so sick of people apologizing to me; it makes me feel like a pawn on everyone else's chessboard, with no choices that are my own to make. "I thought I was doing something good this summer. Sadie's so important to me, and this has been a huge, hard part of her life for so long, and I just wanted her to get closure and meet the people she'd wondered about forever." He takes a rattling breath. His voice comes out quiet. "I had no idea who you were. I had no idea what you'd mean to me."

"Okay," I say. The words bunch up in my windpipe, suffocating me. I force them out bite by bite. "And instead of telling me once you knew who I was, you waited until after I slept with you."

His eyes widen sharp and fast, air punching out of him. His hands twitch toward me like a reflex. "No," he says. "*No*, that's not—"

"That's what happened."

"Audrey, I swear." His words stumble together, his face flushing red. I hate what it does to me, how panicked he looks and the way

I want to reach for him against every decent instinct. "Factually, yes, I mean, that's what—that's how the timing looks, but I swear, I would never— Audrey, I wanted to tell you that morning after Nashville. When I knocked on your door. I knew you needed to know; I could feel us tipping toward this thing, and—"

"What thing?"

He sucks in a breath, gesturing between us. I don't think he's blinked in a full minute.

"So you assumed we would get together," I say, acidic. He was right, but it enrages me—especially after all of this. "That I'd break up with Ethan for you."

"No," he says again. "No, I don't know, I just knew you'd shared something with me that meant something to you and I knew it wasn't some small moment. It wasn't a throwaway." He swallows. "All I wanted was to be close to you. Having that secret between us was eating me alive."

I press my thumb into my pointer finger so hard that my nail threatens to break the skin. It makes me think of my forearm in Nashville, Silas running his fingers over it in the dark. I close my eyes.

"Audrey," he says softly. "I'm so sorry. I hate that I did something that hurt you. I've been dying to talk to you since the show, and to know how you're doing, and—"

"I'm doing bad," I say, opening my eyes. I'm so angry, and I know I'm being unfair, and I'm an absolute mess, but this is Silas. Silas, who's never turned away from a single ugly thing about me. "I'm doing pretty shitty, actually."

He swallows. "Do you want to tell me about it?"

"My family's a joke," I say, and my voice tightens pathetically.

"My mom's a liar and so's my sister, apparently, and it's not like you'd even understand, Silas, with your big, perfect family and—"

"My perfect family?" He leans closer to me, and I don't move away. "Audrey, when my mom died, my dad totally quit on us. He couldn't take care of anything. Not his kids, not himself. My family was a disaster and that's the only reason I know Sadie at all." His eyes don't leave mine, like he's serious and certain and he needs me to hear this. "My cousins are a full pack of menaces. I've never had a single family holiday without someone yelling at someone else. No family is perfect. Every family's awful."

I think of GG, folding Silas in her arms, calling him *baby*. Maren, a tangle of wild affection. The tree house, home to generations of memories on wooden walls. "But you love them so much."

"Yeah," Silas says. "They're awful and I love them. That's family."

I look at him: his face tipped toward me, his tired eyes, his broad shoulders stooped in defeat. I can feel the last thread of resolve vibrating inside me—a guitar string plucked too hard, poised to snap. "I wish you hadn't lied to me," I whisper.

Silas closes his eyes, exhales through his nose like I hurt him. "I am so, so sorry," he says. When his eyes open, they don't leave mine. "I'll never do it again. I'll never stop apologizing, if that's what it takes. I'm so sorry, Audrey." He draws a breath. "I want to make it right so badly. What do I need to do?"

"Tell me what it looks like," I whisper. My eyes are filling with tears—finally, finally I'm going to cry. "This fall, and school, and after. What happens?"

Silas's eyes track over mine. Quietly, he says, "I don't know."

A tear hops the dam of my eyelid and he reaches for it, thumbs it off my cheek before it drips into the space between us. "But you're going to figure all of this out. I'm going to help you, if you let me." Silas takes my hand, tentatively, in his. Looks up at me. "I don't know what's next, but I see us there together."

"I'm scared." It's a relief to admit it, and when a sob hiccups out of me Silas squeezes my hand in both of his. "I feel like everything I thought I knew isn't true anymore."

"Not everything," he says. "You're still you. You're still going to be so badass at school this fall, Johns Hopkins won't know what hit it. Tropical Storm Audrey." He runs his thumb over the back of my hand, and I watch the motion of it. "Mick and Cleo still love you, and so does your mom, even if she's still learning how to show it, and so do—" He breaks off, swallows. We stare at each other, and I watch him wrestle with it, his jaw flexing.

"Fuck, so do I." Silas rubs his forehead and then looks back at me, completely unguarded. "I've fallen in love with you five times just since I walked into this room."

I laugh on a sob, and Silas smiles. It's so good to see it—in spite of everything. I love his smile, that crooked canine, the unrehearsed honesty of it. How easy it's come to him all summer long.

"Some things have changed," Silas says. "Some really big things. And some things won't, ever."

I nod. Swipe my fingers through my tears. When I jerk out of my chair and into Silas's lap, he wraps me tight as he did in Nashville, hand on the back of my neck, rush of air gusting out of him.

"I'm so sorry," he says quietly. I brush my thumb over the ridge of his shoulder blade, close my eyes in the hollow of his throat.

"I forgive you," I whisper. Silas kisses the top of my head, the curve of my ear.

I've been so many people just this summer alone—the Audrey Camilla painted me to be, the Audrey I became through osmosis with Ethan. And this one: honest and afraid. The real version of myself Silas made space for me to be.

"It's going to be okay," he says.

I close my eyes. I choose to believe him.

52

Fallon Martin—wearing a *Colorado School of Mines* T-shirt, surreptitiously eyeing her watch, and, last I checked, still living in Uganda—is standing on the National Mall next to my dad. I'm so excited to see her that I drop Silas's hand and start running.

"Aud," she says, her face splitting into a grin the same moment I launch myself at her. "Hi."

"Oh my god," I say over her shoulder. Her bony arms lock around my waist and she sways us back and forth. "What are you doing here?"

"Ask your dad," she says, and when I catch his eyes he smiles. He got into DC last night. Told me to meet him here for a surprise.

"Thought you might need someone to lean on," he booms, his enormous voice trumpeting across the Mall. When I pull away from Fallon, he yanks me into a bear hug. "Good to see you, mouse."

I squeeze the familiar breadth of his shoulders, still looking at Fallon. "I thought you were in Africa?"

Fallon shrugs, tugging a hand through her short hair. She's tanner than I've ever seen her. "I was supposed to come back in a few days, but we were mostly hanging around waiting for our flight by the end there, anyway. Quick DC detour on my way home to Alabama, as I heard there's been some *news*." Her eyes flick to Silas, who's come to stand next to me with Puddles at his feet. "Who's this?"

I turn to look at him, and his eyebrows lift just the tiniest distance. Fascinated to hear how I'll introduce him, I'm sure. "This is Silas," I say, voice as steady as I can get it. "My boyfriend. And Puddles, his dog." Silas grins, and it moves through me like the best kind of shiver. Like the first warm breath when you come in from the cold. "Si, this is my father. And Fallon, my roommate from school."

"Roommate and *best friend*," Fallon says sternly, reaching her hand out to Silas. "Rude, Aud."

"Best friend," I repeat, hand over heart. Seeing Fallon and Silas right next to each other, occupying the same space in the same city, is nearly too good to be true.

"Silas," my dad says, clapping him on the back. "I remember you from the paparazzi photo."

"Oh my god," I say, just as Silas says, "That's my favorite picture."

I rear back, eyeing him.

"What?" He shrugs, then looks down at Puddles. She's on her back legs, pawing at his knees, and he picks her up. "I think that was the first time you ever gave me your full attention." He waggles his eyebrows at me. "Best day of my life."

I roll my eyes, and Fallon honks out a laugh. "Wow, I *did* miss some shit."

"Oh, this is the tip of the iceberg," Silas says. He bounces Puddles a little, and she lunges to lick the edge of his jaw. "Did Audrey tell you she walked barefoot? Outside?"

"*No*," Fallon says, looking at me. "*My* Audrey? Audrey St. Vrain?"

"Okay," I groan, "enough. Thank you so much, I'm so glad you've met each other—"

"She also jumped into Lake Michigan to save Puddles's life," Silas says. "Even though she—"

"Can't swim," Fallon says, wide-eyed. "No, you didn't."

I sigh. "Unfortunately, I did."

"You don't even like dogs." Fallon reaches out to rub Puddles's ear.

"She likes this one," Silas tells her, and I shrug. "*Loves*, even."

"Let's not get ahead of ourselves," I say, and Dad touches my arm.

"Mouse." He tips his head toward a nearby bench. "Can I talk to you for a minute?"

I glance between Fallon and Silas, and she nods. "We're good here." I watch them lower themselves into the grass, Puddles wiggling with excitement between them. Silas has been so busy editing film for the past few days that I've hardly seen him—as Dad and I walk away, it's like there's a tether inside me, not wanting to stray too far.

"Kiddo," Dad says as we sit on the bench. Our eyes meet, and he smiles in a sad way. "I owe you an apology."

The sun is high and hot over the Mall, tourists moving in waves over the grass. I tilt my head to the side. "You knew, too."

"I did," he says, nodding. It shouldn't surprise me, I know: my parents have always been so close. If there's one person Mom would choose to keep a secret for her, it's Dad. It's Dad and Magnolia, though only one of them turned out trustworthy. "And I'm sorry it all came out this way."

"Why didn't you tell me?"

He exhales, lips pressed together. "It wasn't mine to tell you, mouse. That was your mom's history, from years and years before we knew each other. But I've watched it taking up space there, between you two, for so long. I've wanted her to tell you, but only she could decide when she was ready."

"And Sadie decided for her," I say. "In the end."

"Yeah," Dad says. "That's usually what happens when you wait too long to tell the truth. It finds its own way into the light."

I nod, look out over the grass. Watch Fallon dangle a dandelion puff over Puddles's head and jerk it out of the way just before she bites it.

"Are you angry?" Dad asks. I look back at him, the worried set of his eyes.

"I don't know," I tell him honestly. "I don't think so, not anymore." It's been four days, and the truth of all this has made its home in me. That's what happens—even with the worst news, even with the intolerable things. Days pass and your body absorbs them like air. You learn to live together. "Just trying to figure out my place in all of it, I guess."

My dad shifts toward me. "What do you mean?"

I look at him. "I mean if Sadie's the *someday daughter*, what am I to Mom?" Every day with her has gotten easier, like we've razed it all down and now we have a flat foundation to build from. I'm not my mother's *someday daughter*, but I never was. And now that we aren't lying, it feels like we have our first honest shot at actually knowing each other. "What's Sadie going to be to us? Who am I going to be, I guess, when the tour ends?"

Dad's eyebrows draw together. A kid flits past us on a bike, rainbow ribbons streaming from its handlebars. "You'll be who you've always been, mouse. Your mother's daughter. Not someday—already."

I nod, and when he props his arm on the back of the bench, I scoot closer to lean my head against his shoulder. His hand drops onto my bicep.

"You're going to talk to Sadie," he says, "and figure out what you both want that to look like. You're going to get to change your mind, and course-correct, and do the best you can as you go along. Just like everything in life. You're you, and you're smart, and you're going to be just fine. With your family and with school."

I close my eyes. "I just thought I knew exactly who I was, and now I'm not so sure."

"Then you're in good company." Dad squeezes my arm, and I look up at him. His familiar eyes, the quirk of his smile, the home he's been to me all my life. "Most of us spend our whole lives figuring out who we are, and we're all right after all."

53

"Who's that?" Cleo jerks her chin at the short, angular woman standing next to the stage curtain. She has a headset on and she's holding a clipboard, checking things off a list with such fervor I can only assume she's enjoying herself.

"No idea," I say. "Never seen her before in my life."

Mick glances up from his phone. "That's the new Mags."

Both of us turn to look at him. "*No*," Cleo says. "Did Mags get the boot?"

Mick looks from Cleo to me, his dark eyes catching in the dim lights. "Wouldn't *you* fire her, if you were Camilla?"

"I didn't fire her."

All three of us whip around to find my mom standing a foot behind us, face calm as ever and hair smoothed behind her ears.

"I—" Mick gulps. "Sorry, I wasn't trying—"

Mom holds up a hand. "It's fine, Michael. Could you give Audrey and me a moment, please?"

Cleo reaches for Mick's wrist, grabby as ever, and yanks him into the darkness behind the stage. Mom and I look at each other. Her eyes flick up at the curtain, like she could look right through it to where the audience waits for us—Dad and Fallon somewhere out there, too.

"So, you didn't fire her," I say.

Mom shakes her head. "I sent her home."

"Forever?"

"I don't know yet." Mom adjusts the clasp of her bracelet, like she's nervous.

"You're going to let her stay in your life after what she did?"

She looks back at me, letting out a sigh. "It's not that simple, honey. Magnolia is one of the only people who cared about me before all this." She gestures toward the curtain, the stage, this sold-out theater. It's nearly impossible for me to imagine her without the trappings of her life: the fame, the following, the narrative. But she existed that way once. Just a person, like the rest of us. "She's been my best friend for almost thirty years. And she thought she was protecting me."

"But she was wrong."

"Yes." Mom nods, just once. Final and definitive. "She was wrong. I've been wrong, too."

I bite my lip, nod at her in the quiet dark. She brushes hair from my face and tucks it behind my ear. This is what the past few days have been, mostly: an admission of mistake-making. I've spent a lot of time with Sadie and my mom, talking about what comes next. About what comes tonight.

"Are you ready for this?" Camilla says, her eyes flickering toward the stage and then back to me.

This. By which I know she means being honest. Stepping in front of that crowd and telling them the truth. The lie she's spun since I was born, the *someday daughter* she's made of me, is a fiction. But it's familiar. And I don't know what it's going to look like yet, to be honest together. But this is our last show—the very last chance we'll have to get it right, or to get closer to right.

I say, "Ready enough."

My mother nods, and when her eyes move over my shoulder I turn to see Silas, emerging from the dark in his black shirt, black pants.

"Where's your camera?" I ask, and he glances at my mom.

"Not filming tonight." Silas loops an arm around my waist and reaches ahead of us to part the curtain. Just a little, so the three of us can look out and see the stage. "Just watching."

The theater lights dim and a giant screen glides down from the ceiling. It crackles with static, then fills with color: the floral blur of my skirt, cutting across the stage that first night in Los Angeles. A close-up of Mom's hand on my shoulder during the show in San Francisco. Sadie's face in the audience, thoughtful and focused.

Music swells and it's all cuts of the three of us—Sadie and I bent over notes backstage, my mom laughing with her hand on Sadie's arm, our familiar faces looking at each other and looking like each other.

I look up at Silas, his chin tipped toward me in the dark. Think of the past few days he's spent holed up in his hotel room, editing. "Did you make this?"

Both of his arms are around my waist, his chest warm on my back. He kisses the top of my head and whispers, "Of course."

I can't manage a single other word, watching this montage of my summer. These two women I'm connected to in ways I knew and didn't know, in ways that scare me in all the same moments I want to reach for them two-handed. When the music fades, my mother steps onto the stage by herself.

"Good evening," she says. Her heels echo across the floorboards. Under the single stage light, she looks holy and lonely.

"I'm so grateful to be with you tonight, and to share something I haven't been brave enough to share until now."

She glances over her shoulder, her eyes finding mine. I nod at her. *Ready.* Silas lets go of me, and when I turn to look at him Sadie's here, standing right next to him in the shadows. She smiles.

"If you'll be so kind," Mom says, "I'd like to introduce you to my daughters."

Sadie reaches for my hand and squeezes it hard in the dark. We set our shoulders, mirrors of each other.

And we step forward, together, into the light.

54

Rana hands me her notebook, open to a grid-lined page filled edge to edge with her precise handwriting.

"I mean, have at it," she says. The door to Mergenthaler Hall whooshes shut behind her, heavy wood over scuffed stone floor. "But I doubt I got anything from that you didn't—I think it was just confusing as fuck."

I swing my backpack over one shoulder anyways, tucking her notes inside. "Well, just in case."

Our exam is on Tuesday, right after Halloween. Rana is the smartest person I've ever met—if her notes can't decode that statistics lecture for me, nothing can.

"You going back home?" she asks, pushing dark hair behind one ear to look up at me. The breezeway to Wyman Quad opens up behind her as we move toward the library—all marble steps and fall trees changing color. The heels of our boots click over the brick walkway in tandem. "I have that whack-ass freshman seminar at one but was thinking of hitting a nap first."

"Room's all yours," I say. Rana and I are in a quad in Wolman Hall—two bedrooms and a bathroom and a kitchenette so small there's hardly room for her electric teakettle. Our quad-mates,

Keely and Wren, already left to spend the weekend in New York. "Si should be here soon."

"The elusive Silas Acheson," Rana says. When I cut my eyes at her she laughs—this deep, throaty sound that's always filling our tiny dorm room in a way that's started to feel like home. She waves a hand at me. "I can't wait to meet the guy who signed up for all of this."

"Uncalled for," I say, and she laughs again. The truth is Rana's the best roommate I could've asked for, after Fallon. We share half the same classes, and she always makes extra tea for me, and sometimes she even comes to watch my Saturday-morning swim lessons at the rec center. For moral support. Afterward we get bagels, my hair in a chlorine-reeking bun, and sit on the quad with our coffee.

Oh—and Rana's gone all day every Monday, which gives me plenty of quiet studying time. Because she spends those days at Hopkins Hospital, as the only freshman with a shadowing position in the ICU. The worst part is that I like her so much I can't even stay mad. She deserves it. I did, too. But at least I get to hear about it, every Monday night when she collapses back into our room in crinkled scrubs with stories to tell.

"I'll see you guys in Fells Point tomorrow, right?"

"I think so," I say. We pass the library and start down The Beach, a sloping circle of grass that separates campus from North Charles Street. It's busy with people on blankets with textbooks open beside them, guys in Greek letters throwing Frisbees, dogs with clusters of cooing students huddled around them. The air is crisp and clear and perfectly October. "We don't have costumes yet, but Silas is good at that kind of thing."

"I'm wearing a red dress and horns and calling it a day."

"Perfectly reasonable," I tell her, and then I see him.

Silas is standing at the corner of North Charles and Thirty-Fourth, leaned against a silver hatchback with Puddles's leash looped around his wrist. His hair's tied back—dark, familiar curls, a few strands falling into his face when he stoops to run a hand over Puddles's head. She's staring up at him from the sidewalk. He's wearing jeans and sneakers and a Johns Hopkins hoodie I bought him in August—thick and fleecy and soft on my cheek every time I've fallen asleep with my face pressed against it.

I haven't seen him in a month. Since I took the train to DC in September to spend a weekend with him and Mick and Cleo. He lifts his head, scanning the street and the crosswalk and the red-bricked edge of campus. For me, I know. I want to drop everything I'm holding and dead sprint through traffic to get to him.

"That guy?" Rana says, and I realize we've both stopped walking. "With the man bun and the dog?"

I glance at her and follow her gaze back to Silas. "That guy," I say.

Rana smiles, nudging me with her elbow. "Not what I expected your type to be."

I hear Silas's voice, soft in that tree house in Colorado. Pressed against my ear in the dark at Lady June's. *Not that type of person?*

And I know Silas isn't my type, or any type at all. He's just himself. He's just who I want to launch myself at, bury myself against. I know none of us are types—we're just people, who can change. Who can feel differently.

"I'm going to—" I break off, already stepping away from Rana.

322

She laughs one last time. "Yeah, you go. I'm going to grab something to eat anyway."

I nod, only half listening, taking the rest of the slope down The Beach so quickly my knees ache. When I hit the crosswalk I shout his name and Silas looks up, his entire face illuminating in a grin. He lets go of Puddles and she runs for me—a slow, creaking lope that's so pure and good and familiar I could cry. My knees hit the sidewalk and I wait for her, catch her when she gets to me, squeeze her tight into my chest. When I carry her over to Silas, he wraps us both in his long arms.

"Hi," he says. I draw a deep breath against his throat. "I love you."

"I love you, too." It's a muscle I'm building—saying it to Silas, and Fallon, and my mom. Being brave enough to put those words in safe places. It's one part of a nebulous whole I've been working through in that office a few blocks off campus, where I spend every Thursday afternoon talking about what happened with Camilla and Sadie, about all the stories I tell myself about myself, about the way I hurt in Nashville. About my anxiety—not a possession but a part of me, and one that I'm learning to be kinder to.

I thought once that the kind of doctor I want to be is realer than the kind of doctor my mother is—that the physical of our bodies holds more weight than the intangible of our minds. But in that, as in so much else, I was wrong. And the more I come to understand myself, the more I realize how much I don't understand. It feels good, even when it feels bad, to be getting closer.

"I missed you," I say.

"I still miss you," Silas says, carefully lowering Puddles to the sidewalk and then taking my face in his hands. "And you're right here."

He kisses me—his lips October-cold and soft and searching. I tip him against the car, spread my fingers over his ribs through the thick fabric of his sweatshirt. When his mouth opens under mine, the whole world hazes out—I'm heat and I'm hunger. I'm an infinite ache. I love him so much it could end me.

"Sadie says hi," he murmurs, lips in the hollow behind my ear.

I swallow. Lift a hand to hold his head, feel the curls at the nape of his neck. "Okay." I talked to Sadie just a few days ago; I'll talk to her next month, when we're all in LA for Thanksgiving. "Hi, Sadie."

Silas pulls back, his eyes tracking over mine. We smile at each other and Puddles darts a lick against my ankle and I want to freeze this, just as it is. This suspended moment, with a full weekend ahead of us—fleeting and precious and finite. But how, standing here, it feels hopeful and enormous. Like it's endless enough for now.

"Where to first?" Silas asks. His eyes are golden in the autumn light. "I have a few ideas."

"Anywhere," I say. I slide my palm into his, thread our fingers together. And then I ask him to do what he's done all summer and all fall, what he's done every moment since that first night I met him. "Surprise me."

Acknowledgments

Every book is its own joy, and its own challenge. For me, writing Audrey's story was uniquely challenging—she is so much like versions of the person I've been, and not necessarily versions that are easy to look at in the mirror. Like Audrey, it took me a long time to accept anxiety as a part of myself, and even longer to accept that it was all right to need help with it. If you're in the labyrinth, trying to white-knuckle your way through, please know that you don't need to do it alone. Asking for help isn't weak; it's courageous. You deserve every bright and good and peaceful thing—and there are so many people out there, me included, who want you to have it.

I owe so much to Kaitlyn Topolewski, who's helped me in more ways than there are words for here. Thank you, and thank you for working through Audrey's story with me so that I could tell it in the way that felt the best and most honest.

Thank you to my editor, Tara Weikum, who I was so lucky to work with on another book, and to my agent, Katie Shea Boutillier, for always being in my corner. I appreciate both of you enormously and am so glad to have you as my team.

Thank you also to Sarah Homer, Chris Kwon, Caitlin Lonning, Audrey Diestelkamp, Taylan Salvati, Meghan Pettit, Jessica White, Jill Freshney, and the entire team at HarperCollins. And a squealing, arm-flailing thank-you to Vi-An Nguyen, who captured

Audrey (and sweet, wrinkly Puddles) so perfectly on this book's cover.

Thank you to the early readers who took this manuscript in its messiest form during summer 2022 and helped me turn it into the story I was trying to tell: Crystal, Elyse, Kelly, Laura, Maggie, Matthew, Taylor. And to Andrea, who believed I could write this one and helped me see it through the way she always does—with creativity and care.

Thank you to Betty Culley for the thoughtful sensitivity read and generous blurb. Betty, you're one of my very favorite authors, and I'm honored to have your mark on this book.

Thank you to Destiny Bailey, my Hopkins premed roommate and dear friend, who helped me get Audrey's medically inclined mind right. To Sam Peterson, for helping me get my books out there and being the type of kind, genuine friend we should all aspire to be. And to all my friends at Vermilion, who've supported my work as an author in ways that make me weepy just to think about.

The real treasure of publishing truly *has* turned out to be the friends we make along the way, and I'm so grateful for mine. Kelly Duran, Megan E. Freeman, Matthew Hubbard, Sam Markum, Jenna Miller, Mackenzie Reed, Kelsey Rodkey, Jessie Weaver, every kind author who's gushed in my direct messages or tolerated me gushing in theirs. And Rachel Lynn Solomon, whose warmth and generosity seems to know no bounds. Thank you, all of you, for reading pitches, talking me off the ledge, and making me feel known.

To my parents, who love me equally when I win and when I fail, thank you. I love sharing the triumphs with you, and I know how lucky I am to have you at my back when I need to try again. Thank you for championing me in this new career, and in everything else for as long as I've been yours.

To Tucker, who reminds me in dark moments when I wish I could change myself that I'm worthy just as I am—thank you for taking care of the Audrey in me, and for all the rest of it.

And for this one, especially, thank you to Moose, Puffin, and Lilly—the dogs who've made a home in my heart.